The Fruits
of Our Sins

Jean Mckie-Sutton

Red Lotus Press
Elkins Park, PA

Published by:
>
Red Lotus Press
P.O. Box 11252
Elkins Park, PA 19027
(215) 863-7562
www.redlotuspress.com

Printed by: Color House Graphics
Layout: Jera Publishing, LLC

ISBN: 978-0-9850870-0-5
LCCN: 2012902034

Author's Note:
This is a work of fiction. Any resemblance to actual events, locales, or persons, living or dead, is entirely coincidental. The characters and incidences are used fictitiously and should not in any way be understood or construed as real.

Dedicated

In Memory Of

Louise Humphrey Graham

(1925 - 2003)

Acknowledgments

First and foremost, I give thanks to the Creator for whispering to me my story. It is you who gave me this intense and overwhelming desire to write, and it is you who would not allow me to let it go. With great awe and humility, I submit this work to you.

Rod Sutton -my husband, my friend - you believed in my story even when I wrote those first few fledgling paragraphs. You are light and sustenance, providing levity and solidity throughout life's constant change.

To my dearest friend, Philip Matthews, thank you for being my memory. You reminded me of my purpose and kept me centered when I succumbed to fear and apprehension. "Jean, this is what you were meant to do," you told me countless times.

My love and gratitude to Lori Giancaterino, Nicole Gray, Ladonna Mason, Lakisha Scott and Tracie Upchurch for volunteering to read the manuscript, and providing necessary and honest feedback and suggestions for improvement. You have all been a tremendous source of unconditional support and encouragement.

Sylvia Morris: Your spiritual guidance has been invaluable. Every time we spoke, you shared your belief that God was weaving it all together for my good. In your words, I've found comfort.

To all of my sisters from my dear alma mater, The Cecilian Academy, I am truly grateful for your encouragement to give substance to my dreams.

My sincere thanks to Janet Lipsi - editor, teacher and coach all wrapped up in one. I've learned much during our exchanges and look forward to working with you on future projects.

And finally, my gratitude to the greatest teacher of all: life.

To all of you, and any others I may have inadvertently omitted - peace, light, and blessings.

Every woman has a secret.

Some harbor their secrets in closets, piling boxes and bags atop to obscure them. Others bury them in the recesses of their minds and go on living as if their secrets have no purpose or merit, no right to thrive. Their secrets are relegated to the land of dreams - dreams never spoken, silenced unto death.

Contents

Prologue

1995

Madeline Stovall raised her fists high in the air then plunged them downward forcibly onto Sybil's face. Sybil staggered sideways, dazed and unsteady, yet Madeline continued striking her harder and harder. Sybil cowered at the rage darkening Madeline's eyes, and it was in that moment that she became fully aware of the depth of her fury. Sybil threw a series of futile punches, a few contacting Madeline's chin, most simply sailing through the air, inciting Madeline's onslaught to intensify.

She won't keep fighting someone who won't fight back, Sybil silently reasoned, and she stopped all efforts to defend herself. Trembling and spent, she bent forward with her arms shielding her face, and crouched immobile. Madeline continued her frenzied flailing, and her knuckles, bruised and bleeding, pounded with increasing vigor. Sybil suppressed the urge to cry out for fear of angering her opponent even more. She locked her jaws shut, endured the weighty punches and said nothing at all. She stood erect to lessen the battering to her head and face. Nevertheless, Madeline's blows increased in speed and intensity and the strikes, now aimed at her breasts and stomach, nearly brought Sybil kneeling to the ground. She heard the sickening snap of her own ribs cracking, and grimaced just before the pain punctured her insides. She remained still and rigid hoping that her refusal to fight back might end the battle, but respite did not arrive.

"Stop it! Stop it! Stop it!" she screamed over and over in a rhythmic chant. Her voice was the shrill timbre of a stranger's, yet she could not stop her senseless, cadence of shrieking. Her cries invigorated her opponent. Madeline lunged toward her, fists poised for more. Sybil took several quick steps backwards, colliding with a brick support pillar. There was nowhere to run. She clenched her jaws shut tight, swallowing her shrieking voice into the pit of her stomach. Her teeth sank into her tongue but she dared not cry out again. The metallic taste of her own blood filled her mouth as her body jerked with spasms. She coughed to keep from choking. Blood seeped through her lips, down her chin and onto the concrete below, forming tiny dark circles at her feet. Sybil feared for her life. Weeping openly, she fell to the ground, drew her knees to her chest and rocked back and forth, still shielding her face and head.

In rapid succession, two kicks to her left hip knocked her onto her side, yet she continued her rocking motion until she again assumed an upright position. A damp heat rose from her neck to her forehead and droplets of sweat rolled onto her chest and thighs. Sybil's surroundings grew dim as her senses dulled. But just before she succumbed to the solace of unconsciousness, the assault came to an abrupt halt. For a moment, all was still.

Sybil inhaled and exhaled deeply until she regained lucidness. The warmth of the mid-afternoon sun bathed her neck and shoulders, while the cool rigidness of the concrete cooled her from below. She inhaled the Poeme Perfume she so lavishly splashed on her body before leaving home that morning. A mild scent of lavender with a hint of fresh roses - it was the fragrance all the young women were wearing. It reminded her of springtime and morning rain. But on this day, her favored Poeme pitched waves of nausea spiraling through her stomach. She willed herself not to vomit.

Sybil lowered her arms and examined her surroundings. She was surprised to find that she was kneeling on Madeline's front porch, since the encounter began with the two women having a simple conversation in the living room of the brick twin home. A three foot high stone wall surrounded the rectangular porch, framed by pillars that faced the tree-lined street. Less than six feet away, four concrete steps descended to a path leading to the sidewalk. Adrenaline raced through her limbs, lending her a quick burst of energy. Sybil considered making a run for the steps, but a small group of neighbors clustered on the sidewalk blocked the path that led to a quick escape. She observed the faces of the people in the crowd as they peered back at her. All of them witnessed her brutal humiliation yet did nothing more than watch her suffering. Sybil was alone amidst the dozen onlookers and made a conscious effort to shrug off her self-pity.

I really shouldn't be surprised, she almost said aloud. They were all Madeline's neighbors, and most of them - men and women alike - feared Madeline's wrath. Sybil heard a rumor that she once tried to kill her own husband with a sword while he was asleep. The rumor had never been confirmed, yet no one dared question Madeline about the tale's authenticity.

Sybil shifted her gaze to examine her adversary. Madeline's short, curly hair sat in uneven tufts around the sides and top of her head. A scowl distorted her sharp aquiline features, and one of her large breasts poked through an opening in her silk blouse, twisted where the buttons were torn away. Sunlight glittered off the perspiration on her bare shoulder. Madeline stood with her feet slightly apart and her arms rigid at her sides. She breathed fast and heavy, almost panting, reminding Sybil of a pit bull she once saw mangle a newborn rabbit. She shivered in spite of the intense heat.

I figured talking about the baby would be hard but I surely didn't expect to have a full blown fist fight with this woman.

Just then, the baby, lying in a bassinet in the living room, whimpered softly as a kitten. Sybil's chest tightened. Madeline turned her head in the direction of the baby's whimper and relaxed her stance.

This is my chance, Sybil thought. *I'll take her off guard.*

She sprang from the ground with a frenzied torrent of punching and kicking. Madeline lost her balance momentarily, yet quickly became oriented and battle ready. She pounded her fist down forcibly where Sybil's neck met her shoulder. Sybil folded, collapsing to the ground, and lay motionless. Madeline stood over her, waiting and watching, until it was evident she had fully succumbed. She backed away until she reached the door, and as she stepped into her home, she turned to look at the beaten woman one last time.

Sybil lay flat on her stomach. Splattered blood and tears peppered the ground around her. Shuddering and grimacing with each inhalation, her eyes pled for mercy. Madeline bolted the door.

"Wait!" Sybil screamed from the porch. "I can't leave without my baby." With one arm cradling her abdomen, she crawled across the porch, her knees cutting open on the uneven concrete, and banged on the door with her fist.

"Please! Give me my baby."

Facing the closed door, still on her knees, she waited.

"Please!" she sobbed, her voice now hoarse and raspy.

When Madeline's footsteps retreated farther into the home, she bowed her head and closed her eyes as if in prayer. After several quiet moments, Sybil pulled herself from the ground and faced the crowd of neighbors that was now beginning to disperse. Some whispered with their hands cupped over their mouths, others patronized her with pitying stares, while still others shook their heads disapprovingly.

As Sybil began to depart, the infant's whimper swelled to a persistent wail. She paused with her face tilted toward the sky, but did not turn around, then she dropped her chin to her chest and continued on her way. The wail ripened to a piercing scream, Sybil's sobs now in concert with those of the infant. As she placed one foot in front of the other, knees trembling and unsteady, the crescendo of the wailing symphony commingled in the air. The farther away she crept, the more vehemently the infant screamed, as if bemoaning and mourning Sybil's permanent departure.

Madeline

West Oak Lane sat on the Northwest edge of Philadelphia, nestled in the middle of East Mount Airy, East Germantown and Cheltenham Avenue, the Montgomery County border. It was a friendly, residential neighborhood with larger homes – some detached, modest yards and streets lined with oak and elm trees. Ogontz Avenue was the commercial heart of West Oak Lane. The Route Six trolley ran down the center of the commercial corridor, flanked on both sides by family-owned businesses and Synagogues.

West Oak Lane's distinct colonial architecture was unparalleled in the surrounding city neighborhoods. Homes were built with craftsmanship that many architects considered the pinnacle of domestic design. Constructed of brick and stone, these structures suggested stability, permanence and sanctuary.

By 1969, Oak Lane was thrown into the midst of change. German and Eastern European Jews were beginning the migration across the border into the suburbs of Montgomery County. Reaping the financial rewards of their profitable businesses, most migrated for larger homes with more land, but the more narrow minded fled the city to rid themselves of the sudden influx of middle class blacks buying their pristine homes and infiltrating their schools.

Tucker and Sadie Stovall were among the recent influx, but they could not include themselves among the ranks of the middle class. Tucker worked as a cook at Little's, a diner near the outskirts, and Sadie cleaned the homes of affluent Jewish families in Elkins Park. They were able to afford their three bedroom row home in West Oak Lane solely by chance. Tucker's father, an iron worker at the Alan Wood Steel Company, suffered a fatal accident while on the job, just weeks before his retirement. The settlement paid more than half of Tucker's mortgage. He and Sadie were just able to manage the remainder with their meager salaries. Their home was opulently furnished thanks to the discarded furniture of Sadie's employers. Neither Tucker nor Sadie owned a car, but they lived less than a quarter mile from the trolley, so they travelled wherever they needed to go with ease.

Sadie liked to pretend they were just like all the others – the school teachers, nurses, firefighters, electricians and police officers – and she kept their occupations a secret, as if being a cook and a maid were something to hide in the dark, like a family curse. She cringed when Tucker told their story of chance to their friends and neighbors, and scolded him later when they were alone. Tucker, on the other hand, thought it a gesture of ungratefulness to remain silent about their twist of fate. He was proud to share the truth, for it was his father's death that provided him and Sadie with their way of life.

IT WAS A LAZY SATURDAY MORNING. Beads of frost blanketed the grass, yet the air held the earthy scent of spring approaching. Early blooms stretched through the earth, birds found their songs, and squirrels scurried up and down trees and leapt among the branches. It was the time of day Tucker felt most alive.

There were no sirens, horns, accelerators or people polluting the air with their voices. There was just the solitude of his thoughts, and his kinship with the sounds of nature awakening and stirring.

Every Saturday and Sunday, he rose at dawn to tend to a small patch of grass in the back yard where he planted cabbage, broccoli and onions. Later in the season he'd expand his modest garden to include tomatoes and cucumbers. He plucked the weeds from the soil and watered the seedlings with a homemade Epsom Salt fertilizer he mixed with two parts liquid molasses.

The back door slammed, shattering his morning peace. Tucker winced. Sadie lumbered toward him with her hands on either side of her huge belly.

"This pregnancy is wearing me out." Sadie Stovall fussed and complained about her growing abdomen, the tenacious ache in her lower back, her bulging ankles and the pounds inching higher on the scale, to anyone willing to listen. The bus driver, the cashier at the grocery store, and even the butcher were familiar with Sadie's growing list of third trimester afflictions.

"Good morning to you, too," Tucker told her. He spoke in a soft voice, hoping Sadie would follow his lead. She didn't. Her voice grew louder.

"Some women deal with this torture over and over, having baby after baby," she went on. "Why would any sane woman enjoy carrying a child? Everything's uncomfortable. Bending! Reaching! Stretching! Sleeping! I'll never make it to nine

11

months!" She leaned against the chain link fence that enclosed their back yard until she caught her breath.

He had endured Sadie's complaining since the day she announced she was pregnant. Back then, he scrambled to do whatever it took to make her comfortable, from fixing a small plate of soda crackers to calm her morning sickness, to getting a stool for her aching feet, to rubbing her sore back. He soon discovered that no matter how he tried to appease her, the griping never ceased. Now, instead of scrambling to her aid, he allowed her incessant rants to run their course.

"Get off your feet, Sadie." Tucker smiled, and gestured toward a set of chairs.

"What the heck are you smiling at? If it were up to your kind to carry babies, there would be no human race." She flung her arms wide, knocking herself off balance. Sadie righted herself then settled into one of the green and white striped lawn chairs in a corner of the yard. Tucker turned away to conceal his grin.

When he composed himself and turned back, Sadie's gaze dropped to her belly, then she looked up at Tucker with an expression of sudden surprise.

"What's wrong?" Tucker asked. He stood and walked toward her, his pace brisk.

"Did you see that?" she asked, her eyes wide with the amazement of a child.

Then the rippling across Sadie's belly caught Tucker's attention.

"Let me feel." Tucker discarded his gardening gloves and pressed his fingertips on the place where he saw the movement. "Was that a knee or an elbow?"

The baby shifted to the other side of Sadie's belly. When Tucker placed his fingers over the baby at the new location, the unborn infant moved again.

"I think she can really feel me touching her," Tucker mused.

"You'd move out of the way too if somebody mashed your elbow," she laughed.

"Who do you think she's gonna look like?" Tucker asked.

"Both of us, but he'll get his smarts from you."

"I hope she has your ears and chin," Tucker added.

Tucker's overlarge ears protruded somewhat. He thought they made him appear silly, childlike. Sadie told him they lent him an endearing, vulnerable quality.

"The baby will be beautiful regardless of whom he looks like. I'm more concerned about what this baby is doing to my body. What if I can't bounce back? I haven't seen my ankles since Christmas, and I'm sure I'll greet these stretch marks every day for the rest of my life. And let's not even talk about the weight! I've already gained sixty pounds and I still have three more weeks before I'm due!"

"You're supposed to gain weight. I don't know why you women worry about something that's natural. A skinny pregnant woman just isn't healthy."

After three false starts, Sadie hoisted herself from the chair and waddled back into the house.

"I'm going in to take the sheets and pillowcases off the bed before I start the laundry. I could use some help!" she called over her shoulder.

"I'll be in soon," Tucker told her. He finished watering the seedlings, then trailed Sadie inside a few moments later. He found her resting on the bed, her feet propped up, head nestled in the pillows. He paused at the doorway of the bedroom to admire his beautiful wife. He loved her eyes and considered them her most striking feature. Their almond shape slanted upward somewhat, giving her an alert, sharp expression even when tired. Her clear, cocoa skin emanated health and clean living, and the sharp lines of her chin lent her an air of stubbornness, even when she was making an effort to be perfectly agreeable, which for Sadie was a rare occurrence. She wore her course, wild hair in an ivory barrette with one single braid falling to the middle of her back. A few curly strands broke free at the temple, waving back and forth in the spring breeze wafting through the open bedroom windows.

It was unusual to find her lying so peacefully. She usually bounced and tussled as she struggled to find a position comfortable enough for resting. She complained that her belly was too big to lie on her stomach, and she no longer lay flat on her back because the baby weighed heavily on her spine. She spent most nights alternating sides, and making a very big deal about it.

"Just a few more weeks and you'll have your body all to yourself and our baby here in your arms," he'd try to appease her. Although Tucker didn't dare admit it to Sadie, he enjoyed seeing her big with child. Her growing belly conjured up thoughts of earth, ancestors and the natural order of things, and it filled him with a sense that all was as it should be. At night he wrapped his arms around his wife and lay perfectly still. When he felt the life in her belly move, he held his breath so neither sound nor air disrupted his brief encounter with their new creation. Then he whispered to Sadie in the dark, "did you feel Madeline kicking?"

Tucker guessed that the restless child in his wife's belly was a girl. Madeline was the name he chose for his daughter.

"You know that's Marcus in their fussing up a storm," she shot back. She was certain the child growing in her womb was a boy.

Tucker pulled a fresh fitted sheet from the linen closet. "I thought you needed help putting the sheets on the bed and here you are taking a nap."

Sadie made a big production of getting up, then held one end of the sheet while Tucker pulled the other end over the mattress.

"You put the bedspread on - the one with the red and blue flowers - and I'll get the pillow cases," Sadie said. She stooped to grab a pillowcase from the lowest shelf in the linen closet when Tucker heard her take a deep, sharp breath. He hurried into the hallway.

Sybil grimaced and let out a low moan, "Tucker, it's time!"

15

A puddle of water formed on the floor beneath her. Tucker helped her back into the bedroom where she sat on the foot of the bed. She panted and grabbed fistfuls of the floral bedspread, twisting it into a mound of bundled fabric.

"Hold on, baby. I'm calling an ambulance." He dialed the phone in the hallway.

Sadie's short bursts of patterned breathing quickened.

"The contractions are coming seconds apart. A first baby is supposed to take hours, not minutes! Tell them the ambulance... has to... come soon." She panted a little while longer, until her cheeks grew wan and her eyes stretched wide.

"There's no time," she gasped. "Go get Pearl!"

"Who?" Tucker looked puzzled.

"You know, my friend Pearl," she said, her voice impatient. "She's right around the corner. She's a nurse."

Recognition lit Tucker's face. Pearl lived on the street that ran parallel to theirs. If he walked out of his back door and continued down the driveway and across the road, he'd end up in Pearl's back yard.

Tucker sprinted out the bedroom and down the stairs. He returned minutes later with Pearl at his heels. She'd just finished the graveyard shift and still wore her white uniform and cap. She carried her handbag on one shoulder and held a small grocery bag. She set both on the dresser.

"I already called for an ambulance," Tucker explained. "I appreciate you coming to help, but this baby has to be born in a hospital with doctors, monitors, medication… I understand you're a nurse, and I'm sure you're skilled, but having our baby delivered by a friend right here in the house? I don't know about this."

Pearl rolled her eyes at Tucker then turned her attention to Sadie.

"Let me see what's going on here." She lifted Sadie's skirt and reached in to feel for the position of the baby. Her hand emerged bloody. Tucker blanched, then bolted down the stairs and stood pacing at the front door.

"This can't happen here! Where's the ambulance?" He ran to the kitchen and dialed again. The same operator responded.

"Sir, we've already dispatched a team to your residence."

Tucker ignored the irritated voice on the other end of the phone. "Tell 'em to hurry! My wife is having a baby! Now!" He slammed down the phone and waited at the front door.

"THIS BABY IS COMING FAST, SADIE." Pearl piled pillows behind Sadie's back, then crouched on the foot of the bed.

"Now push!"

Sadie paused to wait for the crushing pain, bore down with the strength of her entire body, and continued bearing down long after the contraction ended. When she thought she could endure the tearing pain no longer, her baby emerged into the world.

"It's a girl!" Pearl announced. "Tucker, come and meet your daughter," she yelled down the stairs.

Tucker instantly appeared and kneeled on the floor alongside the bed, his face nearly touching Sadie's.

"She's perfect," Tucker gushed. "My Madeline is perfect."

Pearl smacked Madeline's fleshy, round behind, then placed her on her mother's belly. Madeline covered her eyes with her fists and her lips pouted as if she were holding back a good cry. Dark fuzzy hair covered her head and her bronze skin shimmered in the sunlight streaming through the window. She was a broad, meaty infant with stout limbs. While pregnant, Sadie crocheted dainty caps and sweaters in anticipation of her baby's arrival, but the delicate clothing would never fit around her wide torso.

"Your first day here and already you've outgrown your clothes," she joked. Sadie cooed, rubbed noses and held Madeline at different angles to coax her into looking in her eyes, but Madeline was more interested in the light fixture on the ceiling overhead.

"Stubborn already, huh?" she giggled. She kissed Madeline on both cheeks.

Pearl sterilized a pair of scissors the old-fashioned way. She dipped them into rubbing alcohol, then held them briefly over the flame of a cigarette lighter.

"Here, Tucker," she handed him the scissors, "cut the cord."

Tucker hesitated.

"It's fine. It won't hurt her."

He winced as the scissors cut through the flesh then braced for the crying that never came to pass.

Sadie's packed hospital bag sat alongside the bed. Pearl unzipped the bag and pulled out a mint green receiving blanket. She wrapped the baby in the blanket and leaned forward to lay her on Sadie's chest, when Sadie sat up fast, her back and shoulders rigid.

"I still need to push!" she told Pearl with a grimace.

Pearl settled the baby alongside Sadie, reached under her skirt again and felt another moist, warm head emerging.

"It's another baby!" she shrieked. "Push!"

"What?" Tucker exclaimed.

Emitting an animal-like moan, Sadie bore down again, this time giving birth to a son.

"Twins? The doctor never said anything about twins!" Wild with astonishment, Sadie's eyes darted back and forth from one baby to the other. "Can you believe it? I have two babies!"

"And this one's name is?" Pearl prompted.

"His name is Marcus."

Tucker's mouth gaped open.

"You okay there?" Pearl asked him, "you look a little peaked."

"Th… this is a miracle," he stammered, "a son and a daughter, both at the same time!"

Trembling from the first gusts of cool air outside his mother's warm belly, Marcus was tiny and frail, the smallest baby Sadie had ever seen. The palms of his hands, the whites of his eyes, and his thin, papery lips were a soft shade of blue. He held his limbs close to his birdlike torso. Fine brown hair covered his head except for a moon-shaped smooth area near his forehead. Sadie kissed him there and his trembling turned violent. Marcus opened his eyes just long enough to get a glimpse of his mother, then squeezed them shut. His body grew still and limp, and his limbs swayed loosely about his diminutive frame. Sadie nudged his cheek with her nose. When he didn't move or open his eyes, Sadie jostled him. Still, Marcus did not respond. She held his face to her cheek, anticipating the warmth of his breath, but there was no air.

"Something's wrong." Sadie shook Marcus back and forth. "What's wrong with him?"

Pearl snatched the baby and placed her index finger below his right ear.

"I'm not getting a pulse." She laid him on her lap, covered his mouth with hers and breathed into his lungs. In between breaths, she massaged his chest. Sadie sat ramrod straight, her arms still outstretched, reaching for her child.

"What's happening?" she asked.

Pearl glanced at the clock in between breaths. Three minutes passed. She massaged his chest and continued breathing for him, her movements growing frantic.

Tucker walked back and forth from one end of the room to the other, his hands folded, his lips mouthing desperate prayers.

"Come on Marcus. Don't you leave me!" Sadie screamed.

Marcus bore the countenance of death but Sadie's distress forced Pearl to continue her efforts. Pearl alternated breathing into the baby's lungs and massaging his chest. When she checked the clock again, ten more minutes had passed. Pearl paused for several seconds, then dropped her hands to her sides. The bustling and stirring of new life gone, the only sounds Sadie heard were the tick of the clock on the nightstand and the beating of her own heart.

"What are you doing? You can't stop!"

With great reverence, Pearl rose to her feet and stood firm in front of Sadie. Sadie's eyes met Pearl's and she understood that Marcus was not coming back.

"It wasn't meant for him to stay, Sadie," Pearl explained, her voice gentle and low, "but your beautiful daughter is alive and well. She's the one who needs you now."

"Please Lord," Tucker now prayed out loud, "bring us back our son. I beg you in the name of the..."

"Give him to me!" Sadie screamed.

Pearl swaddled the dead infant in a soft throw from Sadie's overnight bag. She placed him in Sadie's arms and left the room without a sound. Sadie rocked him, her tears wetting his face.

"How can you be gone from me?" She said to Marcus. "We can't be together, now. They're gonna take you away forever... put you in the cold ground." She looked up toward the ceiling. "My God," she exclaimed, calling on the heavens for mercy. She pulled his blanket tighter then held him to her breast as if expecting him to nurse.

"Is this my fault? Did I do this to you?" Her mind raced through the past eight months – she kept all of her doctor's appointments, diligently took her prenatal vitamins, ate nutritious meals – she could think of nothing that might have caused this.

She laid Marcus on the bed next to Madeline and looked at both her babies side by side. Madeline was plump, round, and nearly twice as large as Marcus. Her head, limbs, and fists were the size of a two month old baby, her large belly nearly obscuring her freshly cut umbilical cord. In stark contrast, Marcus' ribs protruded through his sunken chest, his skin stretched thin over his knees and elbows. He was angles and bones with no soft, fleshy places. *How can they be so different*? She thought. She looked back and forth from one baby to the other, and then the answer struck Sadie so hard her head pounded. She understood with a certain calm and clarity why her son was dead and who was to blame. It wasn't her fault at all. She had done nothing throughout her pregnancy that might have caused this. It was Madeline. Madeline was to blame. Madeline had taken everything for herself, growing large and healthy, and left Marcus malnourished.

That has to be it! The more she thought about it and believed it, the calmer she felt. *How else do you explain the size difference in my babies?* Sadie imagined the struggle that took place in her womb, and she knew Madeline was to blame for the battle that cost Marcus his life. She looked from one baby to the other. Resolute, she nodded.

I'm certain about this.

When Pearl returned, she seemed surprised but pleased at Sadie's quick acceptance of the dreadful circumstance.

Tucker, on the other hand sat hunched with his head in his hands. Pearl grasped his wrist. "I'm so sorry Tucker, but it's time to say goodbye."

As she placed the dead baby in Tucker's arms, sirens wailed in the distance.

Tucker cradled the still warm infant and held him close as he whispered love and goodbyes, then he wept. Not a quiet weeping with soft tears and stifled sighs, but a shameless, open wailing and lamenting. "My son," he cried, "my dear son."

"You have life to celebrate, too," Pearl reminded him. I'll take Marcus, you hold Madeline."

There was a hard knock at the front door.

"Come right in," Pearl yelled, "we're upstairs."

After heavy footsteps pounded the stairs, two paramedics rushed into the bedroom.

"She already had the babies but the boy stopped breathing," Pearl told them. "I tried but couldn't revive him."

Still cradling Madeline, Tucker led them to Marcus' lifeless body. He lay in a bassinet against the wall on the opposite side of the bedroom. A blanket covered him up to his chin, as if he were simply taking a nap. One of the men descended upon Marcus, administering CPR and searching for vitals with monitors and gauges. The other checked on Sadie, who sat transfixed, riveted by the frenzied resuscitation attempts.

"Sadie, here... take Madeline." Tucker tried to distract her.

She peeled her eyes from Marcus to look at her baby girl. Her eyes narrowed to tiny slits and her lips twisted, grotesque and abnormal, but when Sadie caught Tucker's eyes, her countenance returned to its wretched sorrow. She turned her attention back to the paramedics' orchestrations, then leaned over and whispered to Tucker, "I see no need to tell anyone about this."

The paramedic breathing air into Marcus' lungs kept pace in the background.

"What do you mean?" Tucker asked.

"The baby ... no one needs to know about Marcus. All anyone needs to know is that we have a healthy baby girl."

"You mean keep this all a secret?"

"He's gone, and telling folks won't bring him back."

"But what about our family? Our friends? We had two babies and one is ... gone." Tucker held his breath to stifle a sob. "What's wrong with telling them the truth?"

"Telling means I relive this over and over again. It's already in the past and that's where it will stay."

"In the past? Our dead son is still here in our bedroom!"

"Sir, may I speak with you in private?" asked one of the paramedics. The two men walked into the hallway.

"I'm sorry, sir. There's nothing more we can do. I've contacted the morgue. They'll be here shortly. You'll need to provide consent for them to take the body." He handed Tucker a form with an "X" at the place for his signature. Tucker signed.

All too soon, men in white lab coats entered the room. One wrote on a clipboard while the other picked up Marcus' limp body, zipped him into a tiny black bag, and carried him away. Tucker grasped the bedpost to keep his knees from buckling under him. His other hand, he placed on Sadie's shoulder.

"It's gonna be okay, honey," he told her. Pearl stood on the opposite side of the bed with her hand on Sadie's other shoulder - the three of them connected by witnessing the beginning and ending of life in an instant.

"Sadie, we're going to get through this." Tucker kissed the top of her head and squeezed her shoulder. When Sadie lifted her eyes to his, again she was more angry than sorrowful.

Sadie turned and whispered to Pearl, "Not a word of this to anyone!"

ST. THOMAS CHURCH WAS TWELVE MILES away in a remote corner of West Philadelphia, arrived at solely by an intricate maze of one-way streets. Neither Tucker nor Sadie had ever attended St. Thomas yet it was here, in the aged cemetery at the rear of the church, where Sadie chose to lay Marcus to rest.

The minister preached a brief eulogy and administered the final blessing. Tucker bowed his head and prayed a father's prayer for the safe passage of his son's soul, then placed a single white rose on the center of the miniature wooden box. After lowering the casket into the ground, gravediggers piled in shovelfuls of dirt. Sadie requested that there be no headstone to mark his grave, therefore the only evidence of his burial was the soft mound of newly dug soil. After the rain, wind and sun leveled the earth, all visible evidence would be gone.

"We shouldn't have had to endure this alone, Sadie. Our family and friends should be mourning with us, consoling us." Tucker wiped his wet face with the back of his hand. "We can't pretend like Marcus was never here."

"We will move on from this and we will not mention his name again." She turned and walked toward the cemetery exit. Tucker kicked the brake hold free on Madeline's carriage and walked fast to catch up with Sadie.

"It's not normal," Tucker yelled behind her. But Sadie was finished talking about the matter. She left the cemetery and shed no more tears for her son.

Tucker, on the other hand, thought of Marcus every day. Since Sadie forbade any conversation about their deceased son, Tucker's unspoken grief compelled him to write his pain. Every night, after Sadie fell asleep, he wrote a letter to Marcus, telling him how much he loved him and missed having him in his life. He held no illusion that Marcus somehow knew of his letters, but putting his thoughts down on paper was his only path to healing. He kept the letters in a cardboard box under the bed and with each passing day, he added one more to his private letter stash. Several months after Marcus' burial, Sadie found his box of grief. She told him it was an absurd and useless act. Without taking the time to read Tucker's ruminations of love and loss, she lit a match and held the flame to his pile of letters. She watched them burn and disintegrate into ashes, then she continued living as if Marcus never existed at all.

Monday mornings were unbearable. At daybreak, there was the rustle of bed linens followed by a slow sliding, then the thump of naked, chubby feet slapping the hardwood floor. Quick footsteps in the hallway paused at the entrance to Sadie's bedroom. Sadie's eyes popped open. Coiled and tense, she stared at the textured plaster ceiling, and waited for the screaming to begin.

"Dada?" Madeline whispered. There was no use telling her Tucker wasn't home. Sadie tried that countless times before. Madeline had to find out for herself, and searched the house anyway. The footsteps moved to the stairs, then a bump, bump, bump as Madeline plopped her bottom on each step until she reached the first floor. Her quick feet darted through the living room, dining room and kitchen.

"Dada?" she called out again. When she searched every room in the house and discovered that Tucker wasn't home, she collapsed on the floor by the front door, wailing. It would go on for at least half an hour. Sadie covered her head with her pillow. There was nowhere to escape the piercing shrieks. They permeated the walls and floors and even the down pillow she pressed over her head.

Sadie blamed Tucker for Madeline's ill behavior. He indulged her, treated her like royalty, scrambling to her beck and call, anxious to eradicate any frown, fret or discomfort. It started the moment he came home from work on Friday evenings. He swept Madeline into his arms and whispered in her ear, "I'm all yours."

She'd scurry down and tug on her jacket hanging in the coat closet.

"Out!" Madeline demanded. Tucker took Madeline wherever she wanted to go. She had merely to point in the desired direction and Tucker obliged. Friday, like most days, they ended up at a variety store. Madeline picked a box of caramel corn from the shelf and hugged them to her belly. Tucker agreed to the caramel corn but told Madeline she couldn't eat them until after dinner. Madeline nodded in agreement only to beg for the snack the second they left the store. Tucker obliged. She ate a few handfuls of the caramel corn then jammed her arm into the box until she found the prize, usually a ring or some other trinket. Once she had the prize in hand, her interest in the caramel corn vanished.

"Let's go home for dinner," Tucker told her. A tune played in the distance reminiscent of an old jack-in-the-box. As the sound drew closer, Tucker recognized the high-pitched repetitive jingle of the ice cream truck.

"No," said Madeline, "ice cream."

Tucker bought a small scoop of vanilla ice cream on a sugar cone. By the time they walked back home, sticky white streaks plastered her chin, fingers and forearm. Sadie waited for them at the door.

"Tucker, she should've had dinner first," Sadie complained, "now she'll pick over her food."

Sadie was right. At dinner, Madeline ignored the cut up chunks of chicken and vegetables on her plate and demanded seconds and thirds of the potatoes. Again, Tucker obliged. When she awakened in the middle of the night, Tucker ran to her room, and stayed by her side until she drifted back asleep. He carried her whenever she said 'up' and held her arms over her head, fetched her toys, even when she deliberately threw them on the floor, and so it went on for the remainder of the weekend. Tucker was Madeline's entire world... until Monday mornings. Every Monday Tucker left home at five in the morning to open the diner. Madeline woke up at six, discovered her entire world was gone, and erupted into a storm of crying. After half an hour, when Madeline's screaming regressed to sniffles and breathless shuddering, Sadie descended the stairs.

"It's Monday, Madeline. Daddy's at work."

Madeline would not even turn to look at her. She faced the wooden door instead. Sadie moved past her to the kitchen and took the lid off the cake tin. There were two puff pastries left, both sprinkled with sesame seeds, but only one with a potato filling. Sadie bought two dozen from Schwartz's Bakery before the weekend. She couldn't resist a bite of the flaky dough and the warm sweet, salty filling, and ate a half dozen on the way home. Mrs. Schwartz was a tiny, bent woman with a bump on the bridge of her nose and a shock of white hair. She crept about the tiny bakery carefully, as if she were afraid her fragile bones might shatter into pieces, yet she baked the best pastries in all of West Oak Lane. Mrs. Schwartz always threw a few extras in the bag for Madeline. Had it not been for these, there would be none left.

Madeline followed Sadie into the kitchen and opened her hand for the pastry. She squeezed it in her fist, potato filling oozing through her fingers, and shoved her fist in her mouth.

"Juice," said Madeline, still chewing as she handed Sadie her big girl's cup.

"You had enough juice all weekend, thanks to your father. Today, it's milk."

Madeline frowned. Sadie mirrored her sour face.

"That works on your father, but not me." She filled the cup and gave it back to Madeline.

"Drink your milk."

WITH MADELINE FINALLY CALM, SADIE settled into her usual morning routine. She cooked a hot breakfast - Madeline wanted none of it - and watched the morning news. After checking the circulars for specials at the markets, she wrote out a list of groceries, while sipping a cup of black coffee. She didn't realize she'd nodded off until a piercing shriek, followed by objects striking the wall, startled her awake. She ran from the kitchen and found Madeline sitting cross-legged on the living room floor, forming faces out of colored wooden blocks. When her works of art didn't quite turn out the way she imagined, she let out a shrill screech, grabbed a handful of blocks in each fist, and hurled them across the room striking the wall. Seconds after the blocks came to rest atop a growing heap on the floor, Madeline's mouth remained stretched open and her head thrown back, her angry and persistent wail rattling Sadie's nerves.

Sadie glared at the three foot square area of scuff marks and chipped paint on the wall just below a row of portraits - Martin Luther King on the left, a smiling Nixon on the right and their family portrait in the middle. It was Tucker's ridiculous idea. Sadie didn't mind the pictures of King and Nixon in the house, but did Tucker have to hang them in a row like they were all members of the same family?

"Madeline, Stop it! Stop throwing those blocks and stop screaming!"

Madeline stopped yelling long enough to catch her breath and inhale. Then she screamed louder while reaching for another fist full of blocks.

At least she's sitting still, Sadie thought. When Madeline was really angry, she kicked and screamed stormy tantrums from one end of the room to the other, colliding with the legs of tables and chairs in her path and bruising her shins and thighs.

"Madeline, I'm tired and I need a break." She glanced at the clock. "Noon. It's time for lunch." After lunch it would be time for Madeline to take a nap. Lunch was easy. Naps, on the other hand, were more a test of wills than a break for Sadie, since Madeline elected to scream for the duration of her two hour nap time. Pearl told her to stick to her guns and just let Madeline 'cry it out' no matter how long it took her to fall asleep. But Madeline could scream for an hour straight, without pause, and Sadie couldn't bear the incessant yelling without thoughts of harming her own child, so she elected to skip the battle of the nap. Pearl told her she was a fool to give in so easily. Sadie didn't care. Giving up was worth the peace.

After lunch, Madeline resumed hurling blocks while Sadie mopped the kitchen floor and folded the laundry. Then she and Madeline walked to the Farmer's Market for more potatoes and eggs. The Farmer's Market was only two blocks east yet Sadie took a roundabout route that took fifteen minutes longer for the sole purpose of tiring Madeline out. Her tactic proved successful for as soon as the clerk bagged her groceries, Madeline tugged Sadie's slacks and raised her arms.

"Up. Pick me up!"

Sadie slipped the handle of the bag over her shoulder and hoisted Madeline to her hip. The rhythm of Sadie walking lulled her to sleep. She wouldn't sleep for long but Sadie was grateful for even a half hour catnap. Once home, Sadie settled her into her playpen, covered her with a light cotton blanket, and left the room on her toes.

It was Sadie's intention to catch an hour or so of soaps – the characters' lives were far more intriguing than her own everyday existence – but dealing with Madeline was so tiresome, and the house was so peaceful, that soon after sitting on the living room sofa and clicking on the T.V., she dozed off. Keys jingling in the front door lock awakened her.

Sadie rose, her finger to her lips.

"Shh... Madeline's still napping," she told Tucker, while stealing a quick glance at the clock. "I should have started dinner by now."

Tucker followed her to the kitchen. "How'd the day go?" he asked.

"Tough, as usual."

"What happened?"

"It's Madeline. I can't manage her, Tucker. She's headstrong, willful and too demanding for a child her age."

"What did she do?"

Sadie scrubbed and rinsed the potatoes and threw them into a pot of water. "What didn't she do? A toddler's running the house! She resorts to screaming when anything doesn't go her way, she naps whenever she wants to, so I never have a set schedule. She's intolerable on Mondays, after you've spoiled her rotten all weekend, she never goes to bed on time, and she even determines what we eat! We eat the same food over and over because Madeline is so picky. This is the sixth time this month we're having potatoes – all because it's Madeline's favorite."

"So you're throwin' the food around because you're tired of eating Madeline's favorites?" he asked with a mischievous smile.

"Don't be silly. You know there's more to it than that. Her behavior is out of control and there's no satisfying her... ever. If I read her a book or sing a song, she yells until I do it over and over again. If I'm on the phone and not paying her any attention, she kicks me until I turn around and face her. Put food on her plate that doesn't happen to be one of her favorites? It ends up on the kitchen wall. Don't tell me again that it's a phase, Tucker."

"She's a passionate child," Tucker tried to explain. "And she..."

"She's spoiled," Sadie cut in. "Probably nothing an old fashioned spanking can't fix."

"That's saying her problem has to do with discipline. There's more to Maddy than that."

"More to Madeline? She's two and a half years old. How much more could there possibly be?"

Tucker liked fresh lemonade with his dinner. He grabbed some lemons from the fridge, a knife from the cutlery rack and sliced the lemons into quarters. "She's kind to other children her age and generous with her toys. When she's happy she laughs so hard she holds her sides, and she loves to sing. She sings with a grin so big her cheeks almost cover her eyes. Her temper and stubbornness are hard to deal with now, but she'll grow out of it and..."

"Tucker, I can't connect with Madeline. She doesn't understand me and I don't understand her."

"Just because she's headstrong? Aren't all toddlers like this? You know... the terrible two's?"

"It's more than that. I... I don't have the bond that a mother is supposed to have with her child." The words came out too fast.

She said exactly what she was thinking, but she wanted to say it in a different way – a way that didn't bring into question her maternal abilities and instincts.

Tucker set the knife on the counter and turned to his wife. A scowl crept across his face. "A mother who can't bond with her child? Whoever heard of such a thing?"

"You're looking at me like I'm insane, but the only thread of commonality I have with that child is the nine months we shared the same body." Sadie cringed at the sound of her owns words. When she referred to Madeline as 'that child', it sounded as if she were talking about someone else's baby.

"You expect too much from her. You have to take the time to understand Maddy, maybe spend more one-on-one time with her."

"I'm home with her all day, every day. If that's not one-on-one time, then what is?"

"I mean time interacting with her, talking with her, not just existing in the same house."

"She closes herself to me."

"Sadie, a two year old doesn't deliberately close herself to anyone." He appeared pensive for a moment. It was evident he chose his next words with great care.

"You still blame her, don't you?" Tucker asked.

"What are you talking about?"

"You always blamed Madeline, but can't you see it was never her fault? You have to find a way to put this behind you and move on. Move on and accept that it was nobody's fault."

"Blame her? What, for God's sake would I possibly blame her for?"

Tucker took both her hands in his. "You have to stop blaming Madeline for Marcus' death. The doctor told you what happened. He called it twin to twin transfusion, and it can happen to anyone carrying more than one baby."

Sadie snatched her hands away, her eyes stretched wide open and eyebrows raised. "How dare you mention my son's name. We agreed not to do this, Tucker!"

Tucker's face darkened. "No, Sadie. *You* decided we would never talk about him again. You erased him from our lives. I didn't agree to anything!"

"Marcus has nothing to do with this. This is all about Madeline and her terrible behavior." Sadie shifted her weight from one foot to the other, her hands contracted into fists. "Even you admit she's a difficult child to raise. It feels like she's someone else's child, and her mother will be here at any moment to come and get her."

Tucker stared at his wife. His mouth hung open for several seconds.

"Say something!" Sadie implored him.

"All of this is still new to you." He spoke slowly, deliberately. "Maybe you're just getting used to being a mother. You'll adjust as time goes by, and it'll get better... it has to get better."

Sadie nodded her agreement, even though she knew he was not convinced of his owns words. They both turned and left the room without looking into each other's eyes.

Madeline squeezed her eyes shut. Her lips formed words with no sound, words she spoke only for herself. Sadie looked puzzled.

"She's making a wish," Tucker explained.

Madeline took a deep breath, and blew out the candles on her rainbow sprinkled, chocolate cupcakes. There were five in all and each held a single candle.

When Sadie said she was throwing a party, Tucker expected a swarm of kids, a birthday cake, multi-colored streamers and noise makers. But Sadie made it clear she had no intention of having a 'legion of four and five year olds traipsing through the house with sticky hands and clumsy feet, leaving a mess for her to clean up afterwards'. It was just the three of them and Madeline's five cupcakes - what Sadie referred to as a birthday celebration in a neat package.

"What did you wish for?" Sadie asked.

"It's a secret wish, mommy." Madeline was so earnest and innocent, Tucker's heart ached.

Madeline wore a pair of denim shorts, and a white blouse with lace around the sleeves and a bow at the collar. The blouse was the only girly item left in her wardrobe. She'd banned all dresses, skirts and everything pink from her closet the week before.

"I can't believe I'm already five!" She held up five fingers and grinned.

"This is for you, Maddy." Tucker handed her a box wrapped in shimmery red paper and tied with a white ribbon. Madeline ripped off the paper and ribbon and pried open the box.

"Roller skates!" she squealed. They were pale blue with shiny silver wheels and her initials sewn on the sides in fancy lettering. She strapped them on all by herself, then Tucker and Sadie each held one of her arms to help her down the front steps.

"You can let go now," she announced with her chin up and her chest puffed out.

"Not yet," Tucker warned. "First you need to learn how to…"

Before he finished delivering some general skating instructions, Madeline jerked both arms free and moved her legs with long confident strides, like the older kids in the neighborhood. It wasn't long before she was face down, her eyes an inch from the pavement. Her upper lip swelled and blood seeped from her nose. Tucker held his breath waiting for tears or perhaps an angry outburst, but Madeline pursed her lips and struggled to her feet. When Tucker reached out to help her, she turned away.

"I can do it all by myself!" she yelled over her shoulder and started off again. Madeline skated about four strides when she tumbled to the ground a second time. She maintained her resolve, righted herself and gave it one last try. After the third tumble, a skinned elbow, and scraped knees, Madeline sat on the pavement with her mouth turned upside down.

"I can't skate at all!" She cried. She unlaced her skates, hurled them onto the lawn and burst into tears, running to her mother.

Madeline threw her arms around Sadie's neck and clung to her hard. At first Sadie hesitated, then she patted her back awkwardly. Madeline visibly stiffened at Sadie's halting. She tore away from her mother and ran to Tucker, who swept her up in his warm, open arms.

"You are so brave and independent. You can't give up though. Keep trying until you get it," he encouraged.

Tucker carried her inside to bandage her knees and elbows and hold ice to her swollen lip. He turned to look back at Sadie just before going inside and was saddened by the relief and envy etched on her face. Madeline looked back as well. He hoped she didn't notice it too, but more than likely she did. Although Madeline didn't always know how to put her thoughts into words, she had the insight and understanding of an older child.

JUST BEFORE BEDTIME, MADELINE WALKED INTO Sadie's room with an exaggerated limp. Her fingers guarded her lip, as if the air might bruise it. Sadie sat at a dressing table setting her hair on large rollers.

"Mommy, do you love me?"

"That's a ridiculous question," Sadie remarked, "of course I love you. I'm your mother."

"Then why don't we ever talk or do fun things?"

"We're talking now, Madeline. If you want to do something special, let me know exactly what it is. I can't just automatically guess what you want because I'm your mother." Sadie's tone was kind, yet she slammed the comb on the dressing table.

Madeline didn't really know how to explain what she was feeling inside, but she thought a mother should just know these things. "But we don't just talk."

"About what?"

"I don't know. Regular things, I guess."

"You're not making any sense. Just tell me what you want to talk about or what you want to do and we'll make a day of it."

That wasn't really what she meant but they weren't getting anywhere and the ridges deepening on Sadie's forehead meant she'd had enough of her questions. What she really wanted to say was that Sadie was like a brick wall with no cracks or breaks. She wanted to ask Sadie why she loved her only halfway. She wanted to ask her why her hugs felt empty. But she didn't know how to say those things without making Sadie angry.

"I'll talk to daddy," she shrugged, "maybe he'll know."

***

Madeline rose early the following morning, and sat up in bed rubbing her eyes. She breathed in the hearty aroma of the coffee brewing in the kitchen. She wasn't allowed to pour a cup for herself. Tucker told her that caffeine wasn't good for her, yet she found comfort in the daily routine of inhaling the rich aromas.

"There's something I'm supposed to do today." Then she recalled her unusual encounter with the Sadie from the day before.

"Daddy!" she called out.

"He's out back!" Sadie yelled from the bedroom.

She found Tucker kneeling in the backyard tending to rows of sprouting vegetables. Usually, Madeline ran and jumped into Tucker's arms first thing in the morning. Today, she stood there in her yellow cotton pajamas staring at her toes planted firmly in the soft, morning soil, her only movement an indefinable shuddering of her shoulders from the cool morning air. In a group with other children her age, Madeline was easily recognizable. She was taller, faster, louder and braver than the rest. But today, she was somber and still.

"Mornin', Maddy."

"Morning."

She had something important to say and she didn't want to rush. Tucker sat on his heels and waited. Several seconds passed before she lifted her head to meet her father's gaze.

"Daddy, do you ever feel empty?"

"What do you mean?"

"Empty on the inside."

Tucker sat on the ground and held out his arms. Madeline sat on his lap.

"Yes, Maddy. Sometimes I feel empty. There isn't one person on this earth who hasn't felt an emptiness at one time or another."

"What do you do to feel better?"

"I spend time with people who love me."

"And do *you* love me?"

"How could I not love you?" He poked her belly and a smile wiped her serious face away. "You know, Maddy, there are people who love but don't know how to show it."

"*You* show it."

"But not everyone is able to do that."

"Does mommy love me?"

"Yes, she does."

She wanted to ask more questions about Sadie but talking about her mother made her feel guilty in a strange way.

"You come talk to me anytime you feel sad. It doesn't matter what you want to talk about. You just come.

"I will," she agreed, "but I have one more question."

"Go on," Tucker urged.

"Do you know what I wished for on my birthday?"

"Those pretty, blue roller skates?" he teased.

"Of course I wanted those," she giggled. Her smile went away and her mouth set in a straight line. "I wished for mommy to be more like a mommy." It sounded awkward but it was exactly what she meant to say. "Yea daddy, that's what I want."

"Maddy, don't forget what I told you. There will come a time when you'll need to talk to someone. Promise you'll come talk to me."

"I promise."

SADIE WATCHED THE TWO OF THEM in the backyard from the kitchen window. She bristled at her own emotional ineptness when dealing with her daughter but was powerless to control it. When she tried to build a bridge to Madeline, an image of herself holding Marcus' tiny lifeless body loomed before her, and the bonds securing the bridge crumbled into pieces. She closed the kitchen window so hard, Madeline and Tucker winced.

"It's gonna be another one of those days," Tucker sighed.

Sadie glared at them through the window. She'd heard every word.

Tucker wasn't one to eavesdrop, but Sadie talked so loudly on the phone with Pearl, he couldn't help but hear her conversation. This was quite a feat considering she was in the bedroom behind closed doors, and Tucker was downstairs in the living room. At times, he wondered if she actually *wanted* him to know what she was saying.

Sadie's conversations with Pearl were never complimentary of men. She uttered statements you'd typically hear from a woman in the company of other women, like 'men are no good', or 'honey, he's a man – he's not capable of being faithful', or his favorite, 'I should have married for money, not love'. Tucker never took offense at these statements. It was just woman talk, and he'd heard it ever since he was a little boy listening to his own mother's conversations.

"Male bashing, again," Tucker sighed. He rested in his recliner and unfolded the newspaper. Lucy was on the cover again. He found it amazing that a 3 million year old skeleton dug up in Ethiopia grabbed the front page headlines. At least it wasn't Nixon. He was sick of all the news about Watergate and impeachment. He skimmed the news article until he heard Sadie mention his name. He ignored the stereotypical comments she made about men in general, but specifically mentioning his name was worth paying attention to. He sat up straight in his chair. The newspaper fell to his feet.

"Tucker thinks…" her voice trailed off. There it was again. He tiptoed up the stairs and pressed his ear against the bedroom door.

"I'm happy for you Pearl. You have a good man. Tucker used to be a good man. When we were first married, he spoiled me rotten. Now, he doesn't give me the time of day. All he cares about is Madeline, Madeline, Madeline. Sadie, his wife, no longer exists."

Tucker's ears burned hot. *Why didn't she tell me she felt that way?*

Pearl must have changed the subject because Sadie's mood brightened.

"The Ice Capades! I missed them the last time the show was in town. I'd love to go this year."

Tucker eased back down the stairs. He had to admit there was a shred of truth in what she said. Since Madeline was born, their grown-up social life all but disappeared. It would be a nice change of pace to do something special for Sadie. He opened the newspaper's 'Entertainment' section and scanned down the page until he found the Ice Capades show. He reserved tickets for the day after Christmas. It wouldn't be an actual date since Madeline would be there, too. But at least Sadie could enjoy something she'd always wanted to do, if she even enjoyed it at all. She wasn't an easy woman to please.

A BRILLIANT MOON ILLUMINATED THE SKY, while a light, playful snow danced to the earth. To the naked eye, there was no accumulation underfoot, yet their shoes slid over the invisible ice as they waited single file outside the Spectrum.

"I told you we didn't have to leave home so early," Sadie complained.

"You never know how bad traffic will get when it starts to snow. They'll open the doors in just a few moments," Tucker said.

"Daddy, I can't wait!" Madeline's warm breath puffed white clouds into the air. Her hat sat so low, it rested on her eyelids and she held her head all the way back to look at Tucker.

"Maddy, fix your hat," Tucker laughed. The doors opened and Tucker handed over their tickets. They were the first in line at the concession stand.

"Can I get hot cocoa?" Madeline asked. Tucker ordered three.

They sat two rows from the rink still bundled in their hats and gloves while steam from the cocoa circled their faces. "Gym 'n Ice" was the first program of the evening. The performers burst onto the ice with high energy, executing acrobatics that disregarded the rules of gravity. The 'ooohs' and 'aaahs' from the spectators echoed throughout the arena.

During the next part of the show, Happy Birthday Yogi Bear, Sadie laughed out loud, and Madeline clapped her hands and squealed, reaching out to Yogi as he skated by with one foot crossing in front of the other. Later, all the cast members linked arms and formed a circle. They kicked their legs high over their heads one after the other producing a wave effect the length of the rink. Finally, they all skated off the ice and the music tapered to silence. The house lights flooded the Spectrum.

"Oh no, it's over!" Madeline cried.

"The performers are taking a break. We'll see the second part of the show in about fifteen minutes."

Intermission crept by painfully slow. Madeline grew restless. Many times, Sadie had to tell her to sit in her chair. Madeline got on her knees, cupped her hands over her mouth and whispered into Tucker's ear, "I love you, Daddy."

Tucker kissed her on the forehead. "Love you too, Maddy."

Madeline scooted to the other side of her chair and whispered, "I love you, Mommy."

"That's nice, honey," Sadie said as she pat the top of her head.

Madeline flopped back into her seat, inched her way to the side of the chair closest to Tucker and rested her head on his arm.

"Mommy loves you too," Tucker quickly added.

He glared at the side of Sadie's face willing her to turn around, but she sat very still and stared straight ahead at the vacant ice rink, her right eye twitching at random.

All at once, the lights dimmed and the sounds of the orchestra filled the room with sound. The three of them watched the remainder of the show with faces of stone, their smiles and excitement gone, and Yogi's most ludicrous antics failing to elicit any semblance of surprise or glee. They were zombies, eyes open, seeing nothing. They clapped during the finale only after thunderous applause from the crowd jolted them out of their catalepsy.

Neither of them spoke a word during the long ride home on the subway. Madeline sat between Tucker and Sadie with her eyes closed. Tucker knew from the way her eyes quivered that she wasn't asleep. It was her way of letting people know she didn't feel like talking. Her eyes remained closed even after they arrived

49

home and Tucker carried her to bed, slid off her shoes, grazed her forehead with a kiss, and tucked her comforter under her chin.

He closed the door to her bedroom then marched down the hall to the master bedroom and flung open the door. Sadie must have been about to leave the room, for she stood a foot from the door with her hand still reaching for the knob.

"What the hell is wrong with you? You couldn't tell your own daughter that you love her?" Tucker struggled to keep his voice low. He didn't want to alarm Madeline.

"You know I love her!"

"You don't show it to her, Sadie. What good is it if you keep it inside?"

"Madeline's not lacking for anything. I take very good care of her. She's healthy and…"

"That's not enough. Raising a child is about more than taking care of basic needs. What about nurturing, love? You treat her as if she isn't your own kin?"

Sadie paced back and forth.

"She needs you, Sadie. *All* of you! If only you could be honest with yourself, just this one time, and admit that this is happening because you've never gotten over Marcus. If you could get that far, maybe there's a chance at fixing this!"

Sadie stopped pacing. "He has no part in this, and stop mentioning his name!" she spat.

"If it isn't about Marcus then what's going on with you?"

"I just don't know how else to deal with her."

"Are you telling me this is just who you are? A cold, selfish woman who refuses to love her own child?" Tucker knew he went too far, but he wanted to make her uncomfortable. Perhaps then she could see herself as she really was.

Her eyes narrowed and she folded her arms across her chest. "Fine! If you really want to know the truth, *you* are the problem!"

Tucker's shoulders squared. "Me?"

"Yes, Tucker. You're part of the reason I have problems with Madeline. I admit that I don't spend as much time with her as I should, and I could be more patient with her, but you… you shut me out. It's you and Madeline on one side, and me on the other."

"That's ludicrous. We're a family. There are no sides." Tucker shook his head in disbelief.

"You and Madeline are the same kind of people, and you two get along so well. When you're together, I'm on the outside. You don't make any effort to include me. I… I…" she struggled with what to say next. "I don't know how else to explain it." She threw her hands in the air and walked to the other side of the room.

"I don't deliberately exclude you. The problem is that you don't make any effort to get involved in Madeline's life. For me, it's effortless. You, on the other hand, need an invitation!"

Sadie yanked a nightgown from the dresser and slammed the drawer shut. She walked by Tucker into the bathroom and turned on the shower.

"Please don't stop talking. Let's get to the bottom of this."

She closed the bathroom door.

There was so much more Tucker wanted to say. He knew it all boiled down to Marcus. Sadie despised Madeline because Marcus didn't survive, and Tucker made up for Sadie's lack by showering Madeline with the love and affection Sadie was unable to give. With all of his attention focused on Madeline, Sadie felt isolated, alone.

Sadie emerged from the shower wearing only a towel. Droplets of water fell from her hair. Tucker loved the way her hair curled when it was wet. He touched her hair over her right ear. Sadie flinched.

"Listen, Sadie, I would never shut you out. I admit our marriage isn't what it should be. We need time together, without Maddy... time to be a couple again. When was the last time we went out on a date?"

He lifted her chin. "What if we find a sitter for Maddy and go out to dinner - just the two of us - to a classy place with candles, maybe order a bottle of wine and talk... talk about anything and everything, like we did when we were first married."

"And waste money that we don't have? No thank you."

"Well if you won't let me take you out, I'll cook for you at home. Please, Sadie, let me do this for you."

Sadie leaned forward and rested her head on his chest.

"Fine," she mumbled.

TUCKER SPENT THE ENTIRE MORNING PREPARING for Sadie's surprise. After she left for work, he called the diner and told his boss he wouldn't be in that day. Tucker took the trolley to the flower shop, where he selected a bouquet of orchids, half of which he set in a vase as a centerpiece. The others he scattered on the front steps and around the entrance to the house. His next stop was Schwartz's bakery for the puff pastries Sadie loved so much, then he rushed home to cook her favorites - smothered pork chops, green beans, and rice with gravy. He set the table with a linen covering and the china his mother gave them as a wedding gift. They'd never used it. There was no occasion Sadie thought worthy of it. When all the details were in place, he called Sadie.

"Come home right away," he told her.

"What's wrong, Tucker?" she asked. "Is it Madeline?"

"It has nothing to do with Madeline, but I can't discuss this matter over the phone."

"It's noon. I can't leave right now. I have a ton of work to do. What's going on?"

"Just come home as fast as you can, please."

After he hung up the phone, he yanked the cord from the wall so Sadie couldn't call back with an excuse as to why she couldn't make it. Tucker grabbed a chilled bottle of white wine from the freezer, set it next to the orchids, pulled the drapes closed and lit the candles.

Sadie worked twenty minutes away, yet arrived nearly two hours later. Tucker reheated the meal three times and replenished the ice in the bucket twice. Undaunted, he rose to greet her, standing tall and proud in front of the feast he'd prepared.

"Hello, my queen," he said as he presented it all to Sadie with a grand arching sweep of his arm.

Her eyes grazed over the table and her nose tilted upward. Sadie frowned as if inhaling the putrid scent of rotting garbage.

"I came home from work early for this?" She waved her hand through the air. "Now I'll have twice as much work to do tomorrow. I don't have time for these games Tucker."

"I told you I was going to cook for you."

"You didn't tell me it was today. Why not an evening or the weekend?"

"Madeline is home from school in the evening. I wanted us to spend some time together alone. Besides, if I told you what I was up to you would have found a way to avoid it. I know this looks desperate and the timing may not be perfect, but you leave me no choice. I wanted to share a nice meal without Madeline to distract us, talk without interruption, talk about us, Maddy and what we can do to keep our marriage alive. Face it, Sadie, things haven't been rosy between us."

"Candles and flowers aren't going to change anything. This is a waste of my time." She started up the stairs.

"Wait... please... I'm trying here."

"Madeline... us... I don't want to talk about any of it," she told him.

"Then let's have dinner and talk about something else... anything else... whatever you want."

She stopped halfway up the stairs, and for a moment it appeared as if she were considering Tucker's proposition. But something in Sadie's expression remained unyielding. Her face hardened and she continued climbing the stairs.

"I have a busy day tomorrow. I'm taking a nap."

"At least fix a plate and take it up with you."

"Not hungry."

Tucker blew out the candles and opened the drapes. Alone, he ate the dinner he prepared. He fixed a plate for Sadie and covered it with aluminum foil.

"Whenever you're ready, your plate is on the stove. It's three o'clock so I'm gonna go pick up Madeline from school," he hollered up the stairs. Sadie normally picked Madeline up from school but she still hadn't emerged from the bedroom.

"Wasted day, wasted effort," Tucker thought as he walked to Madeline's school.

He heard the dismissal bell ring half a block from the school, and jogged the rest of the way. The second Madeline spotted him, she sprinted across the playground and jumped into his arms.

"I didn't know you were picking me up today!" Mud caked her jeans and sneakers, and her once baby blue jacket was a dull shade of gray.

"Something else for Sadie to be angry about," he mumbled.

"What did you say daddy?"

"Your mom's gonna throw a fit when she sees you."

"Just cause I'm dirty?"

"Just cause you're dirty," he mimicked her voice. Madeline melted into giggles.

On the way home, Madeline chatted about recess, art and playing the cymbals in music. She was telling Tucker about the seedlings her class planted at school, when Sadie greeted them at the front door.

"What were you doing to get so filthy?" Sadie asked.

"Playin' football," Madeline grinned.

"Why would you girls want to play football?"

"Those prissy girls in my class don't play ball. I was playing with the boys."

"You what?"

"And my team won," she smiled. The space that her front tooth used to occupy was empty.

"And when did you lose that tooth?"

"This mornin' when I got tackled," she said nonchalantly, then skipped to the kitchen for chocolate milk and cookies. It was her favorite after-school snack.

"That's my girl," Tucker smiled.

"She likes being tackled? Don't encourage her. She's like having a boy in the house."

"She's making use of her natural gifts. She's tall, strong, athletic…"

"That's bull!" Sadie spat back. "When will she learn how to act like a young lady? Perhaps sit with her legs crossed, comb her hair from time to time or wear something that's remotely feminine. You can't keep encouraging this tomboy crap!"

"There's no harm in it. Besides, you'd find fault in anything having to do with Madeline!" He lowered his voice when he said Madeline's name.

"What's that supposed to me…?"

"Are you okay, Madeline?" Tucker interrupted, as Madeline walked past them to go up the stairs, balancing cookies in one hand and milk, spilling over the rim, in the other.

"I'm fine."

Red blotches formed on Sadie's cheeks.

Tucker made sure Madeline was in her bedroom with the door closed before resuming their discussion. If he allowed it, Sadie would say anything in front of her, even the most hateful of words.

MADELINE HEARD WHAT SADIE SAID ABOUT HER, but she didn't mind. She liked being different from the other girls. She beat all the boys in arm wrestling matches and was the only girl picked to play on the kickball team at recess. She popped a milk-laden cookie into her mouth. It was so soft, it melted onto her tongue.

The conversation downstairs escalated into a noisy argument. Madeline went into the bathroom and turned both faucets on, as far as they could go, so the sound of the running water would drown out their voices. But Madeline didn't have to hear their words to know what they were saying because they yelled the same phrases at each other over and over again. Madeline moved her lips as they spat the words.

"You can't keep treating Madeline like this," Tucker argued. "Why can't you just love her?"

"I do love her!" Sadie screamed. "She's not missing anything! She's perfectly fine! You shutting me out is the problem."

Madeline wondered if it was her fault their marriage was so unfriendly, since she was the topic of their worst arguments. She was puzzled at how she was connected to Sadie's unhappiness, yet she knew that somehow she was responsible. But there was something else that baffled Madeline even more. It felt like a puzzle with a missing piece. This missing piece was the cause of all of their arguments, making Daddy sad and Mommy angry. The missing piece was a stranger. Madeline never met this stranger but the mere mention of his name sent her mind racing for answers. She turned off the running faucet in time to hear Sadie and Tucker speak aloud the stranger's name.

"Can't you see this is all because of Marcus?" Tucker's angry voice cracked.

"Stop mentioning his name! I don't want to hear it ever again!" Sadie screamed.

"Marcus." Madeline whispered to her reflection in the mirror over the bathroom sink. "Who is Marcus?"

Madeline's overnight bag sat by the front door, the zipper bulged at the seams. She'd packed far too many clothes for just one night, but wanted to be prepared for anything that might arise.

"I'm all ready to go," she told Sadie. It was four o'clock on a Saturday afternoon and Sadie still wore her robe and slippers from the night before. She lounged with her feet propped on the living room sofa, a cup of mint tea at her lips.

"Go where?" Sadie asked.

"Don't you remember? Angie Jackson's sleepover is tonight."

The invitation arrived in the mail two weeks earlier. Madeline assumed it was sent to the wrong address, until she flipped the envelope over and saw her own name in bold letters. Why Angie invited her, of all people to the sleepover, was a mystery. They had never shared the same circle of friends and the two had nothing in common besides being in the eighth grade.

Prim and polished with manicured nails and arched eyebrows, Angie never left home without coordinating her outfit with her shoes. She carried a compact in her purse and popped it open several times a day to ensure her curls were tousled to perfection. Although her chest remained flat as a boy's, she wore a training bra and walked with her back arched and her chest jutted out. Madeline thought she looked ridiculous and had no problem telling her such in the event she asked. Who in their right mind would pretend to have breasts?

Madeline preferred jeans, sweats, sneakers and oversized T-shirts, topped off with an occasional baseball cap if she could get out of the house without Sadie noticing. Sadie arranged a standing appointment twice a month at the hair salon for a press and curl, but Madeline had no use for fancy hairstyles. The minute she stepped foot outside the salon, she pulled her hair into a ponytail. Madeline was an athlete. She played basketball and ran the one hundred yard dash. Fancy hair was a hindrance in the middle of a layup or when outrunning her opponents during track meets. The eighth grade boys stole sidelong glances at the changes taking place in Madeline's body – the rounded hips and young breasts – yet Madeline remained unaware of her physical ascent into womanhood.

It was during science class, that Angie and Madeline's paths intersected. Their teacher divided the class into teams of two for the annual science fair project, and Madeline and Angie were partners. The girls had four weeks to complete the project. They agreed to meet on Wednesdays in the library after school, and Saturday mornings at Madeline's house. Angie only showed up for that first Wednesday meeting. Her excuses for being absent the other days were always convincing - cramps, dentist appointment, too much homework, etc. In the end, Madeline completed the entire project on her own, earning them both an "A". Perhaps the invitation to the sleepover was Angie's way of showing gratitude?

"Are you going to drive me or what?" Madeline asked Sadie. Tucker bought a used Toyota the year before. After three failed attempts, Sadie passed her driver's test, but she never drove the car, insisting that Tucker chauffeur her wherever she needed to go.

"Why didn't you remind me?" Sadie complained. "I would have made sure your father was here to drive you to Angie's."

Madeline rolled her eyes. "God forbid you actually get in the car and drive me yourself. It's not like you don't have a license."

"I don't like the tone of your voice!" Sadie snapped.

The front door opened. "Calm down ladies," Tucker intervened. "I'll drop you off at the party."

"You're home from work early! Thanks for not forgetting about me, Daddy," Madeline said as she cut her eyes at Sadie.

"Only for you, my dear. Let's go!"

Outside, he loaded her overnight bag in the trunk of the car. If it weren't for Tucker, she'd have no life at all. He took her everywhere – school dances, track meets, doctor's appointments. He even suffered through hours of shopping with her at the mall.

"Are you nervous?" he asked, during the short drive to Angie's house.

It was Madeline's first sleepover. She always wanted to have one of her own, except that when she asked Sadie about planning a party, Sade always put her off.

"I'm not nervous, just excited."

The Jacksons also lived in a row house in West Oak Lane, except theirs was on a corner lot with a large backyard and a family room addition. The couple greeted them at the front door. Mr. Jackson's bald head barely reached his wife's shoulder. He had cheeks that hung below his chin, and his wide belly covered his belt. Thick, bushy brows framed his eyes. His wife gazed down on him so lovingly, Madeline guessed his beauty must have been on the inside since the outside was not at all easy on the eyes. They were at ease in each other's company, unlike Tucker and Sadie who maneuvered around one another like total strangers, growing increasingly contemptuous with each passing year.

Tall and broad, Mrs. Jackson was a capable mother and wise grandmother all wrapped up in one person. She spoke in calm, comforting tones and had a way of looking at you - as if she understood your worries and fears. In her presence Madeline felt exposed, and wavered between looking in her eyes and turning away.

"It's nice to meet you, Madeline," said Mrs. Jackson. She pulled Madeline into a warm embrace. Madeline resisted the urge to linger in her arms.

"The rest of the girls are in the basement. Go on down."

Mr. Jackson grabbed Tucker's hand and pumped it up and down. "Don't worry Mr. Stovall, we'll take good care of your daughter."

Madeline scanned the group of girls in the basement. There were ten in all. None were the type of girl she'd hang out with. They were part of the pretty, popular 'in' group. They all dressed the same - short skirts and too tight shirts, with hair permed silky straight. She knew what they were talking about before even joining in the conversation – boys and fashion – although she found it hard to believe they could hear each other speak above the music videos blaring from the old floor-model television. Madeline joined the girls on a leather sectional.

Angie made no effort at all to pull her into the conversation, not that Madeline was dying to join in considering they were talking about where to buy the best-fitting jeans. Madeline figured she'd have to be the one to make the effort otherwise she'd likely sit alone unnoticed her entire stay.

She waited for a lull in the conversation, "Angie, we aced that science project, eh?"

"We rocked it!" Angie put her hand in the air for a high five. It wasn't Madeline's thing but she high-fived her anyway. "I've been wanting to ask you," Angie went on.

I knew she wanted something. Here we go.

"So," she said then stopped to pop her chewing gum, "we're allowed to pick partners for the final research paper in science class. How about we partner up again? We're an awesome team!" She held up her hand for another stupid high five.

All the other girls turned to look at Madeline.

Hell no, Madeline wanted to say. Her mind searched for some clever, yet elusive, answer. An awkward silence swelled among them until Mr. Jackson broke the silence.

"I'm coming down," he hollered, then emerged with boxes of steaming - hot pizzas stacked in his arms. Mrs. Jackson followed with two liter bottles of soda.

"Enjoy, ladies," she said in a sweet singsong voice. They finished off the entire batch of pizzas then Angie sent her father out for more.

Mrs. Jackson retreated to the kitchen to bake fudge brownies for dessert. She half- hummed, half-sang to Prince's "Little Red Corvette" on the radio, and stirred the rich batter in a wide plastic bowl. She didn't know Madeline was right behind her and jumped, letting out a small scream when Madeline popped from the basement doorway.

"I'm sorry, Mrs. Jackson. I didn't mean to scare you," Madeline said.

"I didn't hear you come in, honey." Mrs. Jackson paused to catch her breath. "Can I get you something?"

"I'd like to help with the brownies." Madeline looked at her shoes, surprised by the jitteriness in her voice.

"I'm finished with the mixing. I just have to pour this into the pan and let it bake." Mrs. Jackson glanced at Madeline then blurted out, "You can preheat the oven to three twenty five."

Once Madeline turned on the oven, Mrs. Jackson began tidying up. Madeline pulled out a chair and sat at the kitchen table with her hands folded, as if waiting to be told what to do next.

"Well I'm all done in here," said Mrs. Jackson. She folded her arms across her chest.

Madeline took a few steps toward the basement stairwell then spun back around.

"Are you sure there isn't something I can help you with?" she asked again.

"Well I was planning to bake sugar cookies for you girls to take home tomorrow in gift bags…"

"I can do that!"

"You get the butter and eggs from the fridge and I'll grab the rest from the pantry."

Madeline dumped all the ingredients into the mixing bowl. Mrs. Jackson watched while Madeline mixed them all together. Flour powdered her chin, and batter coated her finger tips. Madeline looked up to mist in Mrs. Jackson's eyes.

"Are you alright?"

"You remind me of the first time I baked cookies with Angie. She was four years old then, and had the cutest, tiniest oven mitt and apron."

"Thank you for letting me do this. This is really fun." Madeline told her.

"Don't you bake at home with your mom?" Mrs. Jackson blotted her eyes.

There was a swell of giggling and chatting from the girls in the basement, then the room grew silent as someone turned the volume up for Michael Jackson's "Beat It" video.

"This is the first time I've baked cookies."

"I'm sure you've baked other desserts… cupcakes… muffins?"

Madeline shook her head.

Mrs. Jackson looked at Madeline with her head to the side. "The next time we bake something special, I'll have Angie call and invite you over. It's best to know how to do your own baking these days," she explained. "The best bakery in Oak Lane is closed. As a matter of fact, all those quaint little shops are closing one after another. It was so much nicer when we first moved in."

She donned a mitt, took the brownies out of the oven, and walked over to the basement stairs. "Ladies, dessert's ready."

There were squeals followed by footsteps pounding the stairs. The girls poured tall glasses of milk, consumed all the brownies, and rushed back to the basement before they missed the next selection on the video countdown. Since there was no more work to do in the kitchen, Madeline followed them downstairs.

Mrs. Jackson checked in on them from time to time bearing pitchers of soda and iced tea. The girls were too engrossed in each other's gossip to notice, except for Madeline who thanked her for every kind gesture.

By three in the morning, the giggling and chatting ceased. Mrs. Jackson dimmed the lights, and tiptoed around the room to make sure they were all nestled in their sleeping bags. Only Madeline lay with her eyes wide open. When Mrs. Jackson pulled her sleeping bag over her bare arms, Madeline's eyes filled with tears.

"What's wrong, honey?" Mrs. Jackson smoothed her hair and touched her cheek.

"I don't know. I sort of feel like I miss my mom, but not in the usual sense because she's different, you know. I miss..." Madeline held back a sob.

"Shh," Mrs. Jackson put her finger over Madeline's lips, "I know, my dear," she whispered. She settled on the floor alongside Madeline, and wrapped her arms around her. Madeline allowed herself to be cradled, rocked. She was a little girl, resting in a mother's warm bosom.

Madeline feared one of the other girls might wake up and witness her regression to childhood. Ridicule and shame would surely follow. After all, they were nearly thirteen years old. But Madeline was far more afraid that this warmth, that enveloped her like a healing cocoon, might soon end. She dozed in the woman's arms – the most restful sleep she had ever known - and awakened just as daylight streamed through the basement window. By then, Mrs. Jackson was gone.

***

Tucker picked Madeline up the next day just before dusk. The house was warmly lit and the sounds of laughter and pleasant voices drifted outdoors. Mrs. Jackson answered the door, Madeline by her side.

"How did it go?" he asked.

"You have a lovely daughter. She's welcome to come anytime." She gave Madeline one last hug. Tucker cringed when he saw how Madeline clung to the woman, longing etched on her young face.

"Th… thanks for inviting her," he stammered. "Let's go, Maddy."

"I mean it. Come any time," she told Madeline.

Madeline turned to wave at Mrs. Jackson several times while walking to the car. Once at the curb, she stopped and half-turned with one hand on the car, the other hand continued waving. If she were a little girl it would seem fitting, but now…

"Maddy, get in the car," Tucker told her.

Madeline was pensive, almost melancholy during the ride home. Normally talkative when she and Tucker were alone in the car, she had nothing to say.

"Didn't you have a good time?" Tucker asked.

"The best time ever."

"Why such a long face?"

"Daddy, I didn't want to leave."

What she really means is that she doesn't want to go home, Tucker thought.

He didn't want to go home to Sadie, either. They'd argued nearly the entire night. He was puzzled as to why Sadie told Madeline she forgot about the sleepover, considering he reminded her the night before. When he asked her why she pretended to forget, she had no real answer. She insisted her treatment of Madeline was fair, then accused Tucker of catering to Madeline and shutting her out, except this time she went on to add that she was sorry she ever married him.

"If we had never married, Madeline wouldn't be here," he told her. The expression on her face meant that not only had she considered the possibility, but she'd somehow made peace with it.

No, Tucker didn't want to go home, either.

A roaring wind stripped the leaves from the branches of trees and hurled them to the ground. Shrubs and vines succumbed to the gusts, and power lines dipped and swayed. Flocks of birds migrated southward, their sweet morning birdsong replaced by the discordant calls of migrating geese. Were they cries of sorrow, lamenting their hurried departure from familiar land, or were they cries of exuberance, as they raced toward their new lives in southerly climes? It didn't matter to Tucker. What mattered was their freedom.

His own, he relinquished years earlier. He relinquished the freedom of acknowledging and professing the birth and death of his son, and he relinquished his right to love his daughter without wrath and hostility. No, Tucker knew no freedom. Life with Sadie was bondage.

Tucker had been driving ever since he finished his shift at work two hours earlier. He drove to the city limits and back, stopping once to fill his tank with gas. He had no destination in mind. Driving allowed him to think in solitude. His head pounded from thinking so hard - thinking about Sadie, his marriage, and his weighty, overwhelming desire to be free of it all.

Dusk descended. A fitting backdrop for his thoughts, for just as the day was coming to a close, so was his marriage. *Will it survive another month? Perhaps a year?* What Tucker knew for certain was that the woman he woke up to each day at dawn was not the woman he married, and after more than a decade of pleading, compromising and arguing, it was unlikely Sadie would change. Sadie despised Tucker's relationship with Madeline more than ever, and Madeline paid the price for it every day. Sadie's vengeance, although subtle, was most sinister, for it manifested itself covertly in the form of disdain, neglect and selfishness.

Tucker came to a stop in front of his home and parked his car. The quaint, cottage-like house painted a deceptive picture. Curtains with lace trim hung in the downstairs windows, yellow chrysanthemums lined the steps from the porch leading to the pavement, and smoke circled from the chimney. For several moments Tucker was drawn in. Weary after a long day's work, he wanted nothing more than to slip on his comfortable shoes, stretch out on the recliner and rest his head on a pillow. But Sadie's shadow passing in front of the living room window offered a grim reminder of the task at hand. The time had come to decide what to do about his marriage.

He left his car parked in front of the house in the event Sadie might need it that evening, then walked to the end of the street and turned the corner onto the main road. He boarded a trolley to the bus terminal and caught a subway to center city. There, he checked into a hotel.

"Third floor," the hotel attendant told him in a nasally voice. He held out the room key in one hand. In the other was the newspaper he stopped reading only long enough to swipe Tucker's credit card. It wasn't like Tucker to skip pleasantries, but the clerk lacked the simplest of courtesies.

The elevator groaned and lunged before depositing Tucker on the third floor. He unlocked the door to his room and switched on the lights. Layers of dust blanketing the lampshades cast a dim pallor on the room's off-white walls, the blue and gold draperies were a pitiful contrast to the green and brown floral spread, and the heat was cranked so high, his shirt dampened within seconds. But these drab details were mere trifle disturbances since he came to this place for neither comfort nor pleasure. Tucker turned off the lights and lay in darkness.

"I've done all I can do, Lord," Tucker prayed. "Do I stay in a failing marriage year after year. What if it doesn't change? If I leave, will Sadie make an effort to get along with Madeline, or will she blame her for my absence?" He considered taking Madeline with him, but she was too close to finishing high school to disrupt her life now.

Tucker tossed and turned with his thoughts all night. When daylight streamed through an opening in the drapes, he still had no clear answer. He began his journey home that morning with a silent prayer that the path would soon reveal itself.

BERORE TUCKER COULD FISH HIS KEYS from his pants pocket, Madeline flung open the door. The wind chimes hanging over the front porch clinked and swayed.

"Daddy, where have you been? Why didn't you call?" She looked him up and down.

Tucker became acutely aware that he wore the same clothes from the day before. He ran his fingers over his stubbly chin. He hadn't shaved either.

"I didn't mean to worry you Maddy. I needed some time alone to think."

"You still should have called. I was afraid something horrible happened to you. I couldn't sleep at all last night. I was so worried I even missed school today!" Her eyes were red and rimmed with dark circles.

"Where's your mother?"

Madeline pointed to the kitchen. Tucker walked through the dining room, his footsteps hollow on the wood floor.

"Sadie," Tucker greeted her.

"Mornin'," she replied. Rigid and stoic, Sadie said nothing more after her monotone 'good morning'. She stared into the kitchen sink while she washed and dried the breakfast dishes. Tucker watched her closely for some reaction to his absence the night before. There was none. She was a blank canvas. In that single moment, Tucker decided on the direction of the rest of their lives. If Sadie screamed insults about his failure to be a good husband, and hurled dishes at him from across the kitchen, he would have stayed. If she cussed and swore at him for spending the night away from home and failing to inform her of his whereabouts, he would have stayed. It was her indifference that eliminated any doubt about the path that lay open before him. It was time for freedom.

Tucker stared at the back of Sadie's head and spoke the words he himself dreaded to hear, but desperately needed to say.

"Sadie, there's no use in my staying. I'm gonna pack my things and go."

Sadie picked up a glass bowl, scrubbed it with a sponge, set it on the counter, then picked up another dish one after the other. Sudsy water pooled beneath them.

Tucker said it again, louder this time and waited. The neighbor's car turned over after three attempts to start it, another neighbor called out repeatedly for her cat, Fredo. The sun bounced off of Sadie's gold watch creating a flash of light. He held his breath for some reaction, no matter how small – a tremor of her hand, a bend of her shoulder or perhaps an exasperated sigh. There was nothing.

"Mommy, say something!"

"Stay out of it!" Sadie yelled.

"Tell him to stay!"

"This is not your business, Madeline!"

Tucker left the kitchen and took the stairs to the bedroom. Madeline followed and watched him stuff clothes into a duffel bag.

"I'll come get the rest of my things when I find a place."

"Daddy, you can't leave me."

"I'm not leaving *you*, Maddy. It's just that your mother and I don't get along anymore. I have to go."

Madeline knew it was far more complicated than he told her, but she let him go on anyway. He grasped her shoulders and looked right into her eyes.

"If I thought your mother and I could work things out I'd stay, but there's nothing more I can do. I'll always be a part of your life and I'll let you know where I am as soon as I get settled. You're already in high school. Before you know it, you'll be all grown up and this will all be behind you."

"Daddy, I need you to stay," she pleaded, the knot in her chest growing tighter.

"It might be better for you here if I'm gone."

"I don't want it to be better. I want you here." But even as she uttered the words she knew it was useless. There was a finality in his bearing that would not yield to any pleas, not even hers.

Duffle bag in hand, Tucker descended the stairs, Madeline trailing behind him. At the bottom of the landing, he held her while she clung to him and sobbed. For the last time, he glanced at his wife's stiff back, her face turned to the kitchen window, then left his home.

***

Watching Tucker leave was like ripping off a limb, yet his departure, although painful, was not surprising. Within the privacy of their home, her parents coexisted like total strangers. They survived entire days without uttering a single word to one another, and night after night Madeline watched them eat dinner directly across the table from one another and not exchange so much as a glance. When they did chance to speak, vicious arguments ensued.

Madeline watched Tucker until he was no longer in sight, then she stormed into the kitchen and stood behind her mother.

"Why did you let him go?" she demanded. "He would have stayed if you said something. Why'd you let him go?"

Sadie finally turned around. Her face was twisted, ugly. "Madeline, I'm glad to get rid of him. I'm sick of living with a man who cares nothing about me. All he ever did was cater to you since the day you were born. I was his wife for God's sake, and all I was good for was cooking and cleaning. I may as well have been his live-in maid."

"You're jealous of me, aren't you?" Madeline asked incredulously.

Sadie spun around. Madeline felt the sting of her hand on her cheek, before she even noticed Sadie raise her hand.

"Can't you see this is all your fault? Always needing, whining, complaining, 'daddy I want, daddy I need'. Thanks to you, Tucker had no room for me!"

"Don't you put this on me! You are the problem! You caused him to leave!"

Sadie lunged at Madeline, her hand raised to strike her again. Madeline backed out of the kitchen and ran to her room.

"I hate it that I'm stuck here with you," she hollered down the stairs. "Daddy was lucky to get away."

Apollo Evers' 1987 Mustang convertible rolled to a stop. He closed his eyes, breathing in the scent of the rich, dark leather. Protective paper covered the floor mats, and the manufacturer's sticker adhered to the driver's side window. He'd already hung miniature flags from the rearview mirror. The green, yellow and black striped flag represented the Jamaican heritage passed down by his mother, and the red, white and blue flag, a reminder of how far he'd come considering his father was a laborer from the south with limited means.

Apollo exited his new car and removed his shades. He basked in his own prosperity, for his new car sat parked behind him, and in front of him stood the home he'd just made settlement on that very morning. It was a blur of signing endless documents. He was careful about reading the fine print in the beginning, but at the end he signed his name blindly, eager to end the tedious and endless progression of paperwork. He could have chosen a more affluent neighborhood in which to settle, but this middle income community provided him with a comfortable lifestyle, yet left him with more than enough money to afford a few luxuries.

The home was large for a single man but Apollo imagined it alive and bustling with a beautiful wife and children one day. He was in no hurry, however, considering all the fine women delighting his senses as he cruised the streets of Philadelphia.

At twenty seven years of age, Apollo was more successful than anyone in his entire family, yet he was quick to admit that it was hard work and careful handling of his finances that brought him prosperity, not education or upbringing. He landed his first job at the age of fourteen bagging groceries in a supermarket. By sixteen, he rose at four in the morning to deliver newspapers on his bicycle before school. After school, he mopped floors at a candy store, and was later promoted to cashier. Apollo's father gave him a glass piggy bank when he earned his first dollar. At the end of every week, Apollo fed his spare change to the pig. When the pig could hold no more, he opened a savings account at a local bank and was diligent about depositing half of his earnings each week. Right after his twenty-first birthday, he landed a job as a Merchant Marine, and his considerable savings combined with his keen business sense earned him a twin home in West Oak Lane and his very first brand new car. Apollo accepted no handouts along the way. All that he had he earned on his own, and he was pretty damn arrogant about it.

As Apollo basked in his success, he had the distinct feeling of one who is on the verge of fulfilling a destiny. He recalled a story his mother told of the night he was born. His father, elated at the first sight of his newborn son, fell to his knees and looked to the heavens. He prayed aloud that his firstborn would rise above the fate of his ancestors and fulfill a nobler, loftier destiny. He named his only son Apollo, after the Greek god who drove the mighty sun across the sky in a carriage. His father succeeded in instilling great pride in him, for Apollo was certain that his purpose was just as lofty as the mythical god whose name he bore.

PEARL MANNING HAD A CLEAR, UNOBSTRUCTED view of Apollo from her living room bay window. He bent over to take the 'for sale' sign off of his lawn, then strolled down the walkway toward his front door.

"He has to be handsome with an ass like that," she said aloud, even though no one else was home to hear her. Just before opening the door, Apollo turned and looked in the direction of Pearl's house, as if he sensed someone was watching.

Pearl whistled. "A cute ass *and* he's fine." She picked up the phone and dialed Sadie.

"Girl, a drop dead, gorgeous man just bought the house across the street. He's the best looking thing I've seen in a long time in this neighborhood. Stop everything and get over here!"

"If he looks that good he's probably already married," Sadie argued. "Besides, I have too much to do today, and I don't have a decent thing to wear."

"For someone who's always talking 'bout findin' a man with loot, you sure have a lot of excuses."

"How would you know if the man has any money?"

"How many poor men do you know with a brand new '87 Stang *and* a home? I'm telling you, this one won't last long with all the single women around here. This could be the one, girl. Get your tail over here. And hurry up!"

Moments later, Sadie and Pearl both peered out of Pearl's bay window waiting for Apollo to emerge.

"Pearl, you know we're too old for this nonsense. Look at us sittin' in this window trying to sneak a peek at a man like we're fifteen again. We should be ashamed…"

"Look, Sadie. There he is."

Apollo strolled to the perimeter of his property, looking from one end of the street to the other as if sizing up his neighbors' homes. Sharp, strong lines sculpted his jaw and chin, and his restless eyes darted everywhere, missing no detail. He wore a pair of stonewashed jeans, with a white silk shirt open to the middle of his chest. A camel-colored belt matched his boots. He took long strides with his shoulders back and his head tilted slightly upwards, his gait and countenance divulging his arrogance and pride.

Sadie grabbed her belly, "I haven't had a flutter over a man since I met Tucker. No wonder you called me over here. It's not every day a man like that moves into the neighborhood. I have to meet him," she said, "although he does seem a bit young."

"What's age got to do with it? He's over eighteen, so he's fair game."

Three houses to the right of Apollo, a young, alluring choco-late-skinned woman lifted a bag of groceries from the trunk of her car and walked down the sidewalk with an exaggerated roll of her tight behind with each deliberate step she took. Model thin and nearly six feet tall, it was evident she was clearly working it.

Sadie crossed her fingers, "I hope he doesn't look her way. He'd be a fool not to run after that one."

"Damn," she exclaimed as Apollo caught sight of the young woman.

Just then, the girl glanced sideways at Apollo and conveniently dropped her bag. Oranges and apples rolled onto the concrete. Apollo sprung into action, running to the woman's aid.

"Go stop him!" Pearl yelled.

***

Sadie scurried out of Pearl's house and ran across the street.

"Hello, there!" she yelled, waving both hands in the air.

Apollo stopped and spun around.

Breathless, she stumbled onto the curb. "Welcome to the neighborhood," she said, "I'm Sadie."

He extended his hand to Sadie while simultaneously glancing back at the young beauty. She rolled her eyes and stooped to pick up her own groceries when she realized Apollo wasn't coming to her rescue. He turned back to Sadie.

"Nice to meet you, Sadie, I'm Apollo," He nodded toward Pearl's house. "Do you live there across the street?"

"No, I was visiting a friend but I live on the next street over." Sadie paused. She was still out of breath. "I couldn't help noticing you. You have quite a striking presence."

Apollo smiled. "This will definitely be interesting."

"Pardon me?"

"You seem a little winded. Are you okay?" he asked.

"I'm fine, but you have quite an accomplishment, Apollo," she gestured toward his house. "Congratulations on your new home."

"I'm looking forward to settling in. By this time tomorrow, the moving van will have already delivered the boxes and I'll be in the midst of unpacking."

"When does your family arrive?"

"I'm single," Apollo said with a sly smirk.

Sadie's grin practically consumed her face. She noticed Apollo looking her over from head to toe. She wished she'd had the time to change into something more seductive. At least she wasn't still wearing her work uniform, but the oversized shirt and stirrup pants she wore weren't suitable for a potential suitor either.

"Where are you from, Apollo?"

"I've lived in the Olney section of Philly for the past three years, but I'm originally from the south. My family moved north when I started school, and you?"

"Home grown. Born and raised in the City Of Brotherly Love."

Droplets of rain splattered their faces. Both looked up at the sky as it changed from blue to gray.

"Storm's on the way, we better get indoors," he said.

"Apollo, it was truly a pleasure meeting you. If you're in the neighborhood Sunday at about six, stop by and I'll cook you up a 'welcome to the neighborhood' dinner. Can I leave you my phone number?"

He inserted two fingers into his shirt pocket, pulled out a pen and a slip of paper, and gave them to Sadie in one swift, practiced movement.

"I just might take you up on that. I'll call you Saturday to let you know for sure."

"See you soon." Sadie gave him her best 'I'm available' smile and scurried back to Pearl's house.

"Girl, I've never seen you move so fast." Pearl was laughing so hard she held the sides of her stomach. "I have to admit, if you didn't run to that man, I would have done it for you."

Sadie knew Pearl was joking. Her husband adored her and she him. She envied how he still surprised her with bouquets of flowers and letters proclaiming his love, even after fifteen years of marriage.

"Did you see the look on that broad's face when she realized you stopped him from picking up her bags?" Pearl poured them both a glass of wine. Sadie tilted the glass to her lips and swallowed its contents in one gulp. She held out her glass for more.

"I can't believe that just happened," she breathed. "I do wish I'd had time to change into something more seductive. The best man I've ever seen walks into my life and I look a hot mess!"

"Trivial details," Pearl interjected. "None of that matters. The wheels are already set in motion and the train has left the station. This is just the beginning, Sadie," Pearl told her. "Now let's plan that fabulous dinner you're going to reel him in with."

APOLLO KNOCKED AT SADIE'S DOOR PROMPTLY at six. She greeted him wearing a knee-length black cocktail dress with spaghetti straps that crossed in the back, and a ridiculous red party hat. Her hair, free from the barrette she bound it with every morning, hung loose covering her shoulders. Red and white balloons and streamers decorated the foyer.

"It's nice to see you again." He extended his hand.

"I'm so glad you've come," Sadie said as she took his hand in both of hers and leaned in, brushing her cheek against his.

Apollo followed Sadie into the dining room but not before noticing the two recliners opposite the sofa. The armrests were threadbare and the cushions worn flat. He figured the second chair was once her husband's and she was either separated or divorced. He also noticed, but did not comment on, the framed photos of a young girl in various stages of childhood scattered across the mantel, along with silver trophies with wooden bases for basketball and track and field. The jacket draped over the banister with the class of '88 logo was likely the girl's too, along with the gym bag tossed in the corner.

In the dining room, a magnificent feast adorned the table. Aluminum food pans filled with roast chicken and lamb, potato salad, green beans, yams perched atop chafing stands, Sterno flames warmed them from below. Hot buttered rolls wrapped in linen filled a wicker basket. A two-layer strawberry shortcake was the centerpiece of the feast, and cheese, crackers, olives and fresh fruit covered the buffet. Apollo's stomach roared.

"When will the other guests arrive?" he asked.

Sadie looked perplexed. "Other guests?"

"You couldn't have possibly cooked all this food for me."

Sadie's face grew rosy. Apollo had never seen a woman her age blush.

"I did. It's all for you."

Apollo's eyes widened. "You... Sadie, you've done too much."

"It was truly my pleasure." She batted her eyelashes.

She showed him to his chair then extended a tray of hors d'oeuvres. After he heaped finger foods on the small plate, Sadie took her place at the opposite end of the table.

"How did the move go?"

"Moving from an apartment to a house, I don't have much furniture. All my belongings were in place in just a few hours. I still have a few small boxes to unpack but I imagine those will be empty within the next few days."

"What do you think of your new neighborhood so far?"

"I haven't had much time to truly look around, but I'm surprised by all the vacant store fronts on the main road."

"Most Jewish folks abandoned their stores and shops one right after another. Blacks have started to inhabit a few vacancies - there's the barbershop and laundromat, and a pharmacy. We're gaining some momentum but it will take time. When the banks won't lend you the cash, it's hard raising that kind of capital."

After Apollo finished off the hors d'oeuvres, Sadie filled his dinner plate with the main course.

"So what do you do for a living?"

"I'm a Merchant Marine."

"I've never met a Merchant Marine before. Sounds like hard work."

"The work is bearable. The hardest thing is adjusting to the schedule. I work six months out of the year, then I'm off six months," he answered in between mouthfuls of food. The meal was exquisite. The lamb was tender, the potato salad perfectly seasoned and the hot buttered rolls just out of the oven were both flaky and moist.

"I'm assuming you've travelled many places."

Apollo wanted to savor his food - eat now and talk later - but Sadie pummeled him with question after question. He set his fork on the table and politely answered her.

"My ship departs from the West coast ports - Oakland, San Francisco and Long Beach, and we sail to the Asian ports, like Taiwan, Japan and Hong Kong." He wanted to tell her how he enjoyed watching the waves settle into smoothness after the ship's departure, the drum of the engine lulling him to sleep, and the brilliance of the purple and red sky mirrored in the ocean at dusk. But these intimate details were not appropriate for dinner with someone he'd just met. Instead, he told Sadie of the artifacts and treasures he had collected over the years and spoke briefly of his parents and upbringing. Apollo picked up his fork and resumed eating.

Amazing food. I'll have to find a woman who can cook.

Sadie finally stopped barraging him with questions, and instead began talking about her job. But cleaning houses was not a topic that made for interesting conversation. Apollo almost hoped she'd resort to asking him questions again. It didn't help that her voice had few degrees of inflection, rambling on in an irritating monotone. Apollo eventually stopped listening to what she had to say, but Sadie was too caught up in her own words to notice.

After dinner, Apollo helped clear the table. He considered asking for her lamb recipe, since he hadn't yet perfected his own cooking skills, but Sadie gave him an extra dinner plate to take home, with enough lamb to last the next two days.

"Thank you for an excellent meal. I hope you'll have me over again soon." He was trying to be polite and hoped he didn't give the impression he was interested.

"How about you come over again next Sunday?"

Apollo should have said no. Sadie wasn't at all his type. Forward, desperate women were a turn-off. He preferred a woman who allowed him to pursue her. It was the chase that quickened his blood. He also preferred a woman who held up better over the years. He guessed Sadie was close to forty, and normally age was not a deterrent, but Apollo wanted a woman who was more voluptuous than matronly.

On the other hand, Apollo was a bachelor who hadn't had a home-cooked meal in months, and Sadie could truly burn in the kitchen. Surely he could tolerate her company again.

"See you next week."

SADIE CALLED PEARL AS SOON AS APOLLO was out the door.

"Girl, dinner was a hit. The way he shoveled food in his mouth, I'm sure I'll see him again. He cleaned his plate and asked for seconds."

"You can't go wrong with a good home-cooked meal for a single man," Pearl laughed. "Did you take my suggestion and eat by candlelight?"

"I didn't want to scare the man off on the first date."

"It sets the mood, lets him know you're definitely interested. Anyway, What does he do for a living?"

"He's a Merchant Marine."

"Not bad, girl. Not bad at all. I hope you invited him back."

"I'd be a fool not too. I asked him over again next Sunday and I'm planning the menu as we speak."

"You don't get anywhere these days sitting around waiting for the man to make the next move. Nice work!"

How many weeks has it been?" Pearl asked Sadie. Sadie stood in Pearl's kitchen. It was remodeled the year before, the cabinets still out-of-the-box shiny. All the appliances were jet black, and a rectangular pot rack hung from the ceiling. But it was the double oven that caused Sadie the most envy. She could cook two main courses at the same time, rather than slave in the kitchen all day roasting and baking one dish after the other.

"Apollo's come to my house for dinner five Sundays in a row. I have to get home soon to tidy up the house because he's coming tonight, too. As a matter of fact, that's why I stopped by. I want to borrow your turkey baster. I can't find mine."

"Anything you need to hook that man, you can have."

"Did I tell you about the gifts he bought for me the last two weeks?"

Pearl shook her head.

"It's not anything extravagant of course, but tasteful gifts, like he put some thought into it. Last week he gave me a silk scarf and the week before it was a crystal vase. I can't wait to see what he brings tomorrow. "

"Well you do put a lot of work into those meals. It's nice of him to bring something."

"I'd cook for him, regardless. I really want him Pearl. Not only is he good looking but he makes a decent paycheck. I'll live a far more comfortable life if this works out."

"Has he invited you out on a date yet?"

"Not yet. I'm going to have to talk to him about that. I don't have time to waste on long term dating. I want a serious relationship that leads to marriage, and it needs to happen soon. I'm not getting any younger."

"Men don't always have to take the lead, you know. Ask him out on a real date. Suggest that you meet him at a restaurant next time."

"I don't feel comfortable bringing it up yet, but soon..."

"Has he met Madeline?"

"That's the other problem, Pearl. Madeline's pictures are all over the mantel in the living room, and her fifth grade photo is on the buffet in the dining room. Apollo has a clear view of it from his chair, yet he never asks who she is. So before I start talking about a serious relationship, I have to at least introduce him to Madeline so he knows what he's getting into. I mean, he could be her stepfather one day."

"Hurry up, Sadie. He's a catch. You can't be the only woman out there who wants the man."

DURING THE SIX WEEKS HE'D KNOWN SADIE, she was never at a loss for words. But today, on their sixth consecutive Sunday together, Sadie was mute. Apollo had dealt with enough women during his life to understand what that meant. Sadie wanted something, and she used silence to set the stage for her request. Silverware rang loudly against their plates, ice cubes clinked in their glasses, and the sounds of chewing and swallowing amplified in the quiet room. He enjoyed the eating without talking. Having to stop savoring his food in order to answer Sadie's probing questions ruined his dinner experience.

Unfortunately, the peace lasted only twenty minutes. Sadie, satisfied that the stage was amply set, broke her silence.

"Apollo, I want you to meet my daughter. Her name is Madeline. That's her picture right across from you on the buffet. I'm surprised you haven't already asked about her." She cleared her throat and smoothed an imaginary wrinkle in the tablecloth. When Apollo didn't respond, she went on.

"She's smart, athletic and easy to get to know. She graduates from high school this year. Perhaps I'll have her meet with us for dinner next week?"

Apollo shoved the last forkful into his mouth. He removed his napkin from his lap and pushed his chair away from the table.

"Dinner was magnificent, as usual, but I have to get up early tomorrow," he stood up fast. "How about we call it a night?"

"It's not like you to eat so little. Seconds? A plate to take home?" There was a slight edge to her voice.

"Not this time, watching the waistline," he patted his flat, firm abs.

She escorted him to the door then turned and threw her arms around him, pressing her body hard against his. His body responded, pressing back, his lips found hers. It was at first a slow, hesitant kiss until Sadie pushed it to searching and wanting.

Abruptly, Apollo drew back. It was several seconds before Sadie opened her eyes. Apollo knew what she was thinking. Even though she didn't speak the words, he knew she wanted to know where the relationship was heading. Sadie wanted more.

Damn! I got caught up in the moment. I have to end this.

"I'll see you next week, Sadie." Apollo cleared his throat.

"Bye Baby," she said, batting her eyes.

The warmth of the sun tempered the chill in the air on that cool fall day. Nature had just begun its fashion show of burnt oranges, warm browns and bits of yellow. Sadie opened all the downstairs windows. The fresh, crisp air sailed through the house.

Sadie had a themed table cloth for every season and her favorite was the fall covering. She unfolded the cloth with a corner in each hand, snapped it high in the air and let it billow softly onto the table. A cornucopia decorated the center, and pumpkins danced around the border.

The turkey timer beeped its completion just as Apollo knocked at the door. "Hello darling," she greeted him with a hug, moving her body into his. Apollo took a step backwards to avoid having her body touch his. If Sadie noticed she didn't comment.

"Go on in the dining room and have a seat. I can't wait for you to meet Madeline." Once again she'd gone overboard. There was enough food for ten people. Apollo knew she worked full-time during the week, and she sometimes worked Saturdays too, so he was curious as to how she found the time to prepare Thanksgiving - sized meals on a weekly basis.

"Lovely weather we're having," Apollo said.

"I haven't had the chance to enjoy it. It's dark outside when I go to work in the morning, and dark when I get home. What can I do? Somebody has to put the food on the table. Of course, if I had someone to provide for me, maybe I could enjoy the little things, like this gorgeous October day."

15Jean Mckie-Sutton

That won't be me. "How's Pearl?"

"She and her husband are in St. Maarten on vacation, and…"

"Did you cook the pork roast again?" he quickly interrupted.

Pearl's island vacation with her husband would spark another conversation about Sadie's lack of a man in the house. It annoyed him how she managed to turn a simple, light conversation into a monologue about why she needed a man. Desperation was not becoming.

"I decided on the turkey and the lamb. You had three servings the last time I fixed them so I thought I'd treat you today. We'll start as soon as Madeline comes."

After what seemed like hours, Apollo checked his watch. Six twenty-five. He found the small talk tedious and exhausting, but he was captive, his stomach growling with succulent food just within reach. He waited several moments before checking his watch again. It was six forty- five and still no Madeline. Sadie simultaneously glanced at the wall clock.

"You know how teenagers are. They expect the world to wait for them. Let's just start before the food gets cold. I'll put a plate aside for Madeline and she can eat when she gets in – whenever that is." She threw her hands up in the air.

She stuck serving spoons and forks into the platters and carved slices of lamb so violently, the knife struck the bottom of the dish.

There's no future in this relationship so there really is no need to meet this woman's teenage daughter. This is a better time than ever to

94

tell her it's over. Besides, she's already angry so how much worse can it get? Apollo stood to deliver his farewell speech. He didn't realize how tense he was about meeting Madeline until his shoulders relaxed.

"Sadie…"

"Yes, Apollo?" Expectancy lit her face.

"I've enjoyed your company these past few months. You were the first to welcome me to the neighborhood and I thank you for your hospitality."

Her eyes softened and a smile played at the corners of her mouth.

She actually thinks I have something good to say. I better hurry and get to the point. "I've given our time together much thought and I…"

The front door opened. There was a long sigh, as if coming inside was a great ordeal, followed by footsteps into the dining room.

"Sorry I'm late. I hope you two didn't wait for me," Madeline said.

The remainder of his sentence remained suspended somewhere between thought and spoken word. Apollo's mouth hung open. Not because he had any doubt about what he wanted to tell Sadie, and not because he was interrupted mid-sentence by Madeline's tardiness, but because his breath was taken away by the striking young beauty that stood before him.

She was tall, lean and simultaneously graceful and athletic. Madeline was innocence on the dawn of womanhood, and she possessed an innocent passion only seen in those who are not yet aware of their sensual power. He took her all in from head to toe – the slope of her shoulder, the curve of her neck, and her hands, both delicate and strong.

I could gaze on this woman for the rest of my life and never grow tired. This is Sadie's teenage daughter? He was dizzy with the irony of it all.

Apollo remained standing and extended his hand. "Good evening, princess," he flattered her.

Madeline gaped at Apollo unblinking.

He took her hand in his, bowed low and kissed her fingers. Madeline shivered.

"Good evening Mr..."

"Just call me Apollo." He winked. She dropped her head and stared at her shoes, but Apollo was very much aware of the effect he had on her.

"I told you not to be late. Did you forget your watch or do you have a total disregard for time?" Sadie scolded. "It's rude to keep a guest waiting. I put your plate in the oven to keep warm."

Madeline was too preoccupied with Apollo to respond to Sadie's snide remarks. She lifted her head for another glance at Apollo and their eyes locked.

"In the kitchen! Go get your dinner!" Sadie's shrill voice propelled her into action.

Madeline shook her head as if waking, allowed her eyes one last chance to enjoy the man treat from head to toe, then retrieved her covered plate from the oven.

"And you were saying before the rude teenager interrupted?"

"Ah… I forgot."

"You were saying something about giving our relationship thought? Go on," she prodded

"I… I… It was nothing. It can wait. We can talk some other time."

"I have a feeling you were telling me something I've been waiting to hear. Come on Apollo, get it out," she teased.

But Apollo heard no more of Sadie's words. His thoughts were occupied by the innocent beauty who took his breath away.

He looked toward the kitchen then turned back to Sadie.

"What time should I be here for dinner next week?"

Sybil

S ybil took the stairs by two's to the third floor, with a blue mesh laundry bag flung over her shoulder, bouncing against her hip. She unlocked the door to her apartment and walked into the living room. The stench of stale liquor that blanketed her nostrils used to give her the dry heaves, but now she greeted it with contemptuous familiarity. Her Keds made a slick, peeling sound as she walked across the hardwood floor. The floor needed a good mopping but Sybil could never find the time, considering her growing list of responsibilities, a list she considered far too long for a ten year old. She dropped the clean load of laundry at her feet and noticed Terri's dinner from the night before still sitting on the glass and brass coffee table - a brown and serve roll, green peas and hamburger patties. Terri didn't touch the peas and hamburger at all, and she ate just a few small bites of bread. Terri rarely ate a full meal all at once. She snacked in small spurts throughout the day – a handful of crackers here, a cup of soup there - and sometimes she went the entire day without eating anything at all.

"Terri, are you home?" Sybil called to her mother.

Several pairs of strappy sandals formed a random path leading to a dresser in the corner of the living room, and blue jeans draped over the open drawers trailed to the floor. Sybil stuffed the clothing back into the drawers and arranged the sandals in a row. It was hard keeping the living room neat since it also functioned as Terri's bedroom. The convertible sofa was a couch by day and a bed by night, and the end tables served as nightstands. Sybil continued searching the apartment.

"Terri, are you home?"

To the left of the living room was the bedroom Sybil shared with her baby brother, Shane. A fifth grader shouldn't have to share a room with her brother but this was the only bedroom in the apartment. The narrow, rectangular room held a bunk bed on one side, and a chest of drawers and cardboard boxes filled with toys on the other. Shane was still asleep on the bare mattress of the lower bunk. His pillow, sheet and blanket were in a pile on the floor. Grandmother Rose nicknamed Shane the wild night wrestler, for no matter how diligent she was in tucking his fitted sheet securely under the mattress, Shane managed to wrestle his linens off the bed in the middle of the night, only to awaken in the morning shivering with a smattering of goose bumps on his naked limbs.

Sybil retrieved his blanket from the linen heap, covered Shane's bare legs and continued her search for her mother.

"Terri?"

Finally, Sybil entered the only remaining room in the apartment – the kitchen. There she found Terri lying on the floor flat on her back, her dress bunched over her hips and her legs flung wide open, revealing red panties with lace trim. Wide, hoop earrings dangled from her ears onto the black and white linoleum. A straw handbag still hung on her shoulder, and one of her sandals lay upside down on the far side of the kitchen. Here, the stench of liquor was most pungent. She kneeled on the floor alongside Terri and leaned in close with her face inches from her mother's breast. Sybil's heart beat loud and fast, and her palms grew damp. She inched closer and waited. When Terri's breasts rose and fell, and Sybil felt her warm breath graze her forehead, she exhaled relief. She sat upright, leaned against the cabinet, and forced herself to breathe in deep slow breaths until her heartbeat returned to its natural rhythm. Then Sybil's relief swiftly turned to anger. Terri was drunk and passed out again.

A dutiful daughter might brew a pot of coffee, coax her drunken mother from the floor and encourage her to lie down on the sofa with a cool, damp cloth draped across her temples. But Sybil had played this role countless times before. Weary and fed up, she left Terri on the cold linoleum.

TERRI ANN TAYLOR, A PETITE woman with delicate hands, full lips and high cheekbones, appeared to be older than her thirty-two years. Crow's feet framed her hollow eyes, and loose, transparent skin stretched over the veins in her neck and hands. Once curvy, her body was now frail and thin. Thick, shoulder length hair was her best asset. Whether she permed, dyed, roller set, or flat ironed, it looked salon finished even on her worst days.

She was a self-professed party girl who spent most nights at the Star Mist Lounge on Broad Street. She referred to the Star Mist as 'the club' but it was simply a corner bar with a crowd as down and out as its décor. Streetwalkers, desperate middle aged women, cheating husbands and anyone looking for a one night stand frequented the Star Mist. But Terri didn't mind the crowd. She was at home amidst these people. There were no airs, no pretense, and no one cared if she was three months behind on the rent or couldn't afford to pay her electric bill.

The Star Mist stayed open until two o'clock in the morning and Terri usually partied until the manager turned off the lights and locked the doors. She stumbled home drunk, slept off her incessant hangovers during the day, only to do it all over again at nightfall.

They lived on the third floor of the Pine Square Apartments on the outskirts of Nicetown. Nicetown began its decline in the 1970's after the death of the industrial complex led to poverty and joblessness. By 1981, Blacks and Puerto Ricans struggled with high crime, unemployment, and abandoned building and homes. Perhaps it was the economic reality of the times, or perhaps it was the result of sheer laziness, but Sybil did not recall ever seeing Terri even attempt to look for work. Welfare and occasional checks from Grandmother Rose kept a roof over their heads and food in their bellies. When Terri was careful with money, her modest income provided the basic necessities for her family, and allowed her to pay the rent and utilities on time. But more often than not, Terri spent far too much of her limited income at the Star Mist, leaving little for household needs.

While Terri partied all night and slept all day, ten year old Sybil cooked, cleaned and took care of Shane. She brewed a pot of coffee for Terri every morning before heading to school and placed her mother's pink and white fleece slippers by the front door so she could slip them on as soon as she stepped into the apartment in the wee hours of the morning. Terri never thanked her daughter, but when she drank those first sips of steaming hot coffee, she rewarded Sybil with a wink.

Sybil left Terri in the kitchen and backtracked to the bedroom. She wrapped her arms around Shane just as he sat up in bed, yawning with his head thrown back and his mouth stretched open to the ceiling. The two were only four years apart but Sybil treated him more like he was her own child than her baby brother. She coddled and babied him, and made sure to hug him first thing in the morning and last thing at night. She ironed his clothes, corrected his homework and attempted to alleviate his incessant coughing. Just before she tucked him in at bedtime, she poured him a teaspoon of cough syrup, else he hacked straight through the night. When it was really bad, she ran the shower until the bathroom filled with steam, and sat with him on the bathroom floor until the moist air soothed his lungs. Shane was impatient and temperamental, and had a hard time concentrating on school work. He was easily confused, even during basic alphabet and counting exercises, but all in all he was a sweet, if serious, child.

Shane wriggled out of her arms and rubbed his eyes with his fists.

"Get off me," he whined.

"When did you eat?" Sybil asked.

"Dis mornin'."

"Are you hungry?"

"O 'course!" he yelled.

Sybil made her way back to the kitchen, stepped over Terri and opened the cabinet door. Shane marched behind her with his knees raised high like the drummers he saw in the marching band at school. He too stepped over Terri, not even missing a beat, then flopped down onto the kitchen chair.

"What you fixin?"

"Soup and a sandwich."

"I want peanut jelly."

"You mean peanut butter and Jelly," Sybil corrected.

"Yeah," Shane grinned.

Terri mumbled and rolled onto her side, but neither Sybil nor Shane paid her any mind. It would be several more hours before she came around.

"What are we gonna do today?" she asked, while placing Shane's sandwich on a napkin in front of him. It was noon on Sunday and the laundry was already done for the week. There were always chores to do but those could wait.

"Playgroun'!" he answered through a mouth full of food.

"No, the weatherman said there's gonna be a thunderstorm. We can play out front until the rain starts then we'll come back in for dinner."

The rain held off until seven o'clock. When the two returned indoors, Terri was snoring on the living room sofa, an arm and a leg trailed to the floor. Sybil boiled egg noodles and heated the peas from the night before.

"Your dinner's ready!" she said as she tapped Terri on her shoulder.

Terri rolled over but didn't wake up. She put Terri's plate on the coffee table with a paper towel over it to keep it warm.

"Get a bath after you eat," she told Shane.

"Ok, after Disney goes off," he bargained.

Shane complied and filled the tub with water as soon as the credits rolled at the end of the show. Sybil added a capful of bubble bath to the water then draped his pajamas where he could reach them on the bathroom doorknob. While Shane bathed, Sybil washed the dishes and wiped down the stove and counter-tops. Just as she switched off the kitchen light Shane hugged her from behind. She felt the dampness through his pajamas.

"You didn't do such a good job at drying off!"

"Good night, Sybil," he said, his voice already heavy with drowsiness.

Sybil tucked Shane in and kissed his cheek. He tried but was too sleepy to duck out of the way. She checked to make sure the bolt lock was on the front door, then climbed into the top bunk.

Sybil went to bed that evening not having spoken to Terri at all that day, and when she awakened at dawn, Terri was gone.

This wasn't an unusual occurrence for Sybil. Terri frequently stayed out all night, well into the next day. Sybil had endured Terri's absences for as long as she could remember, but after years of waking to a household without a parent, she expected to be accustomed to it. She expected to be numb and feel nothing. She expected to carry on as if it were any other ordinary day. Instead, a suffocating panic seized her. Air and sound vacated the room, and she gasped and gulped into nothingness, while a roaring – like ten oceans rushing by – obliterated the world around her. Seconds later, all was restored in a rush, leaving her weary and spent. Today was no different than the others. When she discovered Terri was gone yet again, she fell to her knees, breathless in a silent world. It was the vibration of Shane's footsteps reverberating through the floor beneath her that propelled Sybil into calm. She pulled herself from the floor. If she didn't look after him, who would?

Sybil rummaged through the kitchen cupboards for a suitable breakfast. They had no more waffles, eggs, bread or cereal. A package of pork sausages remained but these were frozen solid and there wasn't enough time for them to thaw before school started. She found a package of cheese and crackers at the very top of the cupboard and gave those to Shane. The rumbling in her own belly, she quieted with two tall glasses of water. After they both dressed, she walked Shane to school, then ran home, crossing her fingers and making a wish that Terri would be there. Her wish came true. Terri was sprawled on the sofa. She was passed out again, but there, nonetheless. Sybil ran right past her to the kitchen and flung open the cupboard. Pushed to the rear was a glass jar where Terri stashed money. She slid the jar toward her and lifted it from the shelf. All that remained was spare change. Sybil counted less than two dollars. It wasn't nearly enough. She dreaded what she had to do next, but there was no other choice.

Terri's handbag sat on the living room floor inches from her face. Sybil grabbed a strap, slid the bag toward her, and cautiously pulled out three crisp twenty dollar bills. What if Terri suddenly woke up and caught her? She pushed the thought from her mind and stuffed half the money in her pocket. Terri rolled over and Sybil ran from the apartment. She didn't stop running until she arrived at the corner grocery store. She bought bread, eggs, peanut butter, instant noodles, cereal and milk. She never took money from Terri for frivolous purposes. Mostly it was for food, although a few times she used the money to pay the electric bill. She was sure her mother knew about her stealing, yet Terri never said a word. When she awakened from her drunken stupor, she simply counted the money remaining in her purse, shrugged her shoulders and carried on as if all was well.

THE RUNNING AND THE JUMPING STARTLED Sybil awake. Shane leapt from the furniture and crashed into the walls. He was practicing his fight moves again. His imaginary opponents moved in on all sides, yet Shane defeated them all. Only his super hero pajamas called forth the fighter in him. When he wore his plain pajamas, you didn't even know he was awake on Saturday mornings until he turned on the T.V.

Sybil rolled over and pulled her blanket under her chin to keep out the cold air seeping through the cracks in the window frame. The food she bought a week ago with Terri's money was nearly gone, but there was no need to get up early and there was no need for alarm. Terri was home. Surely Terri would take care of figuring out what to fix for breakfast. Sybil sunk back down into slumber, until the front door opened and slammed closed.

She shot up in bed and darted out of the room.

"Did Terri leave?" she asked Shane

"Yup," Shane said, his forehead dripping from battling multiple legions of enemies.

She ran after Terri, down three flights of stairs and out onto the street in her night clothes. She looked both ways up and down the street. There was no sign of her mother. She sighed and trudged back up the stairs.

"Whas for breakfast?" Shane asked, before she was fully through the door.

Sybil tore through the cupboards. Aside from a few remaining slices of bread, and a small can of creamed corn, the cupboard was bare.

"Just buttered toast." She toasted two slices of bread for Shane and two slices for herself. Whenever Terri came home, she'd take more money from her purse and buy groceries. In the meantime, Sybil kept herself busy sweeping the floors, putting away the laundry, and ironing Shane's clothes for school the following week. She took a nap at noon and watched T.V. until two forty-five in the afternoon. She planned to take another long nap until Terri came home, so she didn't have to keep thinking about her empty stomach, but Shane kept nagging her.

"You forgot to fix my lunch. I'm hungry," he said. "Fix my lunch now!"

"I want lunch, too." She didn't want to frighten her brother but she knew they were in trouble.

At five o'clock, she toasted the last two slices of bread for Shane and warmed the creamed corn for herself. Shane stuffed his mouth with both slices of toast and showed her his empty napkin.

"All finished. I want corn, too," he told her, his mouth still full. Ignoring the empty aching in her own belly, she poured the corn into a bowl for Shane. The two glasses of water she drank did nothing to fill the empty place.

Terri will be home in the morning, she told herself in order to get through the night ahead. Sybil knew all too well that hunger and sleep were not friends, yet she did sleep, for a brief time that night.

She dreamed of Terri. Not Terri as she knew her, but a present and whole Terri. A Terri who knew how to nurture and love, a mother any child might yearn for. She came home from school to an alert and clear Terri who asked her how her day was and actually listened to what she had to say. She said, 'I love you, Sybil' and they weren't just words. She felt loved.

But she awakened at dawn to the grim reality that was her life. She didn't have to search the apartment to know Terri wasn't home. She knew with her entire being that she and Shane were alone. Air and sound took flight as she fell to the floor gasping to fill her lungs. Shane found her there in her room, curled into a ball.

"Sybil, whas wrong?" he asked.

His pleas went unheard in the place where Sybil dwelled. Her mouth opened in a silent scream, her eyes bulged from their sockets.

"Talk to me!" He jumped up and down, with clenched fists. "Sybil!" Shane screamed, his eyes filling with tears.

It was the fear and anguish on Shane's face that yanked her from hysteria. She emerged shaken and trembling.

"I… I'm okay," she told him. Her pajamas were damp against her skin. She sat up and steadied herself until her breathing grew regular.

"Sybil, I'm hungry but I don't want any more toast. I want pancakes."

She considered waiting until the end of the day to see if Terri came home before doing anything drastic, but that would mean an entire day with nothing to eat. She could endure the stomach pangs, but Shane didn't deserve to endure them too.

"Don't worry. I'm gonna call Grandmother Rose. She'll come and get us."

"Yippee!" Shane leapt into the air.

Grandmother Rose lived in Booten, New Jersey on an acre of land. Her three story home sat alone on a wide road, the nearest home a quarter mile away. Sybil imagined herself helping grandmother plant flowers in the front yard while Shane played in the fenced-in back yard. After they all feasted on the pastries that Grandmother Rose brought home from the bakery each week, she'd soak in an enormous bubble bath and snuggle for bedtime stories before Grandmother Rose tucked them into their beds.

It wasn't exactly perfect at Grandmother's house. She was strict about getting to bed on time, rising early, and eating lots of vegetables and she didn't allow them to sit in front of the television all day Saturday watching cartoons. But all in all, the luxuries of living in the big house far outweighed Grandmother's strict routines.

She dialed Grandmother Rose.

"Hi, sweetie. It's so good to hear from you. What's going on?"

"Grandmother Rose. Mommy hasn't been home since yesterday. We're hungry and the food is all gone!"

"When did you last eat?"

"Last night, Shane had the last of the toast and corn for dinner. There's nothing for us to eat at all today."

"Don't worry, sweetie. I'll be right there."

Within just a few hours, there was an angry knock at the front door. Sybil flung the door wide open and began her customary leap into Grandmother Rose's arms, but grandmother's mouth was set in a straight line and ridges furrowed her forehead. Sybil took the bag of sandwiches in her outstretched hand, then noticed Terri standing alongside her, her lips pursed with attitude. Their argument resumed.

"You embarrassed me! I'm a grown woman out having a few drinks. You dragged me out of there like I was a child! Why can't you stay out of my doggone business?" Terri complained.

"Your children should be your only concern." She said 'only' as if it were the most important word in her sentence. "When you fail to take care of your children you leave me no choice. I have to step in."

"My children are just fine. Look at them." She pointed at Sybil and Shane. "Not a thing wrong with 'em."

"You didn't come home in enough time to make sure they had a meal. What kind of mother allows her children to fend with no food?"

"They're not starving for God's sake. They exasher… exaggerate…"

"And you're still drunk." Grandmother Rose added. "You're going back to the clinic."

Sybil understood that this was no ordinary clinic. It was a place where people learned to stop drinking. Terri had gone there once before.

"I can't go back."

"Either you go back and get treatment or I will take these children!"

"But I…"

"It's a disgrace the way you live! Look at this place." She moved her arms in a grand circulating gesture. "Animals live better than this."

"If I go to the clinic, who will look after the kids?" Her anger was gone for a moment. Her shoulder dropped, as if she'd already given up the fight.

"You weren't worried about them while you stayed out all night. Why pretend you have maternal instincts now? And don't believe in any way you have any choice in this! You *are* going back to the clinic!" Grandmother yelled so loud her voice cracked.

Terri stomped out the room. The pictures rattled on the wall. "We were doing just fine without you. Why are you here?" Terri shouted from the kitchen.

Sybil and Shane ate their turkey sandwiches and watched the altercation from the sofa. Grandmother Rose followed Terri into the kitchen and stepped forward until their faces were inches apart. With every word she spat, Terri blinked.

"I'm here to make sure you do *right* by my grandchildren, and I'm *not* leaving until I'm *satisfied*. You will pull this together *my* way – not yours - or I will go to court and file for full custody of these children. If you challenge me, I will *fight* you every step of the way."

Grandmother Rose turned so swiftly her heel scraped the linoleum. She pulled a suitcase from the coat closet and stuffed it with clothes she snatched from the dresser drawers. Then she turned to her daughter and stood firm, looking her right in the eyes. Terri opened her mouth to say something. For several seconds her mouth hung open. Sybil and Shane stopped chewing waiting for Terri's next words. Then she clamped her mouth shut and waited for her mother to make the next move. Grandmother Rose nodded, picked up the suitcase and exited the apartment. Terri followed her without uttering another word.

"I'll be back you two," she called to the children over her shoulder.

Sybil turned to Shane. "Let's get ready!"

"For what?"

"We're going to Grandmother's house."

She packed their clothes in large green plastic trash bags, set them by the front door and waited.

"We're on our way to Booten, Shane."

"I guess mommy's gonna go away for a while," Shane said, his fists opening and closing. It was a habit he'd had since he was a baby except back then it meant he was hungry or thirsty. When he was older the habit surfaced when he was angry or afraid.

"But she'll be okay, and so will we." She rubbed his back just below his neck until his fists stilled.

"Did you pack my super hero jamas?"

"They were the first thing in the bag."

"Toys, too?"

"I packed everything you need, toys too."

The two changed into clean clothes and their best shoes and waited.

When Grandmother Rose returned two hours later, the fire and energy that fueled her ire was gone. No longer firm and standing tall, her shoulders curved and the furrows in her forehead were more worrisome than angry.

"Your momma's all settled in." She spoke in a hushed tone.

"You look so tired." Sybil took her hand and led her to the sofa to sit down.

"Oh I'm fine. It's the two of you I'm worried about."

"Grandmother, how about I fix you a cup of coffee?" Sybil measured the water in the carafe, poured it into the machine and scooped ground coffee onto the filter.

"When did you learn to make coffee?"

"I make it for mommy all the time."

"It's nice that you make your mama coffee, but I suspect you make it to relieve her hangovers." Sybil didn't answer. Grandmother Rose didn't press the matter.

"Is this the first time you two were without food because Terri wasn't there?"

"It's not the first time but usually there's money in Terri... uh... mommy's purse or in the jar in the cupboard, and I take the money and go buy groceries from the store." Even though Terri hadn't earned the right to be called 'mommy', Grandmother Rose didn't tolerate them calling their mother by her first name.

"You buy the groceries all by yourself?"

"Yup."

"Honey, I'm proud of you for doing what you have to, but you shouldn't have to worry about finding money for food. You're just ten years old! You should be out doing what ten year olds do – jumping rope, riding a bike, hanging out with friends. It's a good thing you called me when you did. Hopefully this time around, Terri will change her ways. For now, at least she's in the right place to get some professional help."

"Grandmother Rose, do you really think it will get better for us?"

She took a sip of her coffee. "It's up to Terri. She has to want to change. When you say your prayers tonight, send one up for your momma."

"Is she gonna be okay?" Sybil asked.

"She's where she needs to be right now," Grandmother Rose sighed.

"Well whenever you're ready, we're all set to go!" Sybil told her.

"Go where?" Grandmother Rose looked confused.

"Your house, of course." Sybil explained.

"Oh no sweetie, you're not coming with me."

Sybil and Shane exchanged hurt glances.

"You don't understand now but the most important thing is that you and Shane keep the same everyday routine and continue to go to school. Your mama will be home in a few months, so there's no sense in uprooting you from school and friends for such a short period of time. I'm gonna stay here with you until she comes back home. We have lots of work to do. We'll scrub this place clean, take all the clothes to the Laundromat, organize the closets, but first, grab your jackets. We're gonna go to the market and buy enough food to stock the kitchen from top to bottom."

SYBIL AND SHANE SETTLED INTO A COMFORTABLE and welcome routine. Grandmother Rose made certain they arrived at school on time every day and she made them check and re-check their homework assignments until there wasn't a single mistake. She starched and ironed their outfits for school and they endured her fussing if their socks and undershirts were not a perfect bleached white. Playtime and T.V. time were not to exceed two hours a day, and the lights went out every evening promptly at nine. Grandmother Rose tolerated no deviation from the rules yet was sure to reward them with an extra half hour of T.V. if they complied. After school, Sybil and Shane came home to dinner on the table, and the sweet savory aromas of cookies or pies baking in the oven.

It had been a long time since Sybil felt like a ten year old. It was nice not having to be responsible and grown up. Shane reaped the benefits as well. He was more happy than serious, his runny nose and cough disappeared and his belly hung over his pants. If he needed a hug, skinned his knee or wanted a warm lap to sit on, he now ran to Grandmother Rose, which suited Sybil just fine.

"You're as plump as a turkey," she teased after he downed three servings of dinner. "Maybe we'll cook you for Thanksgiving later this year." Sybil chased him around the apartment with a fork.

"You know the rules," Grandmother scolded them. She sat in the kitchen clipping coupons from the newspaper, her reading glasses perched nearly on the tip of her nose. "No running in the house and stop teasing that boy about his belly. It's better than having to see his ribs poking through his chest."

"Grandmother Rose, can you take us to the carnival today?" The carnival came to town every spring. It was on the site of an old factory that had been torn down years before. There was talk of rebuilding an office complex on the grounds. Men in work boots and hard hats drove bulldozers that dug up a mountain of dirt they piled on the other side of the lot. The project must have been abandoned because the bulldozers never returned to finish the work, and the mountain of dirt remained for several months until the ground was leveled just prior to the carnival unpacking their amusements.

Grandmother Rose took them to the carnival three years earlier. Sybil still tasted the crystalline texture of the melted cotton candy on her tongue, the thrill in the pit of her stomach just as the roller coaster crested the top of the hill, and her elation at leaving the arcade with a fuzzy gray and white shark tucked under her arm.

"Not today. We're visiting your mother at the clinic."

Shane stopped running, and slipped his thumb into his mouth. Sybil's fond memories of the carnival evaporated.

"I thought she couldn't have visitors." She drew closer to Grandmother Rose, the revelry now gone from her voice.

"That's only in the beginning of the program. She's been there now for over a month, so she's allowed visits from family."

Shane ran to his room and buried himself under his comforter.

"When does she come home for good?" Sybil asked with reluctance, as if she didn't really want to know.

"A few more weeks."

Sybil's shoulders slumped.

Grandmother Rose put down her scissors and caressed Sybil's cheek. "She's getting better," she reassured her. "She won't be the same when she gets home. Go on now. Get dressed."

Sybil wasn't sure what made her turn around on the way to her bedroom, but when she glanced back at Grandmother Rose, etched on her face was the worry she tried so hard to keep a secret.

THE CLINIC WAS AN OLD THREE STORY MANSION flanked by immense willow trees, the exterior renovated with gray limestone. Columns stood on both sides of the portico, overhung with a banner that read, "Welcome to Havenhouse".

"Wow!" said Shane, "is mommy on vacation?"

"It's just a really fancy clinic," Sybil explained.

A receptionist sat at a desk straight ahead. She took their names and told them to have a seat in the sitting area. Scuffed wood floors and decades-old furniture told a story of neglect and disregard. Two chocolate leather sofas, patched with duct tape where the seat cushion touched the back of the knees, sat to the left of a bay window. Framed portraits of nature and animals dulled from years of the bright sun streaming into the bay window, hung above the sofas. Fingerprints smudged the eggshell walls while cobwebs nestled high in corners.

"Grandmother Rose, the inside doesn't match the outside. I thought I'd see a crystal chandelier and fancy oriental rugs."

"Things are certainly not what they seem," Grandmother mumbled. "That's the case with a lot of folks, too."

They didn't have to wait for long. Within moments, the receptionist led them down a hall on the opposite side of her desk, and opened the first door on the right.

"You can have a seat. The residents will be in shortly."

They sat in the meeting area on silver metal folding chairs at square tables situated around the room cafeteria style. A door opened on the far side of the room, and one after another, the women and men walked single file into the room, all sharing the same hollow eyes, dark circles, sallow skin and nervous restlessness. Terri entered looking the same as all the others. Her eyes searched the room until settling on her family. Her gait quickened as she approached the table.

"Hey, you two." She gave them each a quick hug.

"Hi mama," they said in unison. Terri cringed as if their voices were much too loud. She took a seat at the table.

"Mother," she nodded at Grandmother Rose. Grandmother Rose looked her up and down. Fidgeting under her mother's stare, Terri turned to the children.

"I hope you're being good for your grandma."

"We are!" Sybil answered. "Are you feeling better?"

"I'm doin' real good. I'll be home soon. I really miss you both."

Terri appeared to be uncomfortable for a time, as if she didn't know what to say next. Then she turned to Sybil and Shane.

"I'm sorry I put you two through so much. You too, mother," she told Grandmother Rose. "Things will get better when I get home. You'll see. I'm making big changes."

Sybil didn't know whether to believe her or not but she hoped Terri was telling the truth. "You look good, Terri... uh mommy." What she wanted to say was that Terri looked tired and drawn, her lower lip trembled, and her hands shook, but for the first time in many months, her eyes were clear, her speech was not slurred and she gave them all her focused attention.

"How's school, Shane?" Terri asked.

Shane clung to his sister and stared at the television across the room. "I'll be home soon, honey, and I promise to be a better mommy." She ran her fingers through his hair. He leaned in toward her but said nothing.

Grandmother Rose inched her chair closer to talk to Terri in private. Sybil couldn't hear a word of what she whispered but it must have been serious because her face was rigid and grave. Grandmother's lips moved fast. Her hands moved quickly too, keeping pace with her words. Terri nodded intermittently, her eyes watering.

A voice over the intercom soon announced that visiting hours were over. The visitors happily shot up from their chairs as if relieved the ordeal were over. Chairs scraped the tiled floor as they were pushed back under the tables. The residents filed out of one exit and the visitors, the other.

Grandmother Rose and Terri remained huddled, Grandmother delivering fiery words, and Terri, uttering an occasional 'yes ma'am'.

Discussing private matters was a pleasure Sybil denied herself. If prompted, she might disclose a little of what she endured, but wasting her time divulging her innermost thoughts was a luxury she could not afford. She chose, instead, to spend her waking hours devising strategies for survival. Fighting to survive ordered her thoughts, defined her way of being. Fighting was noble, valiant, worthy. Confiding, complaining was for the weak.

Her entire life, she buried her secret fears, depriving them of a voice. But the width and breadth of the accumulation of fears had grown year after year. There was no more room. The seams she'd sewn so carefully could no longer contain them. Seized by surges of violent nausea, Sybil vomited the contents of her stomach and continued retching, her insides contracting and releasing long after her stomach could produce no more.

There was a tap on the bathroom door.

"Come in," Sybil said, her voice weak. She hovered over the toilet, perspiration dripping from forehead.

"This is the third time this week I've heard you in here retching and vomiting. It's a wonder you have a stomach left." Grandmother Rose put a palm on Sybil's forehead and cheek. "Is it a virus?"

Sybil shook her head.

All at once, Grandmother looked as if she were in a panic.

"Are you pregnant?" she blurted out.

"I've never even kissed a boy! Why would you think that?"

"A friend of mine told me her granddaughter, same age as you, was sick only to find out later she was pregnant. She was throwing up in the morning everyday for two weeks and they thought it was a stomach virus."

"No, Grandmother Rose, I'm not pregnant." Sybil was annoyed but too drained to be angry.

"Then what is it? Is it something you ate?" she asked as she poured a tablespoon of antacid.

Sybil's stomach lurched, sending her into another fit of violent retching. She wanted nothing more than to keep her secret fears buried, but she had to let some of it go. She had no choice but to tell Grandmother Rose.

"I'm scared," Sybil said, in the soft, tentative voice of betrayal.

"Scared of what?"

"Mommy's coming home today. I'm scared that our lives will go back to the way it was. I'm scared of not having any food, being home alone, worrying about Shane…" She covered her mouth with her hand. She'd already said too much.

"Don't hold back. Go on."

"What if it doesn't go well?" Sybil asked.

"We'll deal with it *if* the time comes. For now, all we can do is give Terri our support and hope for the best."

She searched Grandmother Rose's face for the assurance that was lacking in her words. She found none.

"It's still early. Why don't you go on back to bed and get a little more rest, I'm not picking up your mom until noon."

"I can't sleep. I was up all night last night."

"Come in the kitchen, then. I'll make some tea."

The whistling teapot bought Shane to the kitchen too.

"Good morning, my wild night wrestler." Goose bumps covered his naked limbs. "It's a special day, Shane. Your momma comes home."

Shane blinked hard then stood on a chair to reach the cabinet. He pulled out a box of cereal. Behind it was cake mix.

"I wanna make a cake," he said, his morning voice still gruff.

"Shane, honey, it's seven in the morning."

"Maybe he's on to something," Sybil said brightening. "What if we have a welcome home party for mommy? We could bake the cake and I could make decorations. Then maybe she'll see how much we love her and not have to go back to that clinic ever again."

"She already knows how much we love her, and there's nothing you can do that will change whether or not she stays sober. That being said, a party sounds nice."

After breakfast, they baked a pound cake and hung balloons. While the cake was in the oven, Sybil and Shane made their beds, lined their shoes against the wall, and stacked their toys in the boxes in their room, so the apartment would be perfect for Terri's arrival.

"Grandmother, we're all done." It was half past eleven.

"I'm gonna go pick up your momma. She slung her handbag on her shoulder. I'll be back in about an hour." She went out the door then stuck her face back in. "And kids… don't look so somber. It's a happy occasion."

"It's a happy occasion." Sybil repeated Grandmother Rose's words. On the back of the door in her room was a full length mirror. She made faces in the mirror, practicing different types of smiles with which to greet Terri. Perhaps a surprised, 'you look great' smile, or maybe a casual 'hey, how are you' smile, or her personal favorite, the zealous, 'I couldn't wait to see you' smile. But when the doorknob turned, her face fell flat. Sybil forced the corners of her mouth to turn upward into a semblance of delight. She couldn't have Terri coming home to her dread.

"Hi mom!" she said, forcing exuberance into her voice.

Shane, too young to understand the importance of keeping up appearances, barely looked up from playing with his action figures. He sat on the floor with his back to Terri. Grandmother Rose pried the toys from his hands, grasped his shoulders and spun him around to face his mother.

"Hi," he said quickly then held his hand out for his toys.

Terri turned around in a complete circle. "I can't believe you did so much! The decorations, the cake, the apartment so clean, and the poster! Sybil did you make this?"

Sybil outlined 'welcome home' letters on poster board with silver and gold glitter, and decorated the border with flowers and stars. The poster hung directly across from the entrance so it was the first thing Terri laid her eyes on when she came home.

"All da laundry's done too," said Shane.

"And I hope it all stays that way," added Grandmother Rose. Her voice was harsh but her eyes, gentle. "Your children worked hard to get this place looking so good."

Sybil was pleased at the changes in Terri. Her stay at the clinic had turned back the clock. Her eyes and skin were clear, curves filled out her frail body, warmth colored her cheeks.

"You look great Terri, uh... Mom."

Grandmother Rose passed Sybil a knife. Sybil sliced the cake while Grandmother Rose scooped ice cream into plastic bowls. Sybil expected Terri to have more to say after being gone so long, but after asking them about school, and complimenting them on their spotless room, she fell silent. Grandmother gathered the dishes and stacked them in the sink.

"I'm going to get on the road," Grandmother Rose announced, while slipping on a jacket.

"Can't you stay a few more days?"

"I'm afraid this place is way too small for the four of us and Granny is too old to sleep on the floor," she chuckled.

"You can sleep on the sofa bed again!" Shane chimed in.

"That mattress is too thin for these old arthritic joints. I've had enough of tossing and turning."

Her face grew serious as she put her hands on Terri's shoulders. "Terri, I'm proud you, honey. You cleaned up real good. You just have to find a way to keep it all together. It won't be easy but you have to make it work for these children of yours."

"I'm on the right track now, mom."

"I'll call to check on you all in a couple of days." She kissed Sybil and Shane.

For a fleeting moment, Sybil thought she saw relief wash over Grandmother's face, but Grandmother Rose covered it with a smile, and waved goodbye.

SHANE BEAT THE BOTTOM OF AN EMPTY coffee can, keeping pace with the drummer in the Easter parade. It was a wonder the parade actually took place. A blizzard a week ago dropped over two feet of snow, closing schools and businesses and tying up traffic for hours. Whoever heard of a blizzard in April? Old folks called it a sign of the times. What was so special a time about 1982?

Sybil refused to watch the parade. She hated the over-zealous commentators ruining the views of the floats and muting the sounds and the music. Watching the parade on T.V. was a tease. She would have preferred to see it in person.

Terri wasn't watching the T.V. either. A newspaper was spread open on her knees. She marked it intermittently with a pen.

"We should go and see it next year," Sybil suggested.

"The crowds are annoying," Terri mumbled. She circled something else in the newspaper.

"Are you doing crossword puzzles?" Sybil asked.

"I'm circling jobs."

"Jobs?" Sybil walked behind the sofa to peek at the classi- fieds section over Terri's shoulder. She couldn't see the paper at first. It took a moment for the cloud of smoke to disperse. Terri chain-smoked two packs a day, more if the day was particularly stressful. Sybil hated the scent of tobacco in her clothes and hair. Terri reeked of it no matter how many times she washed her hair or changed her clothes. But it was a small price to pay, and well worth the tradeoff, for Terri had been home now for seven months, yet remained sober, her cigarette habit quelling her desire for alcohol. Instead of waking to a household devoid of a mother, Sybil and Shane woke to the sounds and smells of breakfast cooking, a spotless apartment, and dresser drawers stacked with freshly folded laundry. Smoking was definitely a reasonable trade-off. It was because of Terri's two pack a day habit that they maintained some semblance of normalcy.

"You're looking for a job?" she said incredulously. "What are you applying for?" She squinted at the small print. "You circled… cashier and receptionist and hostess. Does this mean we'll have more money? Maybe we can move into a better apartment or even a house like Grandmother's. You can buy a car…"

"Hold on, Sybil," Terri said, her irritation mounting. "It's not that easy. First of all, none of these jobs pay much, I have to get through the interview, and I have too little work history to compete with other folks."

"Still, it would be different for us if you had a job."

"I already have an interview two weeks from now. My chances aren't good, so don't get your hopes up."

"I hope you get it!" Sybil clapped her hands and jumped up and down. "I can't wait!"

"Sybil, I mean it!" Terri scolded.

TERRI CHOSE HER CLOTHING WITH GREAT CARE. Black pants, a white, button-down blouse with a collar, and sensible black shoes – stiff, boring and sexless, but necessary if she wanted a chance at having a job. Although far more comfortable and flattering, the hip-hugging, breast-baring wardrobe she'd lived in most of her adult life was inappropriate for an interview.

The phone call from Schaefer & Dougherty came as a surprise considering her scant work history. How was she going to survive the interview with so little to talk about? She'd held a job as a telephone operator right after high school but quit once Sybil came along. That was over eleven years ago. She hadn't worked since.

Terri looked at herself in the full length mirror on the back of the door in Sybil and Shane's room. She was amazed at how business-like and confident she looked on the outside, while inside, terror raged. She'd failed at so many things. Would this interview add to her growing list of failures? Was it even worth putting herself through the stress of preparing for and sitting through the ordeal only to be told she'd never have the job?

She shook her head, dismissed her thoughts, and tucked a new gray clutch under her arm, its only adornment a petite flower embroidered beneath the clasp. Sybil talked her into buying it, complaining that her big, oversized bejeweled handbags were too gaudy for the business world. Terri thought they had personality. She turned off the light and left to take the train downtown.

Terri was gone when Sybil and Shane came home from school. It was the first time in nine months Sybil could not account for her whereabouts. An opened letter from Schaeffer & Dougherty was tossed on the kitchen counter. Sybil didn't have to read the letter to know what it said. Terri's absence explained it all. Sybil lurched forward, cradling the sudden and acute pain in her stomach.

"Are you okay?" Shane asked her before slipping his thumb into his mouth.

"Go play in your room. I'll let you know when dinner's ready." *Maybe she's running an errand, visiting a friend or at the store buying a pack of cigarettes,* Sybil tried to reassure herself. The pain worsened. She slid down the wall and crouched in a corner. She concentrated on the hum of the refrigerator and the drip of the leaking faucet to keep her mind from racing and rehearsing the worst. Minutes, hours, she was oblivious to the passing of time.

Footsteps in the hallway stopped at the front door. It was Terri.

She walked into the apartment carrying a familiar oblong brown paper bag. Not noticing her daughter huddled just a few feet away, she slipped the bottle from the bag, filled a shot glass and held it to her lips, savoring the pungent aroma before swallowing the sweet burning down her throat. A second shot followed quickly after the first. She picked up the bottle to pour a third when Sybil sprung from the floor and grabbed her wrist.

"Please don't drink anymore," she begged.

Startled, Terri dropped the shot glass. It shattered into tiny shards in the sink.

"Please, Terri," Sybil implored her again. The two locked eyes. Precious seconds ticked by. Then Terri turned away and poured the remaining Vodka down the sink drain.

"There'll be other jobs," Sybil told her. "Come with me." She took her mother by the hand.

Like a docile child, Terri allowed her daughter to lead her.

"Sit down," Sybil said, as she gestured toward the sofa.

Kneeling in front of Terri, she pulled off her mother's shoes and swung her legs onto the cushions. She fluffed a pillow for her head, then covered her with a blanket.

"Get some rest. You'll feel better in the morning."

THE FOLLOWING MORNING, THE POTS AND pans in the kitchen were silent. Sybil tiptoed to the living room. Terri still slept with a blanket pulled over her head. An empty two liter vodka bottle lay at her feet. Either she had the bottle hidden in the apartment or she slipped out to the liquor store while they were asleep.

"Terri, we're hungry. Are you gonna fix pancakes?"

"Get what you want." She mumbled. She didn't even bother to uncover her face.

"Are you sick?"

"Just tired. Get on to school before you're late."

Sybil pulled back the covers to get a good look at Terri. Her eyes were half closed and dried saliva trailed from the corner of her mouth to her chin. Terri raised her arm with a finger pointed for several seconds. She moaned something incomprehensible then dropped her arm heavily on the sofa. Sybil put the covers back and looked at her own hands, palms open to the ceiling. They trembled.

Sybil cooked the pancakes eggs and sausage that morning and put a plate on the coffee table for Terri.

"Here's breakfast," she told her mother. "The coffee is brewing. It'll be ready in a few minutes."

"Uh huh," Terri mumbled, her head beneath the blanket again.

"I'll see you after school. Shane, grab your book bag and let's go."

Sybil cried all the way to school, and on and off all day every time she thought of her mother. She didn't understand why she was so sad. After all, Terri was at least home this time, and she'd certainly left her mother in far worse condition, yet the melancholy persisted.

It wasn't until the following morning that she understood her sadness. She and Shane were alone in the apartment once again. In the midst of abject silence, Sybil fought to fill her lungs with air and nearly passed out from her hysteria. Not even Shane's anguished stare could pull her to the surface this time. Her body convulsed, starved for oxygen until the panic released its steely grip. Several moments passed before she mustered the energy to move.

She crawled to the kitchen and grasped the handles of the cabinets to hoist herself to standing. She lifted the jar from the cabinet that held their remaining money. Gone was the hundred sixty dollars that was there at the beginning of the week. Shane, who was right at her heels, knew exactly what was going to happen next.

"Momma won't make us pancakes no more, will she?" he asked Sybil.

"I don't know," she told him. But she did know. They were back where they started. Terri staggered in just before they left for school, her eyes bloodshot and glazed.

"Where were you?" Sybil demanded.

"Wh…where do you think?" she stammered. "My usual spot at the club."

"But you said our life would get better!"

"It's not the end of the world. I went out for one night." She held up a finger. "I'll be back to my normal self tomorrow."

Sybil snatched the handbag from Terri's shoulder. "What are you doing?" Terry screamed, lunging for her bag.

"Don't pretend like you don't know I take your money," Sybil said, while backing out of reach. "I've been doing it for years." She searched the bag and found two one dollar bills and a pile of spare change pooled at the bottom.

"This isn't enough!" Sybil cried, "How are we going to eat?" It would be another week before Terri's welfare check came in the mail and there wasn't enough food to last that long. To make matters worse, Shane was getting sick and he'd complained of not being able to swallow without his throat hurting. He coughed through the entire night, even after she gave him the last two doses of cough syrup.

"When I come home from school, I may have to call Grandmother Rose."

"Don't you dare!" Terri spat back. "I don't need her!"

"Maybe you don't need her, but we do." She took Shane by the hand. "Let's go!"

IT HAD BEEN FIFTEEN MINUTES SINCE THE DISMISSAL bell rang. The throngs of children leaving school thinned to a trickle yet Sybil didn't see Shane anywhere. It wasn't unusual for Shane to stay after school for detention, thanks to his occasional bouts of stubbornness. She figured he got himself into trouble and was stuck once again paying the price for his poor behavior. She walked down the corridor to the Kindergarten wing. The door to his classroom was open, so she peered inside. Shane's home room teacher sat at a massive desk at the rear of the room, writing on a tablet.

"Excuse me, Mrs. Drummond."

Mrs. Drummond, never lifting her head, peeked above her reading glasses, her hair a salt and pepper bird's nest.

"May I help you?" She asked.

"I'm looking for Shane. He's supposed to meet me at the gate after the dismissal bell rings."

"Ms. Taylor picked him up at noon today."

"My mother picked him up? Why?"

"Shane didn't feel well this morning and spiked a fever. The nurse called your mother to come and get him."

Sybil figured he was catching a cold but had no idea about the fever. Maybe Terri took him to see a doctor.

"I hope he feels better," Mrs. Drummond added.

It was the first time in quite awhile Sybil could walk home alone and not have to keep an eye on Shane. Shane was so easily distracted by the silliest things – an ant hill, a beehive, or even condensation dripping from an air conditioner. She had to remind him to look both ways before crossing the street, and constantly tell him to tie his shoelaces so he wouldn't trip and fall. What should have taken ten minutes swelled to thirty when walking with Shane. Sybil skipped the entire way and arrived at the apartment her fastest time ever.

Terri was ironing an outfit in the corner of the living room. It was a floral halter top and jeans that fit like a second skin. She was going out to party.

"Mrs. Drummond said you picked Shane up early."

"Uh huh."

Sybil looked into the bedroom and was surprised to find he wasn't there.

"Then where is he?"

"Shane is fine," Terri mumbled.

"But where is he?" Sybil insisted.

Terri started to repeat the same answer until she turned and saw the look on Sybil's face. "Shane is visiting Nona Jenkins on twentieth street. He's gonna stay there for the next week or so."

The Jenkins? Sybil had to think hard to remember who the Jenkins were. *Twentieth Street...* then she remembered. They owned the G&N candy store on the corner three blocks west. Their home was right next to the store. They were in their mid forties and had no children from their marriage. Sybil once heard Terri tell a friend that Nona couldn't bear children because of a "procedure" she had when she was in high school, however Nona was not one to wallow in self-pity. She kept a house full of nieces and nephews on holidays and during most of the summer. On Halloween she arranged a costume party for the neighborhood children, and the year before she hosted a slumber party for the Girl Scout troop she led.

"Did you say a week!" Sybil hollered.

"Yes, Sybil," she answered, her voice exasperated.

"Why?"

"Because that's the best place for him right now."

"But why so long? Why can't he come home today?"

"Shane can't come home until the beginning of the month when I get more money. The nurse thinks Shane has asthma and maybe strep throat. A lot of the other kids are out of school because of strep too. I can't afford a thermometer or even cold medicine. I got some food today but it's not enough for the three of us. Shane is better off where he can eat well and get the proper medicine to get better."

"You don't even talk to the Jenkins. Shane barely knows them. Sending him there is like sending him to live with strangers!"

"I've known them for over eleven years. Anyway, you can't undo it Sybil. Shane's gonna stay with them until he feels better and I can feed him properly and that's that."

"If you get money before then, can I go pick him up?"

"You can get him in a week."

Sybil checked the calendar on the fridge. It was exactly eight days until Terri's check came in the mail - Saturday, July 1st to be exact. She circled the date on the calendar and wrote in black magic marker, 'pick up Shane'. She tossed the marker on the kitchen counter and folded her arms. "If it's so much better at the Jenkins house, why didn't you send me too?" she asked while sucking her teeth, her head bobbing side to side.

Terri waved Sybil away. She slipped on the too tight jeans, swiped her lips with gloss and left for a night at the club.

ON THE FIRST OF JULY, SYBIL WAITED until just after noon to check the mailbox on the first floor. She unlocked the tiny metal door and peered inside. There sat Terri's monthly welfare check atop a stack of envelopes which were most likely bills. Terri didn't bother to take the pile of bills from the mailbox until she had the money to pay them. A tall pile meant they were in danger of having the electric or gas cut off. Today's stack was short. She took out the envelope with the welfare check and charged up the stairs to the apartment.

"I have your check right here in my hand." She waived the envelope in Terri's face. "Now you can buy food, a thermometer, medicine, whatever you need. I'm picking up Shane today." Terri snatched the envelope from her hand.

"I'll get him when I'm ready to get him. Not when you tell me to."

"But you said he could come home after you got more food. Now you have the money to get everything he needs."

"Not now, Sybil!"

"If you're not going to pick him up, at least go and check on him. How do you know he's alright?" Sybil questioned.

"If I thought Shane was in any danger, I wouldn't allow him to stay there. Now mind your business and let me take care of it!"

"If you won't do it, then I will. I'm going to the Jenkins house to make sure he's okay, right now!" Sybil bolted out the door.

"Get back here!" Terri called after her. But Sybil didn't stop running until she was standing on the welcome mat on the front porch of the Jenkins residence, her fist raised to knock on the door. Nona Jenkins opened the door so fast, Sybil wondered if she weren't expecting her.

"Hi. Ms. Nona. I really miss Shane. When is he coming home? Is he okay? Can I see him, please?"

"Do you realize you just asked me three questions back to back without pausing to take a breath?" She laughed loud and hearty from her belly, like a man. "One thing at a time, honey.

Shane is taking a nap right now, but you're welcome to stay until he wakes up."

Nona wore an ankle length, blue and beige prairie dress and dreadlocks pinned in a loose bun at the base of her neck. Bronze bangles layered her wrist to her elbow. Her feet were bare. Nona walked over to the fridge, her dress swaying from side to side. She pulled out leftover containers of food and warmed them on the stove. Then she fixed Sybil a heaping plate of fried pork chops, greens and corn muffins, and poured a tall glass of fruit punch.

Halfway through shoveling forkfuls of food in her mouth, Sybil realized Nona never even asked her if she wanted anything to eat. She simply pointed Sybil toward a chair and sat the plate on the table before her. Sybil was ashamed of her hunger, but not enough to turn down a meal. She hadn't had this much good food since Grandmother Rose was in town.

"Thank you Mrs. Jenkins," she murmured between burps and hiccups, her plate clean. She slid her chair back to get up from the table when Shane came running into the room.

"Sybil!" He leapt into her arms, knocking her clear from the chair. They sat on the floor giggling and hugging.

"I missed you too." He ducked out of the way with an impish grin when she puckered her lips to kiss him. Sybil sat back and looked Shane over.

"Is that a new outfit *and* new sneakers? You smell good, too, and I like the new haircut."

Shane ran his fingers over his hair from front to back. "I'm hansome, ain't I?"

Sybil bent to kiss him again. He ducked a second time, but not before she planted one in the middle of his forehead. He pretended to wipe it off then got up running toward the stairs.

"Come see my new room!"

Sybil followed him upstairs. Shane had his own bedroom full of books, toys and games, and photos of whales and dolphins decorated the walls. A desk with a globe was to the left of the bed, and to the right were colorful bins stacked in five neat rows, all with white labels identifying their contents - art supplies, blocks, action figures, etc. Blue and white curtains displayed a nautical theme with sailboats bobbing at the hem. A full fifteen seconds went by before Sybil closed her mouth.

"This is a really cool room!"

"And guess what I did, Sybil."

"What?"

"I went to the zoo, then I went roller skatin', and dis mornin' I had a check up at the dentist. I got six cavities." He held up his fingers and grinned like cavities were a thing to be proud of.

"Wow," Sybil exclaimed. "It's not fair that you get to stay here in this big nice house while I'm stuck in the apartment with Terri."

They sat on bean bag chairs and drew pictures in Shane's sketchbook until Mrs. Jenkins called Shane for dinner.

"Shane, I have to go now but it shouldn't be much longer until Terri comes to bring you home."

"Please come back soon." He wrapped his arms around her, his head buried in her shirt.

"I'll come visit every day, and I promise to spend the whole day with you on my birthday. It's next Saturday, you know. As a matter of fact, if Terri doesn't bring you home by then, I'm gonna take you home with me. You'll be my present."

"Sybil, you sure you promise?"

"I'm sure."

"Wake up Sybil," Terri jostled her. "We're going out to get you a new dress today. Happy Birthday!"

Her last two birthdays came and went without any acknowledgement at all. Terri was either too drunk or too hung over to remember them. Nevertheless, there she stood over her bed - awake, sober, fully dressed and ready to take her shopping. Sybil wondered if she were dreaming.

"Is this for real?" she questioned.

"Hurry up and get ready. The store opens at ten. I want to get in and out before the crowds get too big."

"I haven't had a new dress in ages!"

She and Terri took the bus downtown. Sybil sat closest to the window. She bounced up and down as the bus travelled over the uneven roadway. Exhaust mingled with someone's pungent cologne made her eyes water. She watched the passengers boarding and disembarking and wondered where they were all scurrying to. Perhaps they were all going downtown to buy something special too. As they approached center city, the buildings grew taller, and more and more cars and buses filled the roadway. City Hall loomed ahead. Terri poked her with her elbow.

"We're getting off the next stop."

The bus came to an abrupt halt just as she and Terri stood up. She held onto the support pole with both hands and nearly landed back in her seat. Sybil and Terri pushed their way through a crowd clamoring to get on the bus, then Sybil skipped right over to a street vendor selling pretzels, hot dogs and sodas. They shared a soft, salty pretzel and a grape soda, then Terri let her hold a soft, round kitten in the pet store across the street from the hot dog stand. She snuggled the tiny, warm animal close to her cheek and imagined how it would feel to have one of her own.

There were a few more blocks of twists and turns before Terri finally opened the door to Tina's world, a dress shop with the widest variety of dresses in town, from newborn to adult. Sybil squealed and clapped her hands.

"Look at all these pretty dresses! I've never seen so many in one store. And they're all brand new!" For once she didn't have to resort to worn thrift store finds. She walked down the aisles with her arms outstretched, feeling the textures of the many fabrics between her fingers - silk, taffeta, chiffon, wool. Sybil grinned so hard her lips stuck to her teeth and her cheeks hurt.

"I wish we could do this more often," Sybil told Terri.

"Maybe we will," Terri told her in a flat voice.

Sybil smelled the alcohol on Terri's breath. Terri downed a Vodka and tonic before they left home. Sybil was sure it was just one drink since there wasn't time for much else that morning, and it took far more than that to make Terri drunk.

Sybil tried on several dozen dresses, including long, straight, plain ones and short a-line dresses with layers of ruffles and ribbons. She took her time, even trying on dresses they could never afford just to see how she'd look. She finally settled on a gray wool jumper and a blue cotton jumper with tiny white flowers.

"It's too warm for the gray one, but when school starts, I can wear a sweater underneath or a blouse for special occasions. I'll take them both but I need the gray one a size up, please," she told the store clerk.

"I'm afraid we don't have any more of those in your size."

"Sybil, maybe we should come back next week. I'm getting tired," Terri told her.

Sybil knew that what she really wanted to say was that it was almost half past two and she wanted to get home to take a nap before going out to the club. Sybil wanted to drag it out, make Terri sweat a little, take her time trying on dozens more. But she didn't want to make a scene on the best birthday she'd had in a long time.

"Just the blue one then," she told the sales clerk.

After leaving Tina's World, they stopped at a deli where Sybil picked the fattest, juiciest pickle from the barrel to eat with her sandwich, then boarded the bus to go home. She hugged the dress close to her belly during the entire ride.

"When you finish hanging up your dress, start the laundry, clear the dishes from the sink, and mop the floors," Terri told her before she even put the key into the door lock.

Sybil opened her mouth to complain that she already had plans to see Shane, and didn't think it was fair to have to do chores on her birthday, but she didn't want to appear ungrateful.

Terri did buy her a dress for the first time in years. By the time she finished her chores, nightfall approached. It was too late to visit her brother.

"My birthday was wonderful, but it would have been even better if I spent some of it with Shane," she murmured into her pillow, drifting off to sleep. "I'll make it up to him tomorrow."

SYBIL ROSE EARLIER THAN USUAL THE FOLLOWING morning, so she'd have the entire day to spend with Shane. She went to the kitchen to make breakfast, opened the refrigerator door, and stood back in awe. Stacks of luncheon meats and cheeses, produce, fresh fruit and several gallons of milk and juice filled the shelves. The freezer was likewise stocked with frozen meats and vegetables and ice cream. She opened the kitchen cabinets and they too were stuffed from top to bottom with cases of soup, noodles, and canned vegetables. What did not fit on the shelves lined the floors and sat atop the cabinets.

"There's enough food here for a year!" she squealed. She checked the jar that held their money and it was stuffed so tight with bills and coins the lid sat on crooked. "Now it's really time for Shane to come home!"

She put on her new blue jumper, curled her bangs – who wants to wear a new dress without a nice hairdo - and slipped past Terri who was still sleeping on the sofa. Sybil felt unique in this regard. She didn't know anyone else her age who could get away with leaving the house at seven o'clock on a Sunday morning without being noticed.

The morning was still and clear. It was too early for the neighborhood children to fill the streets with bicycles, skateboards and the sounds of laughter and play. The old folks made their way to sunrise service with their Bibles tucked under their arms, the birds greeted the morning with song. Sybil smoothed her new dress and skipped up the steps to the Jenkins' porch. She paused at the top of the landing, her head to one side. Something was odd about the house that day, but she couldn't quite figure out exactly what it was. An uneasiness sent a shiver through her bones. Sybil shrugged it off. She walked up to the door and rang the bell. Chimes echoed down the quiet street. When no one answered, she knocked, softly at first then gradually harder. She waited a full minute before lifting her fist to bang on the door yet again, when a familiar gnawing seized her belly. Only fear caused her to have a sudden ache. *Why am I afraid?* Finally the realization of what stood before her, registered in her brain. Every window in the house was bare. There were no curtains, no blinds, no shades - just the smooth, barren glass bordered by wooden frames. Sybil's heart beat loud and fast in her ears. She pressed her face against the living room window and saw clear through the house. It was completely empty. No chairs, no lamps, no pictures on the walls... nothing at all. Sybil opened her mouth to scream and choked on her sobs. She stood frozen, immobile before the empty home until an unraveling set her free. She broke loose, running back and forth across the porch, banging on the windows and door.

"Shane, where are you!" she yelled. "Where's my brother! Shane!" She ran to the Jenkins' store but that too was vacant so she hurried to the house next door and kicked the door until a red-faced man with a thick mustache opened his window.

"What the hell are you doing?" he growled.

"I can't find my brother. He was staying with the Jenkins. Where did they go!" she screamed.

"I didn't even know they were moving until yesterday when the moving van came. Took up almost half the street. But I'll tell you this… If I ever catch you kicking my damn door again I'll…"

Sybil raced to another stranger's house, but they too knew nothing, except that the family had moved away. Neighbors heard the commotion and came out of their homes onto porches and sidewalks, wearing nightclothes, head scarves and house shoes. Sybil raced up and down the street sobbing and questioning people at random.

"Does anybody have an address?" she asked a young mother holding her infant child. "Did they leave a number?" she asked a middle aged man hanging out of his bedroom window. "Somebody help me!" She pleaded.

The neighbors shook their heads with bewilderment and pity, but they knew nothing. The only certain fact was that the Jenkins cleaned out their store and moved out of their home the day before. Barely containing her panic, Sybil paced the sidewalk in front of the empty house, tears darkening the white flowers on her new blue jumper.

She had no recollection of her walk home, yet all at once she flung open the apartment door and threw herself at Terri who sat on the sofa facing the door, as if waiting for her to return.

"I know you did this!" Sybil cried. She straddled her mother, their faces inches apart, and grasped her shoulders, shaking her so hard, her head snapped back and forth. "How could you let him go! I could have taken care of him. I've always taken care of him," she sobbed. "Why?"

"I'm sorry," Terri choked, eyes stretched wide. Her hands were folded in her lap, knuckles taut, and her knees bounced nervously up and down.

"He wanted to come home! I promised him I'd bring him home!"

Terri stood, knocking Sybil to the floor. "I'm so sorry," her voice echoed as she ran out of the apartment and down the hall.

"I could have taken care of him!" Sybil cried after her mother.

"I could have taken care of him!" she cried over and over.

"**G**randmother Rose, Shane is gone!" Sybil gasped into the receiver.

"What do you mean gone?"

"Terri left him with Mr. and Mrs. Jenkins, and…"

"Who's that?" Grandmother Rose interrupted.

"They own the candy store down on Twentieth Street. Terri sent Shane there to stay for awhile, and when I went to visit, the whole house was empty. They moved, Grandmother Rose. They moved! And mommy won't look for him. Nobody will look for him!"

"Lord have mercy, what has she done. I'm coming baby."

"Hurry, Grandmother, please hurry!"

"Sybil, let me talk to Terri… Sybil!" Sybil had already dropped the phone and took off running back to Twentieth Street, still searching, sobbing and questioning strangers.

"How can nobody know anything? Please help me!" She screamed.

"Go home, child," one woman told her. "You've been here all morning. You're makin' yourself sick."

"I have to find him. He's my baby brother and he's only six."

"Where's your mother? Did you tell her?" someone yelled.

"I did tell her, she won't look for him!"

After awhile, she gave up asking questions - no one had any answers anyway - and walked the streets. She walked for the next two hours. She walked because she couldn't remain still. The feel of the ground under her feet gave her solidity. Movement gave her purpose. Glued to her forehead were the bangs she'd neatly curled that morning. Her swollen eyes burned in the fiery July sun, and her parched, cottony tongue adhered to the roof of her mouth, yet still she walked.

"Sybil, baby, it's time to go home."

The familiar voice broke the spell of her pacing. It was the voice of comfort and safety. Sybil turned around and folded into Grandmother Rose's arms, resting her head against her breast.

"He's just a little boy and I don't know where he is," she murmured.

"I know, sweetie. For now, just come with me."

***

"Where is he, Terri?" Terri sat in a kitchen chair hunched over with her head in her hands. Grandmother Rose stood over her with her hands on her hips.

"I don't know."

"He's your child, a young child at that. You're his mother, it's your job to know where he is."

"I... I really don't know," she stuttered.

"Have you called the police?"

Terri shook her head.

"Then what the heck are you waiting for? You should have called hours ago!"

Terri's eyes widened. "Wait!"

It was too late. Grandmother Rose was already dialing.

A patrol car must have been close by because an officer knocked on the door within a few minutes. He was a tall, thin, severe man with a harsh jaw and an accusing stare.

"My grandson is missing," Grandmother Rose explained to the officer. "My daughter allowed him to spend some time with her neighbors, the Jenkins, and no one can find them. They moved and we believe they took my grandson with them. We don't have an address, phone number or even a next of kin."

The police officer looked at Terri. "Is this correct, ma'am?" His voice was cool, lacking any inflection.

"Yes," she said, small and trembling.

"Did you consent to the Jenkins couple taking your child?"

"No, but..." Terri looked at Sybil and Grandmother Rose then looked back pleadingly at the officer.

"Can you two leave the room?" the officer asked. "I'd like to talk to Ms. Taylor alone."

"But he's my grandson and…"

"Please, ma'am." The officer interrupted with a pointed stare.

She grabbed Sybil by the arm and the two waited outside in the hallway. Sybil pressed her ear tight against the door. She heard Terri mumble something about guardianship, then the police officer left the apartment.

"You're leaving so soon?" Grandmother Rose questioned. "Did you get the Jenkins' last address? A list of people who last saw Shane? Don't you need a picture of my grandson?"

The police officer held up both his hands. "There's nothing I can do, ma'am."

"It's your job to do something. A child is missing!"

"You'll have to talk to Miss Taylor about the details, but there's been no wrong done here, unless you consider the fact that Miss Terri left her son in the care of someone she obviously didn't know well." His voice sounded angry then quickly returned to its detached state. "The Jenkins are the legal guardians of the child. Ms. Taylor has the appropriate paperwork. I'll turn this over to social services for further review, but if they confirm a legal and valid transfer of guardianship approved by the court, there's not much else anyone can do."

Grandmother Rose and Sybil rushed back into the apartment.

"What is this talk of guardianship?" Grandmother asked in a hesitant voice, as if she didn't really want to know.

"What did you do?" Sybil demanded.

Grandmother Rose held a palm up in front of Sybil. "Hush. Let her speak."

"I would never have agreed to it if I knew they were gonna move away. It's just that Shane needed more than I could give him and I knew he'd be in a better place if he could just stay with them for awhile, eat healthy and get the medicine he needs."

"And the groceries and money?" Sybil spat.

"Yes, they did offer to take care of him, and they gave us groceries and money, but it wasn't all about the money."

"You never cared about Shane! All you cared about was the money! All of a sudden we have all this food and then Shane is gone! You sold my brother!" Sybil screamed so loud her voice went away for a moment.

"No!" Terri countered. "There was so much more to it than that. I can't take care of him the way he needs to be taken care of. Sybil, you can fend for yourself. But Shane..."

Sybil could no longer bear to look at Terri. Disgust and horror forced her to avert her stare. Of all the things Terri had done over the years this was the worst of all. She looked to Grandmother Rose for comfort, but Grandmother's eyes were full. She blinked and a single tear rolled down her cheek. She had so much more gray hair than Sybil remembered, and the wrinkles around her eyes deepened, aging Grandmother Rose beyond her sixty-two years.

"You had plenty other options. Why, Terri? Was it so bad you had to give up your child? A child you birthed into this world?" Grandmother's hands were outstretched, pleading. "Why didn't you send him to me? Ask for help? He's my grandbaby, and I wouldn't deny him anything."

"I didn't expect them to move, Mother."

"How do you live with yourself?"

Terri pulled a lighter from her pocket and attempted to light a cigarette, but her hands were too unsteady. She tossed both on the kitchen table.

"Maybe Nona will call and let me know where he is. Maybe..."

"Think, Terri. They moved without telling a soul. They don't want to be found. She's a barren woman and you provided her with her one chance to have a child. And now you think she's just gonna call you up and say 'here he is, take him back'? He's gone and you better hope to God you find that child, or you will have to live with this for the rest of your life. You will wake up every day and wonder, 'where is my baby' and there is no one to blame but you."

Sybil stepped forward. "It's my fault, too. I didn't visit him when I was supposed to. If only I..."

"Hush, Sybil. You have no reason to blame yourself. This was Terri's doing."

Grandmother suddenly had a hard time catching her breath. She held her hand over the middle of her chest. Sybil pulled a chair behind her.

"Sit down."

She grimaced then eased down onto the chair. "Oh my grandbaby," she moaned, still clutching her chest. Sybil stroked her hair.

"We'll keep looking for him, Grandmother, just you and me."

During the weeks following Shane's disappearance, Sybil remained planted on the porch of the vacant Jenkins home for so many hours on so many days, that years later she still recalled in vivid detail the breaks in the porch's concrete floor, the brown-gray shade of the mortar that separated the bricks, the chipped almond-tinted light fixture suspended from the ceiling, and the contrast between the newly laid cemented steps and the old porch and landing. She couldn't bear to leave lest someone brought word of Shane's whereabouts, and she felt an overwhelming need to be near the last place she saw him.

It was all that the neighbors talked about on Twentieth Street that summer, but as is the case with all tragedies, folks eventually moved on to other happenings. They stopped speculating about "that poor, missing Taylor boy," his grieving sister and their drunk negligent mother, and moved on to gossip about the local house fire, a rape, and an upstanding neighbor arrested for a murder he committed sixteen years ago. How could they just forget about poor Shane?

Sybil felt cast off, disregarded. She didn't believe that her circumstance was worse than all the others, but didn't it at least warrant equal consideration? In return, she gave them indifference. She wore her indifference like a crown, with her shoulders back and her head held high. She enveloped her grief and anguish so deeply within the recesses of the cocoon of indifference, people wondered whether she grieved at all. Over time, the indifference fit so comfortably it transitioned seamlessly from the outside to the inside. Sybil soon became what she wanted the world to see.

She was an automaton, observing her robot-like life from the outside. Days, weeks, months passed with staid adherence to her new world view. Nothing penetrated her exterior of indifference. Nothing, that is, until that first Christmas season without Shane. That was the day the darkness descended. The darkness ushered in all that Sybil shut out – anguish, pain, fears and memories. Suddenly, everything became insurmountable, even the daily tasks that gave order to her days.

She heard the sounds of music that Christmas morning, carols sung to an old, out-of-tune piano. It was the family in the apartment next door. Children cheered and clapped as the song came to a close, then the pianist began an introduction to yet another lively carol and the singing began all over again. Had she not lacked the strength, Sybil would have banged on the walls to shut them up. She filled her lungs with air to scream – drown out the frivolous merriment that drove her further into a dark place – when she heard a tapping on her bedroom door, followed by Terri's voice.

"Merry Christmas, Sybil, there's a gift for you under the tree."

A gift? How ludicrous.

Sybil wanted to flee the darkness that consumed her, run to her mother's arms for respite, nurturing, and light, but Terri was just Terri. She was no giver of light. Sybil just lay there on the bottom bunk where Shane used to sleep and stared at the springs of the bunk overhead.

At noon on Christmas day, Sybil still lay in bed. Terri tiptoed by her room and checked in on her from time to time, yet didn't rouse her. When Sybil didn't rise the following day or the next day, Terri called Grandmother Rose.

"She hasn't been out of bed since before Christmas, she barely eats and only gets up for the bathroom."

"Is she sick?"

"Not in the normal way. Not a fever or cold. No complaints about aches or pains. Just... blue."

"She's grieving her brother. She needs you to take care of her."

"Mother, I can fix the ordinary stuff, give her aspirin for a headache or a bandage for a scrape or a cut, but what am I supposed to do when it's on the inside... and it's my fault." Her voice faltered.

"Terri, she's all you got left. Reach out to her."

"Please, just come."

THE APARTMENT WAS VOID OF THE customary sounds of a household. There was no radio, no television, not even the drip of a faucet or the creak of a door opening and closing. All was still. Terri crept about timidly, deferring to her daughter's grief with reverence.

Grandmother Rose let herself in with a spare key. She insisted on it after Shane disappeared so she could check in on Terri and Sybil at random. She hung her coat on the hook behind the door, strolled past Terri without a hint of acknowledgement and headed straight for Sybil's room. She slipped off her shoes, climbed into bed with Sybil, wrapped her arms around her and rocked her like she was still a little girl.

"It's gonna be alright," she whispered.

Sybil had long since run out of tears. All that was left was a bottomless, relentless ache. Her entire body ached. She trembled there in her grandmother's arms while she rocked her with endless, fluid motion. The night ushered in memories of Shane, his first day of kindergarten, the time she held his hand while he took his first steps, and the day he learned to utter her name. In the midst of her torturous memories, the gentle rocking, a salve for her soul, endured.

When the night yielded to dawn, Grandmother Rose fed Sybil warm pudding from a spoon and read passages of comfort from the book of Joshua. Sybil was too lost in her own anguish to heed the significance of the biblical passages, but the rhythm of Grandmother's soothing voice and the old world cadence of the King James, provided her some comfort.

Grandmother Rose left her to rest while she cooked a pot of chicken soup. She returned with a bowl and a spoon and fed her again. She wiped Sybil's face and hands, then took her back into her arms. It was then that she spoke.

"What's ailing you, sweetie."

"I feel a darkness."

Grandmother Rose placed her hand on Sybil's cheek. "Go on."

"I feel it all day and all night. When I go to sleep at night I expect it to be gone when the sun comes up, but when morning comes, it's still there."

"You're grieving is all."

"But we grieve when someone dies. Do you think Shane is..."

"Oh no dear, I'm not saying that. There are many reasons people grieve. We grieve when someone we care about goes away for a long time, when friendships end, when children grow up, and sometimes when we grow from young to old. There are all types of grieving."

"When will it go away?"

"I don't think grief ever really goes away."

"So how will I feel better?"

"You live with it. You carry it with you. It's heavy at first, but as time goes by, it gets a little easier to bear."

"So ten years from now I'll still feel like this?"

"In a way, 'cept it won't hurt the same way it does now. But you don't worry about ten years from now. You just focus on gettin' by day to day. If you can't see through to the next day, take it hour by hour."

Grandmother Rose allowed Sybil an entire week of coddling and soothing, an entire week to be a little girl again. Then she woke Sybil up one morning with conviction and authority in her voice.

"Enough is enough! I know you miss your brother, but now is as good a time as ever to learn how to carry on after suffering.

That's what life is you know... carrying on. Besides, all this wallowing isn't good for someone your age. Get dressed! We're going outside. And bundle up. It's twenty- five degrees."

"I don't feel like going outside."

Grandmother Rose yanked the blanket off of Sybil and stood over her with her arms folded. Sybil's body retracted to the fetal position from the sudden whisk of cool air.

"I'll go out tomorrow."

"Get up now! Sybil. I've been here a week and you've barely left this room. If I thought you'd do it on your own, I'd leave you alone. But you won't. So get up!"

Sybil slid out of the bed and dressed in layers. She sat along-side Grandmother Rose on the front steps of the apartment building. The wind stung her cheeks, her fingertips grew tingly and numb. She pulled her hat down over her hears, then tilted her face to the sky, inhaling until her lungs were full of the winter air. She exhaled slowly then continued breathing in massive gulps of air until her mind was alert and clear.

"Looks like we got a dusting of snow," Grandmother said.

Sybil snapped into awareness of her surroundings. A thin layer of powder covered the streets and cars. Styrofoam cups and broken beer bottles littered the ground. Bits of silver streamers sparkled in the intermittent sunlight and the burning residue of firecrackers from the night before stung her nose.

"I slept through it all?"

"I'm afraid you did, although I don't know how with all the shooting and yelling going on out here last night."

"But granny, it's a New Year. Nobody woke me up to celebrate the New Year, and I missed the first snow of the season."

"Your rest was far more important. Besides, you have all year to celebrate."

"Nothing is worth celebrating without Shane. Valentine's Day is next month. Did you know that was Shane's favorite day of the whole year? He painted hearts with my picture in the middle and told everybody I was his valentine. I got him his very own box of chocolates last year. He ate them slow, one each day, to make them last for the rest of the month. I hope we find him in time for Valentine's day."

"I pray for that every day, sweetie."

Sybil knew that Grandmother did more than just pray. She worked harder than anyone to find Shane, driving to playgrounds, hospitals, schools and even calling all the Jenkins listed in the White Pages.

"Do you really want to know what I think? I don't think I'll ever see Shane again." She thought of how she took care of Shane and it comforted her somewhat. "I hope he knows how much I miss him."

"He knows."

"Why did it have to happen and how can Mommy go on like things are okay?"

"You think it doesn't bother her? There is no mother on this earth who wouldn't hurt if the baby she birthed into this world just up and disappeared. She may not show it on the outside, but it's eating away at her on the inside."

"It's eatin' away at me too. I think about him so hard…" Her voice trailed off.

"Put Shane in God's hands. We have looked everywhere, worried night and day and done all we can. It's God's turn."

"What if God wants him to stay where he is?"

"That's God's choice. We have no say in the matter."

Sybil remembered the last time she saw Shane. He was clean, healthy, happy and boasting about his fancy room and his trip to the dentist and the zoo. Sybil didn't quite smile, but the lines around her eyes relaxed and her lips were no longer in a straight line. *I have to believe that wherever he is, he's okay.*

"You're gonna be alright, Sybil." Grandmother Rose wrapped an arm around her and pulled her close. "Yes, my dear. You'll be just fine."

"But my dear Terri," she said as she looked toward the sky, "may God in his infinite wisdom help you. I no longer can."

ybil leaned out of the kitchen window. Misting rain popped tiny droplets of water on her nose. Although it was early June, the cool breeze was reminiscent of fall.

"What if she isn't coming?" She asked Terri, who'd just tidied up the kitchen in preparation for Grandmother Rose's arrival.

"She's coming, Sybil. She wouldn't miss your graduation for the world."

"But it's only eighth grade. She may not think it's a big deal."

"She'll be here."

The gray Buick rounded the corner and pulled into the parking space alongside the apartment building. Grandmother Rose emerged wearing one of her ludicrous church hats, the one with the overlarge bow and feathers that stuck straight up in the air. She even managed to find shoes with identical bows to match the hat. She opened the back door to the car and draped two garment bags over her arm.

"She's here with the dresses!" Sybil squealed.

As soon as Grandmother Rose came inside, Sybil grabbed the garment bag with the white dress peeking from the bottom, and pulled it over her head atop her slip right there in the living room. It was narrow at the waist and flared at the hem with tiny beading around the neckline and sleeve. For Terri she bought a pale pink suit with short sleeves and cream satin pumps. Terri appeared nearly functional with her hair pulled back into a low curly ponytail. Grandmother warned Terri to 'be sober and ready to leave' when she arrived, and Terri complied.

"Okay, ladies, let's go!" Grandmother Rose announced once they were ready.

"It doesn't start for another hour," Terri explained.

"Which is why we're leaving now, I don't want a leftover seat. I wanna choose where I sit."

Grandmother Rose's Buick inched along in fits and starts, drawing the ire of inpatient drivers who honked their horns and glowered at her through their windows as they sped by. In spite of her snail's pace, and the constant braking and accelerating, they were so early for the promotion ceremony that Grandmother Rose and Terri snagged the best seats in the center of the first row.

The graduating class sat on the stage of the school auditorium on padded folding chairs arranged in neat rows. After the principal opened the ceremony with a congratulatory speech, the names of the students receiving special awards were announced. Sybil's name was not among this group. She earned no special honors. Her grades were average at best and her attendance sporadic. She was grateful simply to be promoted to the ninth grade. After the awards were given out, all the students' names were called in alphabetical order. It took awhile to get to the 't's' but finally Sybil's name was announced. When she rose to accept her graduation certificate, she heard Grandmother's voice above all the applause.

"That's my grandbaby," she yelled. "My grandbaby! Go on, girl!"

Sybil held her head high and took her time walking across the stage, taking in all the sights and sounds of that great moment, a moment she never wanted to end. Her certificate in hand, she turned to the audience to smile for the photographer. Right in her line of vision, to the left of the photographer, sat Terri. Terri smiled and clapped and winked at her daughter, and Sybil noticed something for the first time.

Pride? Was that pride on Terri's face? The flash of light from the photographer blinded her. She closed her eyes to recover from the flash then opened them fast. *There it was again! Pride!* Perhaps she had it wrong all these years and maybe she meant something to Terri. Perhaps she really was someone special, someone to be proud of. It wasn't a feeling she recalled ever experiencing before, even when she deliberately set out to impress her mother. Grandmother Rose made her feel special, and she was special in Shane's eyes, but the pride and recognition that came from a mother had eluded her. She missed out on it her entire life. She wanted to wrap her arms around it, and never let it go. Sybil couldn't stop herself from grinning. The rest of the graduation was a hazy jumble of names, applause and flashing cameras, that one act of pride the defining moment of the day.

The three of them celebrated at a diner not far from the apartment. Sybil sat right across the table from Terri. Throughout the entire meal and dessert she tried her best to catch Terri's gaze so she could get a glimpse of more pride, feel how special she was to her mother. Terri's shifting gaze landed everywhere except on Sybil.

"So how does it feel to be a graduate?" Grandmother Rose asked while adding too much sugar to her tea.

"It feels great. I can't wait to go to high school."

"Considering what you've been through, this is a big accomplishment," Grandmother Rose told her in between sips. "Now don't get to high school and start messing with boys. You concentrate on your studies and keep your grades up."

"You did well." Terri interjected. Her words were stilted and awkward and her head was down. Grandmother Rose and Sybil both turned to look at Terri. Sybil pretended not to hear what she said so her mother could speak those sweet words once again.

"What did you say?" she asked in her most innocent voice.

"You did well… keep going to school. These days you can't survive out here without a high school diploma."

Sybil grinned.

GRANDMOTHER'S BUICK CAME TO A JERKING HALT outside the apartment building. Sybil was glad to be home. She hated how rude the other drivers were to Grandmother Rose.

"I'm not coming in. I have a long drive ahead of me, and I wanna get home before it's too dark. My night vision isn't what it used to be."

"Bye Mother." Terri got out of the car first and walked ahead of Sybil in a hurry.

Sybil leaned into the passenger window, her promotion certificate held with two fingers, so it wouldn't get wrinkled or creased.

"Grandmother Rose, I hate for you to go. Things work better when you're here."

"I'm just a crutch for your mother. She won't learn from her mistakes if I'm around to patch things up. I won't be here always, you know."

"Don't say that. I can't imagine not having you here with us. Besides, you're only sixty five, sixty five years *young*."

Grandmother Rose chucked, "I like that, Sybil." The sky darkened followed by rumbling and a quick flash of light. "You go on in before the storm starts. I'm gonna get ahead of the traffic, and hopefully ahead of this storm, too."

"You'll have to drive a little faster and give the brakes a rest if you hope to get ahead of anything at all," Sybil giggled.

"Go on, girl." Grandmother Rose shooed her off before starting on her way.

Sybil couldn't wait to get inside to hear Terri tell her more of what she was missing, share her dreams for Sybil, encourage her to go far and make something of herself. Normally she ran up the stairs by two's but she took her time going upstairs so her promotion certificate wouldn't get damaged in any way.

"Terri's proud of me." Her voice echoed off the walls in the landing. Saying it out loud gave her butterflies in her stomach. She opened the door with great anticipation, her certificate clutched to her chest, only to find Terri lounging on the sofa with a Vodka and tonic in one hand and the telephone in the other.

"So what time do you want to meet at the club tonight?" she spoke into the receiver.

She barely glanced at Sybil. Not a quick smile or even a lingering gaze. Her eyes passed over her daughter, just as they did any other inanimate object in the room. The pride, the encouraging words, all of it was gone. Once again Sybil was ordinary, regular, her specialness disintegrated.

Terri took a sip of her drink, crossed her legs and laughed into the receiver.

Was it all a farce? A flash of rage propelled Sybil into action. She snatched the phone from Terri.

"To think I believed for just one moment that you were really proud of me. Admit it! You couldn't wait for my graduation to be over so you could go out and get wasted. You only stayed as long as you did and said those nice things because Grandmother Rose was here!"

"What are you doing?" Terri hollered

"Admit it, Terri! Admit it was all fake!"

"You're being ridiculous. You know I care about you. Now give me the phone."

Sybil tossed the phone to her mother so hard, it flew past her and landed on the floor behind the sofa.

Terri stood her ground, as if she expected Sybil to get the phone.

When Sybil didn't budge, Teri got it herself.

"I'm sorry about that," she spoke to the person on the other end. "There's no telling what's gotten into that girl. You were saying?"

Sybil stepped forward inches from the phone receiver and yelled at the top of her voice. "You walk around pretending everything is alright. You live like Shane is still here and you had nothing to do with his being gone. I'm not like you. I can't pretend that everything's perfect. I hate it here, I hate the way you treat me, I hate that Shane is gone because of you and I can't live like it's all okay anymore!"

"I gotta go. I'll call you back." She slammed the phone onto the receiver. "You're pissing me off, Sybil!"

"Good! It beats you treating me like I'm invisible!"

"What do you want?"

"Admit you only pretended to be proud of me because Grandmother was here."

"That's not true. I am proud of you."

"And that's that? Three words of encouragement - 'you did well'. That's all I've gotten from you my whole life. I need more!"

"Sybil, I don't know what else you expect from me. It's unreasonable for me to spend every moment doling out compliments. We had a really nice day. It's over now and I'm trying to relax."

There was so much more Sybil longed to say. She wanted to tell Terri that she just wanted to spend time with her and have her say once again how proud she was. Hearing it once in a lifetime was not enough.

Terri picked up the phone and dialed again. Sybil sat cross-legged on the floor in front of her, directly in her line of vision. She ripped her promotion certificate into pieces, leaving them in a confetti pile on the floor.

Look at me.

Terri continued chatting on the phone, her eyes avoiding her daughter. Sybil turned away and fought to hold back the tears pushing their way to the surface. Terri didn't deserve anything, least of all her tears.

THE FIRST OF JULY CAME AND WENT - another birthday disregarded or perhaps forgotten. Grandmother Rose, of course, never forgot. She sent a card in the mail with fifteen dollars and phoned first thing in the morning. Grandmother sent a crisp one-dollar bill for every year. It wasn't much of a big deal when you turned six or seven but fifteen dollars when you turned fifteen was pretty good pocket change.

But from Terri there was no acknowledgement at all. In previous years, Sybil clued her in by humming Happy Birthday, or asking, "who knows what today is?" Terri would feign embarrassment and shower her with birthday wishes. On her fifteenth birthday, Sybil ceased dropping hints. A mother shouldn't have to be reminded to honor the birth of her own child.

But when July fourteenth came and went, and Terri took no heed to any form of acknowledgement, Sybil was mad enough to get even. With a nasty smile, she sauntered into the living room with large strides and arms swinging wide.

"Terri, there's something you should know."

"What, Sybil." Terri cringed at the sound of her own voice. She had come in from the bar just a few hours earlier. She nursed a hangover with a cup of coffee, soda crackers and a cold compress draped over her forehead.

"I'm moving out." She watched Terri closely, gauging her reaction.

"Where could you possibly be moving to?"

"I'm moving in with my boyfriend, Hasan. He has a duplex in Logan." It was quite a stretch. He wasn't really her boyfriend. In fact, they'd met just a few months earlier.

"Since when do you have a boyfriend, and how old is he?"

"We've been dating for two months. You didn't notice all the nights I've come home late? Oh wait, you couldn't have possibly noticed," she said sarcastically. "You were too busy drunk, hungover or partying to notice anything I was doing. And by the way, he's twenty six."

Sybil waited for a response, any response. Perhaps anger, surprise or even curiosity, but the expression on Terri's face never changed. She maintained her steady gaze at the television set.

"I'm leaving ! I'm moving out right now!" Sybil yelled, as her bold positioning swelled into indignation. It never crossed her mind that Terri might let her go with no resistance at all. But she'd already said it. She had to follow through. Void of the excitement she'd previously imagined, she packed clothes in a suitcase, and left a slip of paper with Hassan's address and phone number under a refrigerator magnet. She carried the suitcase on the side closest to Terri, to be certain she didn't miss it, and walked out.

She stood outside the door in the hall for ten minutes, waiting for Terri to yank her back inside and remind her she was only fifteen and in no way ready to move in with a man, tell her she was out of her mind to think she'd allow her to leave. She put her ear to the door. Terri didn't call her to come back. No footsteps approached. She checked her watch, waited another five minutes then made her way to a pay phone to tell Hassan she was on her way. Surely Terri would come for her when she saw the address on the fridge. Her indignation and anger seeped away, like air escaping a taut balloon. Sybil was alone and afraid.

***

Sybil met Hassan three months earlier while standing on the corner waiting for the bus after school. He pulled up to the curb in front of her in a silver Chevy Cavalier, rap music pumping through the speakers. He drove with one hand on the steering wheel and the other draped over the passenger seat. The sun bounced off his wedding band, creating a star of bright light, cigarette smoke twirled from the ashtray in the center console.

He turned down the stereo volume and stuck his head out the window. Dark shades obscured his eyes.

"What's up! I couldn't help but notice you. You look so innocent standing here on the corner with those big, beautiful eyes."

"Is that a ring I see on your finger?" Sybil shot back.

"Yea, I'm married but my wife walked out on me."

"Sounds like a pick-up line to me."

"I give you my word. If it helps, the ring is gone." He pulled off the ring and shoved it in the glove compartment.

"What did you do to make her leave you?"

"I didn't stop over here to talk about my ex. I'm here to talk to you. Get in and I'll drive you home."

On and off for the next two months, his Cavalier was waiting for her at the same spot by the curb. Some days they stopped for burgers and sodas. Other days they hung out at his place watching movies on his VCR. For Sybil, Hassan was a diversion, an excuse not to have to go home and deal with Terri. Sybil wasn't exactly clear on what his interest was in her. Was she a friend? A potential girlfriend?

She called Hassan from a pay phone, her suitcase leaning against her shins.

"Can I stay at your place for awhile?" she asked hesitantly. She hadn't thought it all through, but she was determined to shock some sense into Terri.

"Stay here? Why?" Hassan asked her.

"I'm having some problems at home." She expected him to ask her what was going on that would make her want to leave her own home. Instead he asked her how old she was.

"Seventeen going on eighteen," she lied.

"Sure," he told her. "Come on over." She knew from the flat tone of his voice he didn't believe her, but all that mattered was that she was getting away from Terri and she had a place to stay.

HASSAN WAS A PLUMBER BY TRADE. Tired after a hard day's work he popped up the footrest on his recliner, leaned back to nearly horizontal and watched sports on his projection T.V. while sipping a forty until late in the night. He wasn't particular about which sport he watched. He loved them all – basketball, football, baseball, even golf. He permitted no interruption while he watched the games and demanded that there be no noise in the house at all, including heavy footsteps, doors opening and closing or even a running faucet. Disobeying evoked a torrent of cussing and fussing that went on far longer than the infraction warranted.

Sybil was astounded at the transformation in Hassan. Once a friendly fast talking man with quick, albeit ineffective, pick-up lines, he was now nearly mute. His conversations were relegated to 'get me a beer', or 'fix me another plate of food'. It wasn't that Sybil didn't attempt conversation. Her eager, 'how was your day' was met with 'fine' or 'ok'. She resorted to deliberately asking him open-ended questions – mostly just to have someone to talk to, but 'what are we gonna do this weekend' was met with 'nothing' or 'I don't know'.

She slept on the sofa undisturbed the first seven days. On the eighth day he came to her in the middle of the night. He slid under the covers beside her and coaxed her on her back. She resisted but was unable to fend him off. He forced her legs open with his knee and took her virginity brutally and swiftly. The ordeal over, Hassan rolled over with his back to her and snored. Sybil, bleeding and torn, moved as close as possible to the opposite edge of the sofa bed so their bodies wouldn't touch. There was no need. He didn't stay long, anyway. After a quick nap, he walked naked back to his bedroom, his boxers still in a ball at the foot of the sofa bed.

She'd dreamed of what her first time would be like. She'd imagined a man madly in love with her, long full kisses, bodies intertwined and trembling beneath. With Hassan, there was no warmth, tenderness, or soft whispers, but then again, she wasn't even officially his girlfriend. Still, a girl had dreams.

Hassan's duplex was hell for a girl her age. Without spelling it out, he'd made it clear she was there solely to fulfill his needs, but she couldn't bear to suffer though many more nights like the last one. She wanted to bolt from that place, return to the familiar, even if it was home with Terri, but she didn't want to go home to Terri at her own urging. She wanted Terri to deliver her, barge in one day raising hell about how she was too young to be shacked up with a man. She left Hassan's address and phone number in full view for Terri to see. It beckoned Terri every time she opened the fridge. Why didn't Terri come or at least call?

DELIVERANCE CAME FIVE WEEKS LATER. Early on a Saturday morning, Sybil woke to a persistent banging on the front door, followed by a redundant, angry voice yelling through the open downstairs window.

"Hassan! Come open this door! I can't believe you had the locks changed!"

Hassan raced to the living room with a pair of pants his hands, his eyes spread wide as saucers.

Sybil shot up in bed. "Who's that?"

"That's Angel, my wife." He hopped on one foot, pulling his pants over his boxers.

"Wait," Sybil called after him. She wanted a moment to slip on her clothes, but it was too late. The front door flew open. She darted to the bedroom, her suitcase in tow.

"Daddy!"

Sybil peeked through the opening in the bedroom door, and watched as a little boy with Hassan's eyes, hugged his leg.

He has a kid?

"What are you doing here?" Hassan asked Angel.

"What do you mean what am I doing here. I'm still your wife. I heard your player ass had a woman up here in my house, and she better get the hell out!"

"Baby, it's seven 'o clock in the morning. Can't this wait?"

"I'm cleaning house right now! Where is she?" She went straight for the bedroom.

Sybil threw on a pair of sweats and pulled a jersey over her head just as Angel kicked the door open. Angel wore a wife beater and jeans low on her waist. Her asymmetrical hair covered her left eye, and a rhinestone sparkled near the tip of her nose.

"That's right, bitch. Get your crap and leave!"

Sybil skirted by Angel, then turned to Hassan as she headed to the door.

"He ain't stoppin' you! Your services are no longer needed." Angel pointed outdoors. Hassan shook his head as if he didn't approve with the way it was all going down. It was his first and only gesture of kindness since she moved in.

"Go!" Angel bellowed again.

Ears burning hot, Sybil felt like an errant child. She dropped her head and left the duplex.

"How old is she anyway?" she heard Angel ask Hassan.

Sybil stood on the corner and searched her purse and pockets for change. Just as a bus came to a halt in front of her, she realized her purse was empty. She waved the bus on and walked the two miles to Terri's apartment. It was the last place in the world Sybil wanted to go but there was no place else. She thought about Grandmother's house in New Jersey. Grandmother Rose would welcome her with open arms, but she felt strange about being so far away. Moving out of the house was one thing, but who would look after Terri if she moved out of state?

She found Terri seated at the kitchen table, staring into her mug while waiting for the coffee to brew. As she drew closer, the oniony scent of Terri's armpits filled Sybil's nostrils. It was unusual for Terri not to bathe, even during her drunken bouts. Her hair was matted at the nape, her collar stuck inside her shirt. Stacked in the sink were dishes with dried food residue, the contents of the trash can overflowed onto the floor. Flies buzzed overhead.

"I'm home," Sybil announced.

Terri lifted her head. "Are you visiting or are you here to stay?"

"I'm here to stay but only because I have nowhere else to go."

"What happened to your boyfriend?"

"It didn't work out."

"You're too young to be involved anyway."

"Why didn't you stop me?"

Terri shrugged her shoulders.

I'm not worth the effort. Sybil washed the dishes and carried the trash outside to the dumpster. When she came inside, Terri was filling the bathtub with water.

"YOU ARE ONE GORGEOUS LADY. I CAN'T believe Terri's so much younger than you, yet looks so much older."

Sybil couldn't help but talk back to the television. The music channel showed a clip of Tina Turner accepting her star on the Hollywood Walk Of Fame.

"I hope I look as good as you when I'm almost fifty."

All of Sybil's clothes were spread out on the bed. She was taking an inventory for back to school. She was a sophomore now, so it was important to make a good impression on the first day. Tomorrow was Labor Day and school started the day after that, so there was little time to get ready. Once she separated her clothes into piles - too small, out of fashion, and ripped or stained - there wasn't much left over for a decent school wardrobe.

I bet Tina Turner's wardrobe is hotter than mine.

She counted the money in the jar on the kitchen shelf. Eighty dollars. She'd need at least half. It wasn't much money but with the back to school sales, she could find something decent for forty dollars. It was three thirty in the afternoon and the shopping mall didn't close until nine. There was plenty of time.

"Terri, can I have forty dollars from the money jar to buy a pair of jeans and a shirt for school? There's a sale at the mall today."

"Ah, sure. I'll give you a couple of bucks." Terri was lacing her shoes. They were her usual spiked heels except these were strapped all the way to the knee. *Hooker shoes.*

"I'll go get a shower and get ready." Sybil had an idea of what she wanted – straight leg jeans and a short sleeve baby doll blouse. She saw a girl about her age wearing a similar outfit on the cover of a catalog that came in the mail. There wasn't enough money to buy sneakers but her hi-tops from last year would be fine once she ran them through the washing machine. After slipping on a tank top and sweats, an outfit easy to pull on and off when trying on clothes at the mall, she went to the kitchen to get the money from the jar. It was too late. All that remained were a few coins.

"Terri!" she yelled. But she knew before she called out her name that she'd already left.

Dizzy with rage, Sybil's jaw clenched, her teeth grinding together. If Terri were still there she'd scream out her rage to her face. She paced the tiny kitchen then abruptly stopped. I *know. I'll show her.* She'd give Terri some of her own medicine, make Terri feel what she was feeling.

Sybil ran into her room, tore off her clothes and donned one of Terri's snug mini dresses, the fuchsia one that revealed the deepest cleavage, and her mother's spike heeled sling backs. She coated her lips ruby and layered Terri's mascara and liner. After straightening and curling her hair into a sleek bob, she painted her nails blood red. To complete the look, she grabbed one of Terri's coordinating gaudy handbags. She walked to the Star Mist, teetering on her heels and prayed no one asked for I.D.

A nearly seven foot tall bouncer opened the door when she approached.

"I.D. please," he said, looking her up and down.

She rummaged through her bag, pretending to look for it. "I must have left it home."

The bouncer folded his hands behind his back and stood tall.

She snapped the handbag closed and mustered bravado. "Are you gonna make me walk all the way back home in these four inch heels for a silly old I.D.? Look at this body." She turned in a full circle. "Is this the body of a child?"

"Only because I'm in a generous mood today," he told her, "next time, bring I.D. or go somewhere else."

It took a moment for Sybil's eyes to adjust to the dim lights and the cloud of cigarette smoke. The floor was sticky as if someone sprayed it with beer, and a deep crack in the ceiling stretched the length of the entire room. There were certainly nicer places to hang out in. Why would Terri want to come here?

She scanned the room for her mother and found her sitting on a stool at the bar. Terri put a shot glass to her lips and threw her head back, downing its contents. The bartender promptly replaced it with another. Sybil sat on the vacant stool next to Terri and tapped her on the shoulder.

"Mother!" she said, dripping with defiance.

Terri's eyes opened wide. She set her glass down so hard, its contents sloshed over the side of the glass and pooled in the coaster.

"What are you doing here?"

"I thought I'd hang out with you for a change." She motioned to the bartender, "I'll have whatever she's having."

"Coming right up!"

Sybil downed her drink in one swallow, ignoring the burning from her chest into her belly, and ordered another.

"Terri, who's the pretty young lady?" the bartender asked.

"My daughter," Terri said, the corners of her mouth nearly upside down.

"I didn't know she was all grown up. I thought she was a young girl."

Terri opened her mouth to answer him, then decided otherwise.

"Are you trying to humiliate me?" She leaned over and whispered to Sybil.

"Why would I do that?" she answered in a sugary child-like voice.

"You know you're not supposed to be here."

"What are you gonna do, mother, have the bartender throw me out?"

"It's time to get this party started people!" The DJ announced. A crowd gathered on the dance floor as the tempo of the music quickened. In the center of the dance floor, a middle-aged man with a patch of gray hair at each temple danced alone. Eyes half closed, he staggered, barely maintaining his balance. Rope-like gold chains layered his neck and his damp shirt clung to his chest. A glitzy ring sparkled on his pinky, fake lizards in his feet. Sybil danced with him. She danced close, allowing her hips to brush against his body. He held Sybil at the waist and ground his body into hers. Her instinct urged her to pull away, but horrifying her mother was far more important. She threw her head back and thrust her body into his. From time to time she glanced back at Terri just to make sure she was still watching the show. Terri held her glass out for another shot.

When the music stopped, Sybil walked up behind Terri, yanked the glass from her hand and gulped down the shot of Vodka as if she'd been drinking for years.

"Sybil, you have to leave. You're only fifteen, for god's sake." Terri sounded annoyed.

"Now you want to stop me? Now I'm supposed to act like I'm fifteen? But it was okay for me to move out and live with Hasan?" Her speech was beginning to slur. "Why didn't you stop me then?"

"Be glad I'm such a lenient mother."

"Lenient, you are, but a mother? You're no mother," she slurred. You're just T… Terri."

"I'm going home." Terri got up from her bar stool and stumbled.

"Looks like she's had enough," Sybil directed her comment to the crowd on the dance floor, but no one heard her over the music. "Guess I've had enough, too." She spun around and waved to the bartender. "Put my drinks on her tab. I didn't get a new outfit today, but I had the privilege of having a few drinks with my mommy dearest." She stood and put her arm around Terri's shoulder. "Mommy dearest," she said again, to be sure Terri understood her reference to Christina Crawford's tell-all book turned movie. Terri jerked free and hurried toward the exit.

"Leaving so soon?" Sybil yelled behind her. "How about we meet here again tomorrow night?"

Terri walked home at a brisk pace. Sybil could barely keep up, her heels rubbing the balls of her feet raw. They walked in silence all the way, Sybil trailing by several feet. Inside the apartment, she grabbed Terri's wrist and jerked her around until she faced her.

"You're so busy getting drunk, and hanging out at bars, you don't care where I go or what I do. You allowed me to sit right at that bar and drink liquor. You allowed your teenage daughter to move in with a man almost thirty years old, then you agreed to give me money for clothes – which, by the way, I rarely ask for - then took it to spend at the bar. Why don't you care about me?"

"What is it you want me to say? Admit I'm a failure? Tell you you're all screwed up because of me?"

"That would be a good start!" Sybil retorted

"If it makes you feel better, then fine! I failed!"

"Saying you failed doesn't make it all better. You live like I don't even exist. If I were to die tomorrow I'd be one less burden to you, wouldn't I? Why didn't you just send me away with Shane?"

Terri leaned back and rested against the wall. She no longer yelled, her voice now at conversation level. "I should have never had children. My life is garbage, and I've ruined your lives too, and it's too late to fix any of it. I tried to love the two of you, and I took care of you the best I could."

"That was the best you could give?" Sybil asked incredulously. "People tend to their animals better."

"The problem is that I didn't know how to really love you and Shane and deal with my own demons," Terri went on as if Sybil said nothing. "I'm sorry," she said, looking directly into Sybil's eyes.

Sybil backed away and sat on the sofa. It was the most Terri had ever shared of her feelings.

"You are a pathetic, lost miserable woman. You never deserved us." She wanted to say more but the anguish on Terri's face both startled her and brought forth a gentle sympathy. Sybil felt an overwhelming urge to embrace Terri and walked toward her mother. Terri opened her arms. Sybil did the same until she caught a glimpse of Shane's kindergarten photo on the wall behind Terri. Sybil stopped short. "I can't," she said, backing away.

Terri dropped her arms and fled the apartment.

Sybil turned off the light and wept in the dark.

***

Terri stayed away three days and three nights. All Sybil could do was worry and wait. On the fourth day, Terri dragged herself in from the streets. She wore the same clothing she'd left in, wrinkled and stained. There was a musty, dirty odor from her body mingled with nicotine and rank alcohol. Fury and rage should have greeted Terri at the door. To Sybil's dismay, there was only relief when she set her eyes on her battered mother.

"Come on in," she told Terri, "I'll brew a pot of coffee."

The light, fine drizzle turned into torrents of rain in an instant. Cars slowed while windshield wipers sprung into action, windows slammed shut and children playing outdoors ducked inside.

Sybil walked home from the market with a large brown paper bag filled to the top with groceries. Normally she'd pull them in a shopping cart, but she left the cart home because she'd only planned to pick up a few items. But the supermarket was holding a stock-up sale Sybil had to take advantage of, and a few items turned into a bag overflowing. She tried carrying the groceries in one arm and an umbrella in the other, but the parcel was far too heavy to carry with just one hand. She stopped, set the bag on the ground, folded the umbrella and stuck it in the bag atop her groceries. She then carried the sagging parcel in both arms, and commenced walking in the fierce, wind driven rain, her sopping hair lay flat on her forehead, her clothing saturated.

A man walking behind her observed her dilemma and quickened his pace until he walked alongside her. He reached in front of Sybil and pulled the umbrella from her bag. Before she could react, he pushed the button, releasing the umbrella open into the air, and held it over her head, shielding her from the soaking rain. Finally, he took the groceries from her arms so her hands were free, and grinned, revealing his amusement at his own adeptness. Sybil smiled.

"Why, hello..."

"The name's Johnson," he said with a slight nod of his head.

"I'm Sybil. As you can see, I'm soaked down to my socks, so I really needed this umbrella. Thank you."

"You're quite welcome, Sybil." He flashed another quick smile.

"So Johnson, does everyone call you by your last name?"

"The name's Cashwell Johnson so I guess you can say I have two last names and no first name."

"Well, Cashwell Johnson... again, thank you."

"Do you always shop for groceries in the middle of rain storms?" he teased.

"Why not? I get to meet handsome men like you who carry my groceries and hold my umbrella." He was, indeed, handsome. Broad and barrel-chested with a lean, tight torso, he walked with a smooth and steady gait. His lips were full – a waste in a man – and his hands were calloused, as if he made his living with them. Johnson's eyes were guarded, almost secretive, yet his smile was open.

"Well, this is my place." Sybil stopped at the entrance to the apartment building.

"Can I see you again? I'd love to take you out."

Sybil sized him up. She was wary but also quite attracted.

"What do you say?" He urged with a confidence that indicated he already knew she'd say yes.

"And I'd love to have the chance for you to see me looking halfway decent, dry hair and clothes for starters."

"Tomorrow, then? I'll pick you up at seven."

"SO WHERE ARE YOU TAKING ME?" Sybil asked Johnson.

"It's a surprise."

He wore dress slacks and a white button down shirt, so Sybil guessed they were going somewhere fancy. But she did not expect, in her wildest dreams, that a first date with a stranger would be so memorable. Johnson took her to the Tap Revue at the Uptown Theatre. Sybil saw a similar show on public television once but had never seen anything like it in person. After the show, he pulled two backstage passes from his pocket and Sybil got to meet the cast and crew one-on-one.

It was the first of many dates. They frequented dance halls, concerts, movies and sampled the eats at many downtown restaurants. Sybil credited Johnson for expanding her world view. He made her aware of things she'd never heard anyone talk about. Johnson celebrated Mandela's release from prison after twenty-seven years, and complained when George Bush waited until Jesse Owens was dead for ten years before awarding him a medal of honor. Until Johnson came into her life, Sybil's world was small. She welcomed the departure from her own banal existence.

Sybil quickly grew fond of Johnson. Kind, gentle and more willing to listen than talk, he was the best man to ever cross her path. He was calm in the midst of turbulence, clarity in the midst of confusion. After six months of dating, Sybil found herself dreading what her life would be like if Johnson were to suddenly depart. She wanted him in her life for the long haul, and hoped he felt the same way about her. But there was no need to rush toward commitment. Their relationship was still relatively new. They'd take their time getting to know each other, allow the relationship to grow at its own pace.

That all changed the day Sybil missed her period.

At first, she convinced herself that her cycle was just running a little late and put the matter out of her mind completely. But when her cycle also failed to appear the following month, she bought a pregnancy test at the pharmacy. It took a full week to muster up the courage to take the test. She waited until Terri left to go to the club, ripped open the box and carefully followed the instructions. The results confirmed what she already knew. Sybil studied her startled reflection in the mirror over the bathroom sink.

What am I going to do? She asked herself. *Is he going to leave me?* She sunk to the bathroom floor. *My first and only good man and I've blown it. I should have gotten on the pill instead of relying on that darn sponge from the drug store.*

Sybil weighed her options. An abortion would provide the cleanest, neatest solution. Neither of their lives would be disrupted . Johnson wouldn't even have to know about the pregnancy. But being riddled with lifelong guilt about a child that could have been, was an invitation to despair. Perhaps adoption? Adoption was benign enough. The child would not be deprived of a home and a family, but what if the child ended up with a mother like Terri? Sybil shuddered at the prospect. She considered raising the baby on her own and not involving Johnson at all, but raising a baby alone with only a high school diploma and no job on the horizon, wasn't the most optimal of circumstances. Even if she tried to find a job, her chances of getting hired while pregnant were slim. If only she'd listened to Grandmother Rose and applied to college. She'd have been nearly finished her freshman year in community college by now, her life on a completely different course.

The only remaining option, although she ran the risk of driving him away, was to keep the baby. She had to tell Johnson. She picked up the phone and dialed his number.

"Johnson here."

"So do you ever just say 'hello'?"

"Hello to you, Sybil. I'm glad you called. I was thinking of you." She heard a smile in his voice.

"Look, Johnson. I have something to tell you and I'm just gonna get to the point."

"Okay, go ahead."

"I didn't plan for this to happen but it did. Before I tell you what it is, know that I'm sorry. Women try to trap good men like you all the time. It was never my intention to trap you."

"Just blurt it out."

"I'm pregnant."

Johnson didn't say a word.

"Are you there?"

"I'm here," he said. His voice was calm, almost too calm. "Look, I can't do this over the phone. I'll be right over."

Johnson lived ten minutes away, but it seemed to Sybil he was knocking on her door right away. Thankfully, Terri wasn't home so they could sort it out without Terri's two cents.

"I hesitated on the phone because I was really surprised. I didn't expect this."

"I hate to do this to you."

He took her hands. "It's okay. I'm here for you and the baby."

She wanted to hear that he loved her and maybe one day down the road, they could talk about marriage. She wanted the ring on her left hand that told the whole world somebody cherished only her. She wanted him to say that everything was going to be alright, but that was asking for too much from someone she'd met just over six months ago.

He lifted her chin. "Don't worry, we'll manage."

"THERE'S NO MORE SPACE. WHAT DO you say we look for a bigger apartment. The baby could have his own room if we had another bedroom."

Sybil spent most weekends with Johnson at his apartment on the other side of Nicetown, near Tioga. Her small stash of clothes, shoes and toiletries multiplied threefold in just a few months. She wasn't deliberately trying to move all her things into his place, it was just easier to keep some items there rather than lug them back and forth from Terri's place.

"Are you sure about this?" she asked humbly, masking her excitement.

"It makes sense," he said as he handed her a bowl of butter pecan ice cream. "You're here on the weekends anyway."

Thanks to Johnson, butter pecan ice cream was now her favorite. During her first trimester, she'd had a craving for something sweet in the middle of the night. Johnson went out and bought a gallon at a twenty-four hour convenience store. Since then he kept a steady supply in the freezer and fixed a bowl topped with caramel sauce for her every day. His thoughtful gesture, however, did not come without a price. She attributed at least ten pounds of her thirty pound weight gain to the daily vice.

Sybil was six months pregnant when Johnson asked her to move in. She still hadn't heard the 'I love you' she wanted to hear, but moving in together was certainly a step in the right direction.

"We'll look for a place right away so we're settled when the baby comes," he told her.

She wiped her mouth. "Pass me the newspaper. I'll start checking the classifieds." She perused the rental section while Johnson got ready for work. He worked in construction, operating heavy equipment. His work site and shifts changed regularly. That day he worked the second shift.

"Call me if you find anything worth looking at," he said and headed out the door.

She circled a few that looked promising but she wasn't sure if Johnson could afford them on his salary. He worked his regular hours and volunteered for overtime, but construction work was unstable, especially during the winter months. She made a note to call the landlord in Terri's building to price their two bedroom units as well.

Halfway through his shift, Johnson called. It was hard to hear him over the noise at the construction site.

"Honey, I searched every listing in the newspaper. I can't find anything reasonable that's not too far from your job." She explained. Johnson took the subway to work so it was important to find a place close to the subway route. "By the way, when did rent get so high? The rent for some of these apartments is outrageous."

"You can stop looking," he told her. "I found a place. The brother of one of the guys I work with is a property manager over at Lynnewood Terrace." He yelled above the lumbering growl of the jackhammer. "I made an appointment to see the place on the seventeenth at six thirty in the afternoon. It's apartment eighteen. I'll leave early from work so I can be there on time. If you like it we can sign the lease that same day."

"Hold on." Sybil scrambled to find a note pad to write the address on. "That's Oak Lane, isn't it?" she said after reading the address back to him for accuracy.

"Yea, not a bad place to raise children. After we sign the lease agreement, I want you to meet my parents."

Sybil hung up the phone and stood stock-still, absorbing his words. He wanted her to meet his parents. A slow smile spread across her face, and then she laughed out loud. There was hope for her after all.

"Sybil Johnson." She said and repeated it two more times. She liked the way it sounded.

Terri wasn't the type to come right out and tell you she was sick. She kept her illnesses to herself like they were a coveted family secret. Even with a simple head cold, she muffled her coughs in towels and buried soiled tissues in the bottom of trash cans. Sybil once heard Terri tell Grandmother Rose she remained discreet about her ailments because she didn't deserve to be fussed over.

If you weren't the observant type, you could easily overlook the signs Terri was so careful to hide. But Sybil was observant of everything having to do with Terri, and realized right away that something was terribly wrong. Sybil unearthed a trail of hidden clues and elected to stay home that weekend to keep an eye on her mother rather than spend the weekend with Johnson.

First, there was the row of four prescription bottles tucked neatly behind the paprika, onion salt and parsley in the kitchen cabinet. Sybil picked them up one by one. All were dated a week earlier and were eligible for refills. This meant that whatever was going on with Terri was long term.

The second clue was water. All their lives, they drank water from the spigot. While putting out the trash, Sybil happened upon a pile of empty water bottles in the trash can. She found two unopened cases of water stacked in the far corner of the kitchen partially obscured by the refrigerator. Terri was notorious for guzzling soda, and several cups of strong coffee a day, and of course never went too long without a shot of Vodka, yet that week she sipped only water - spring, sparkling, mineral, but water nonetheless.

The third and final clue was the obvious change in Terri's daily routine. She was home every day for a week and a half and remained sober the entire time. Rather than spending her days at the bar, she curled up on the sofa with a fleece throw tucked around her.

Sybil still held the prescription bottle in her hand as she tried to decipher the name of the drug when Terri shuffled into the room wearing her slippers and robe. It was rare to see Terri without makeup. She often woke with it on, smudged in the morning, having neglected to wash her face the night before. *Old* is what immediately came to Sybil's mind. The outer edges of Terri's eyes were crinkly, and lines etched her forehead. The skin on her cheeks was paper thin, giving them a translucent quality, yet sagged beneath her chin. Terri poured a glass of water and swallowed a pill from three of the four bottles. She held out her hand for the fourth bottle.

"What is all this medicine for?" Sybil asked.

"Just a few aches and pains."

"I know you're hiding something from me." Sybil checked her watch. It was almost time to meet Johnson to see the apartment. "I'll be back late this afternoon. Maybe you'll tell me then?"

Terri didn't answer.

"You have to tell me, Terri. I'm the one that's stuck taking care of you if you're sick! So yes! We will talk about this later."

She shoved the remaining prescription bottle at Terri and slammed the door behind her.

She and Johnson were to meet at six thirty to see the apartment at Lynnewood Terrace. Sybil arrived earlier, closer to five, to familiarize herself with the area. She found the local supermarket, post office, pharmacy, dry cleaners, the elementary school and playground, and all were within walking distance. After checking out the neighborhood, she walked the perimeter of the complex. She expected a high rise building like the one she grew up in, but to her surprise, these were garden apartments, each with their own private entrance. The entrances surrounded a courtyard bordered by rows of tulips. A fountain in the center of the courtyard sprung streams of water into the air, cascading down into perfect arches on all sides.

She waited outside of apartment eighteen until a white-haired gentleman with a matching mustache walked over and introduced himself.

"I'm Gus, the rental agent. Are you here to see the apartment?"

"Yes, I am. Cashwell Johnson arranged the appointment. He should be here any moment. If you don't mind my asking, sir, what do you think about the area?"

"It's a decent place to live. Quiet, good schools, and the streets and parks are clean. Lots of teenagers but they stay out of trouble." Gus sorted through a ring of what looked like a hundred keys. "You wanna go ahead and look at the place?"

"I wanted to see it with my boyfriend. Can we wait a few more minutes?" They waited a little while longer, but when Johnson still wasn't there by a quarter past seven, she asked Gus to unlock the door.

The apartment smelled of fresh paint and wood cleaner. The main living area was wide and airy with three floor-to-ceiling windows that flooded the room with natural light. Polished maple cabinets graced the eat-in kitchen, and shades of brown, beige and cream warmed the ceramic tiled floor and the mosaic mini-tiles in the back splash. There was an adjoining bath in the master bedroom, with a second bedroom across the hall from the master.

"I love it!" She clapped her hands. The baby kicked in her belly.

By now it was seven fifteen. *How could Johnson forget this?* Sybil scheduled another appointment for Johnson to view the apartment the following evening and walked home.

Breathless, she jumped onto her bed, picked up the phone and dialed Johnson's number. An automated recording came on the line. *The number you have dialed has been disconnected.*

"I must have dialed the wrong number."

Sybil called again and heard the same annoying message. It wasn't like Johnson to forget to pay his phone bill. She sat and thought a moment. She told herself that since they were going to move in together anyway, it made perfect sense that he probably had the phone cut off already. She checked her watch again. He should be home by now. She'd walk to Johnson's place and tell him how wonderful the apartment was. There was an extra room for the baby, the walls had a fresh coat of paint, new carpets, it was spacious, it was… perfect.

During the walk, she imagined Johnson and the baby together with her in the new apartment, her very own family. She found strange comfort in imagining herself engaged in what others considered drab routine - grocery shopping, vacuuming, washing dishes. In the day-to-day chores of running a home, Sybil found a certain civility. But she was also feeling anxious. Why didn't he show up or at the very least call to tell her he wouldn't be there? She shrugged it off and told herself it was probably just an oversight. Besides, wasn't everyone forgetful from time to time?

She used her spare key to unlock Johnson's door. An old familiar terror seized her, and Sybil grasped the door frame to steady herself. Her knees buckled as she lowered herself to the floor. The room rocked back and forth, engulfing Sybil in waves of vertigo. She leaned forward to calm the spinning in her brain, then willed herself to look up and face what was before her. The apartment was completely empty. Everything was gone. Chairs, tables, lamps, pictures - gone. Slowly, she rose to her feet, walked toward the bedroom and opened the door. Aside from two plastic trash bags filled with her clothes and shoes, that room was empty as well. Her belly suddenly heavy, she had an overwhelming need to sit down. There was nothing to sit on.

Footsteps passed outside. *Johnson?* Sybil ran through the living room and outdoors. It was the janitor leaving for the day.

"Have you seen Johnson?" she asked. "He's gone. Everything's gone!" She had trouble catching her breath.

"No ma'am. You might want to check with his buddy Mitchell two doors down. I saw the two of them chatting earlier in the week."

Sybil didn't know Mitchell very well but had seen him in passing. Johnson introduced the two but they hadn't engaged in much conversation. She banged on Mitchell's door with both fists.

Slow footsteps moved to the door, lacking urgency. Mitchell appeared yawning and stretching, as if just waking from a nap.

"Mitchell, Johnson's apartment is empty. We were supposed to look at a bigger apartment today, and he told me he wanted me to meet his parents, and we were moving in together and now he's gone and I don't know where to find him and..." She babbled on, her chest rising and falling at rapid speed.

"Calm down, Sybil." He placed his hands on her shoulders until her breathing slowed. "Listen, I'm sorry to be the one to have to tell you this, but Johnson was talking about taking a higher paying construction job in Maryland. He rented a truck and moved this morning."

"Did he leave an address, phone number or something?"

He shook his head.

"Did he tell you exactly where in Maryland?" She was oddly aware of her eye wild and shifting, yet was powerless to control it.

"Somewhere near Baltimore, he wasn't specific."

"That's it? What about the name of the construction company?" Sybil raked her fingers through her hair, which now stood on end in all directions.

"He never mentioned the name," he told her, shifting from one leg to the other then back again.

"Do you know his parents? Where they live?"

"His parents live in Maryland too, but I don't know their names."

"How could he just... leave? It was all going so well. I thought he was the real thing."

"Johnson and I only met about a year and a half ago, right after he moved in. I don't know much about him."

Sybil's mind suddenly went blank and for a brief moment, she disconnected, venturing off to some other place, far from the present.

"Are you okay?" Mitchell asked. He looked back into his apartment to make sure the phone was nearby in the event he needed to call for help.

"I've been here before." She mumbled in a dead tone, eyes staring ahead past Mitchell.

"What?" Mitchell looked puzzled.

"I've been here before," she said again, this time looking up into the air.

"I'm not sure what you mean."

"Not here in this place, just... here."

Sybil turned around, zombie-like, until her back to Mitchell. She stopped, as if contemplating what to do next, then stepped forward with one wobbly foot in front of the other, like a baby just learning to walk. Mitchell closed his door softly, so as not to startle her. She walked back to Johnson's apartment and wandered from room to room, searching for a sign or clue as to what went wrong.

Perhaps there's a letter explaining everything. She combed every inch of space until she heard heavy breathing - almost panting.

"Is someone there?" She spun around to see who entered the room, only to meet her startled reflection in the mirror. It was her own heavy breathing that reverberated throughout the hollow room.

"What the hell happened?" she screamed, her voice bouncing off the empty walls. Why didn't she see this coming and how the hell was she going to raise a child alone?

She knotted the tops of the plastic bags, retrieved her lone toothbrush from bathroom sink and trudged home, dragging her belongings behind her, her large belly leading the way.

"Last Round," Hank announced. A line formed at the bar as patrons called out their final drink requests. Hank popped the tops off of beer bottles, salted the rims of margarita glasses, and poured the final round of shots. He couldn't help but notice that Terri's glass was empty. He grabbed the vodka in one hand and the tonic in the other and centered them over Terri's glass.

"Oh no, Hank, none for me." She covered her glass with both her hands.

"That's not like you Terri. You've had nothing but soda and ice water all evening."

"I'm trying to cut back."

"You feel okay?"

Before she could answer, someone flagged Hank down for a beer. Terri was relieved. She didn't want to tell Hank her personal business, but at the same time, she didn't want to lie. She'd visited her doctor for what she thought were flu symptoms – persistent nausea, fever and occasional dizziness. During the exam, her doctor pressed a tender area below her ribs that she didn't even know was sore until his fingers expertly palpated her pain.

"Possible liver damage," he told her matter-of-factly. His pre-liminary diagnosis was like a blast of icy water on an already cold day. The test results weren't due until the following Monday but she didn't need the test results to confirm the diagnosis. Her never ending nausea was proof enough. But what bothered her more than the diagnosis were her doctor's last words as she turned to leave his office.

"If you don't stop drinking, this can have fatal implications."

"Fatal?" she repeated, spinning back around.

"Terri, I'm talking about cirrhosis. This can end your life."

"End my life?" *I've never even lived.*

Terri spread five one-dollar bills on the bar. "I'm heading out, Hank."

"I remember when you used to party until I put you out," he joked.

"Getting a little old for that."

She lifted her handbag, draped over the back of the barstool, and flung it over her shoulder. It was a gift from her mother two years earlier. The black leather satchel with bold silver accents was crisp and sleek when she first pulled it from the gift box. It was only now she noticed the discoloration bordering the clasp, the worn and tattered areas connecting the metal hoops to the leather, and the fading where her purse rubbed against her torso. This was the case with everything since her doctor's appointment. Her shoes, their furniture, even her reflection in the mirror had suffered deterioration. Drunk, she thought herself beautiful with her red lipstick, skin smoothing foundation and false eyelashes. Sober, the reality of how alcohol robbed her of her youth stood glaring back at her from the mirror, skin rough as fresh plaster, furrows and ridges deepening and widening. Her problem wasn't with aging. Aging and living were intertwined. Aging meant you'd survived whatever life handed you. But this was not the gentle, natural process of aging. This damage was self-imposed. Years of pouring poison into her body stripped her of her good looks much in the same way rust corroded and distorted the surface of shiny, smooth metal, and she had no one to blame but herself.

She walked home quickly, a route she'd taken many intoxicated nights, except today the street lights were far too dim, and the pitch black alleys threatened unseen menaces. She checked over her shoulder every few steps, and cowered at the sounds of the city night. Never before had she been so relieved to reach the safety of home. She put her key in the lock and turned. Loosened from years of use, the lock nearly popped out of the door when she removed her key. Dirt and debris blackened the base of the knob which hung loosely due to a missing screw.

"Anyone can break in here with this useless lock and a knob barely hanging on. I have to call the landlord to fix this." She closed the door behind her and flipped the dead bolt. Right away she noticed the two large trash bags leaning against the wall alongside the entrance. She tore open the knotted tops. Inside were Sybil's clothes and shoes.

She and Johnson must have had a fight.

She peeked in Sybil's bedroom. She was already asleep. Curled on her side with her hands tucked under her chin, she looked like a child. Would Sybil tell her what happened with Johnson? She and Sybil were never close. Just like everything else, her relationship with her daughter was worn and deteriorated, likely beyond repair. Sybil was already grown and she barely knew her. Where did all the years go?

She took the pillows off the living room sofa and rolled the inner spring out flat for her bed. Her body was so accustomed to being awake nights, sleep didn't come easy. Her thoughts ran out of control, like cars racing down a highway, with no traffic lights or yield signs. And always, it was Shane that occupied her thoughts. *My baby boy, where are you?* It was during the solitary nighttime hours, with no distractions from the mistakes of her past, that she craved a drink the most. Alcohol had a way of banishing all dreams, whether day dreams or the dreams of slumber. Or perhaps this was just an illusion and alcohol merely banished the memory of those dreams.

***

Sybil's bedroom door creaked open. Seconds later, the fridge opened as she hunted for a snack. Terri was grateful for the diversion from her thoughts, and joined her in the kitchen.

"I noticed the bags in the living room. Did you and Johnson break up?"

"We were supposed to meet today to see an apartment. He never showed up."

"Did you call him?"

"He's gone, Terri."

"What do you mean, gone?"

"His apartment is empty and I don't know where he is or how to find him."

"He moved?"

"He left town and left nothing behind, no address, no phone number, not even a note explaining what the hell happened." Sybil set a carton of orange juice hard on the table.

Terri struggled with what to say to Sybil. It wasn't that she didn't want to be supportive. It was just that kind words made her feel weak, vulnerable even. But Terri feared death. Not the act of dying itself. Marching toward that final act with each passing hour was allotted to every man. She was afraid of death robbing her of the chance to fix all that she had ruined. In the end, it was the fear of death that propelled her to speak aloud what she felt.

"Y… you can do this on your own. You never needed Johnson." She stared down at her slippers, her speech halting.

"I just want to know why. How can a man be so loving and kind one moment, then abandon me the next? There were no clues. He was here one day, loving me, taking care of me, and gone the next. I doubt I'll ever find him, and I wonder if I even wanna look for him given that he went to so much trouble to disappear…and now this," she looked down and rubbed her growing abdomen.

"We'll just have to make room for the baby."

Sybil looked at Terri a long time before responding.

"Terri, are you dying?"

"Why would you ask me that?"

"Because you never have anything nice to say. Are you dying or what?"

"I… uh… well, not exactly. I'm waiting for my test results. They should be in on Monday."

"What exactly did the doctor say?"

Terri dropped her head.

"Look, Terri, it's just the two of us. I'm all you have. You have to tell me what's wrong. You can't afford any secrets!"

"It's my liver."

"I figured it was serious after seeing all the medication in the cabinet."

"The doctor says I have to stop drinking. But, ah… back to you and this baby on the way. I can help out a bit. Maybe with babysitting later on when you're ready to look for a job. When this baby comes, I want to spend some time with him. I want him to know me. As a matter of fact, I bought some things this morning." She left the room and returned carrying a small gift bag.

Sybil peeked inside. There was a package of yellow newborn socks and plaid rompers.

"You bought something for the baby?" Her eyes widened, then she quickly grew sullen.

"Why now, Terri?"

"What do you mean?"

"Why now with all the encouragement, baby clothes, offering to babysit. Why weren't you ever there before? Why, after all these years, are you now doing all of this? Is it because you're sick?"

"Partly. Being sick forced me to stop runnin' and take time to think."

"Running from what"?

"Runnin' from problems, pain, heartache, responsibility, maybe even runnin' from myself."

"But we needed you. We needed a mother. What you're offering to do for my child - spending time and attention - I wanted that," she said in an angry voice. "Hearing you tell me the kind of relationship you want with my child makes me want everything I missed growing up."

"I wish I could fix it all but I can't get any of it back. All those wasted years are gone." Torment and regret, deep as a canyon twisted her delicate aging features, her eyes begged for mercy.

"I have many sins, Sybil. Can you ever forgive me?"

Sybil didn't answer one way or the other.

"I can't believe you're going to the Star Mist! Didn't the doctor tell you to stop drinking?" Sybil argued.

"I'm not going there to drink. I..."

"It's a bar, Terri. Why else would you go there?"

"Hank's retiring so they're throwing him a party. I've known him nearly twenty years. I have to go."

"You're an alcoholic, Mother," the word 'Mother' she spat thick with sarcasm. "You, of all people, should reconsider going to a place where everyone around you will be drinking, likely till they're drunk, or have you suddenly developed will power after all these years."

"I'm not staying, just popping in long enough to wish him well. I'll be right back."

"If they were really your friends, they wouldn't let you past the front door."

Terri slipped on her jacket.

"Today of all days, Terri? It's my due date for God's sake. What if the baby comes while I'm here alone?"

"I'll call you every half hour to check on you. If you're in labor I'll come straight home."

"Do you really think you're going to remember me after your first Vodka and tonic?"

Sybil was way out of line. Back when Terri grew up, children, even grown children, never talked to their parents the way Sybil talked to her. She didn't speak on it though. In many ways, she deserved it, and would rather have her disrespect than her hate.

"When was the last time you saw me drunk?"

Deep in thought, Sybil looked up in the air.

"I'll be fine, but if you're that worried, just call Hank and tell him to give me the message. They all know I'm expecting my first grandchild."

"It's annoying when you talk about those people like they're your family. They're just people you hang out with at a bar."

"Call them whatever you want. Just be sure you call Hank if you go into labor."

"I'm not comfortable with this. I should have asked someone more reliable to go with me to the hospital."

Terri started out the apartment and was halfway down the hall when she heard Sybil cry out.

"Terri, come back. The baby's coming!"

Terri thought she was joking until she saw Sybil bent and leaning against the wall, holding her abdomen through another contraction.

"You willed this baby to come so I wouldn't leave, didn't you?"

Sybil's victory smile vanished as another contraction swept her into pain.

"Let's get you downstairs so I can hail a cab," Terri told her.

SYBIL THRASHED AND TREMBLED THROUGH SEVEN hours of labor, yet never cried out. Her only sound was a prolonged sigh when Brianna Lynn Taylor finally released herself from her pain-wracked body, screaming and kicking, fists and toes curled.

After she was clean, dry and swaddled, Brianna snuggled quietly against her mother's breast. Her features were sharp and petite like her grandmother's, but her wide forehead and gentle eyes were Shane's.

"She's beautiful." Terri stood alongside her bed and caressed the newborn's soft, fine hair.

"Thank God she doesn't look anything like her father." Sybil said.

A nurse came in the room to check Sybil's blood pressure. It was unusually high when she arrived at the hospital the evening before.

"Here, Terri, hold her." She placed her baby in her mother's arms.

Brianna wrapped her tiny hand around Terri's finger. Terri held her close, feeling Brianna's heart beating next to hers and experiencing her first moment of true bliss in decades. Cradling new life in her arms, she puzzled at why she'd numbed herself from such pure, simple pleasures for so long. What else had she missed out on all these years? Her daughter grown and still a stranger, her sweet, sweet son missing from this blessed scene.

But in spite of her transgressions, Terri was thankful for the blessings that rained down on her - blessings in the form of forgiveness. Sybil never spoke forgiveness out loud, but Terri knew forgiveness in the way Sybil looked after her, in Sybil's free-flowing conversation and in the way she so tenderly placed her firstborn child in her arms. And although Terri now possessed a clear understanding of why forgiveness set people free, she was not yet ready to forgive herself.

Fallen

minah's Cafe was a quaint, family-owned restaurant on the corner of a shaded but noisy street in West Philadelphia's residential district. Low hanging leaves of a fully mature Oak tree grazed its roof. Miniature ficus with blinking lights strewn through flanked the entrance. Slow jazz hummed from the speakers, one of which perched above the doorway, bestowing upon the neighborhood a taste of the café's musical ambience. The lights dimmed down as dusk arrived, the restaurant illuminated by single candles in blue and black glass mosaic bowls on the center of each table casting long, flickering shadows across the ceiling.

Apollo and Madeline faced each other across a table for two at the rear of the cafe, the coffee and pie between them untouched. Although she had never in her life held a cigarette to her lips, Madeline felt a compelling urge to smoke. She imagined the smooth texture of a cigarette between her fingers, inhaling the menthol coolness into her lungs, and her mouth forming a perfect 'o' as she released the stream of smoke through her lips.

"Madeline, I know this isn't easy. I can't imagine what it must be like for you to have to come clean to Sadie, but we can't go on like this," Apollo told her.

They'd met at Aminah's for dinner every Thursday for the past six months. Sadie assumed Madeline stayed after school for glee club practice, but Glee Club ceased to be a priority once Apollo entered Madeline's life.

"I'm just having a hard time with the timing of it all. Why do we have to do this now?" She sliced a sliver of pie with her fork, and held it to her lips. Her stomach threatened to bring up its contents. She dumped the pie on the saucer and dropped the fork onto the table.

"Why wait? I know you're afraid, but I have to sever ties with your mother. She still thinks there's a possibility that she and I have a chance at being together, and that's never going to happen. If nothing else, I owe it to her to be honest."

"Can't we wait just a little while longer?" Madeline reasoned. She hated that he was so sure and confident and harbored none of the trepidation that churned her insides. "Just yesterday she told Pearl she wanted a serious relationship with you. She's planning on telling you she wants more. She says you're the one."

"All the more reason to come clean. Keeping our affair a secret is leading her farther astray."

"But you have your own home to go to afterwards. I have to live with her no matter what the consequences. I'm not ready." She picked at the bobby pins securing her hair behind her ears. "Please wait."

"Wait for what? There is no perfect time to break off a relationship, and there will never be a perfect time to tell the woman who wants me for her own, that I'm in love with her daughter. I have to do this, Maddy."

Tears sprang to her eyes when she heard the nickname only Tucker called her.

"I shouldn't have to hide a relationship with the woman I love," Apollo went on. "I'm a man, yet I'm sneaking out to see you like some schoolboy. I can't go on like this. Sunday, I'm telling her everything."

"Give it another week," she pleaded.

Apollo shook his head so hard, his entire torso swayed his denial.

"She invited me for dinner again on Sunday and I can't bear to sit another day across the table from Sadie pretending that I'm interested in her."

"What if she forbids me to see you?"

"You're not a child. You're nearly nineteen. Stop worrying about what your mother thinks and live your own life. You graduate high school in just a few months anyway, so you can always move in with me if things get too bad."

"What if..."

"Shh. Whatever happens, we're in this together." He reached across the table and took her hands in his. "You're not facing this alone."

"Please, Apollo."

"Sunday, Madeline."

She pulled her hands from his and slumped in her chair. "Ok, Sunday it is."

MADELINE WORE BLACK. BLACK SLACKS, BLACK penny loafers and a black crew neck sweater. She wore no jewelry or adornments and applied only a thin coating of gloss to her lips. In the pocket of her pants, she stuffed a folded row of tissues. She took her place at the table promptly at five.

Sadie fluttered about the dining room assembling silverware on folded linen napkins, her breasts nearly popping out of her powder blue, v-neck sweater. She wore blue eye shadow. It was the first time she'd ever matched her shadow with her clothes. Nail extensions, like talons, tapped the table.

"You're a half hour early for once in your teenage life. Grab the pepper from the kitchen so I can fill the shaker." Madeline stood up too quickly and knocked over her chair. She bent over to right it and nearly passed out from a wave of adrenaline. She closed her eyes to steady the rush.

"You okay?" Sadie asked.

"I stood up too fast," Madeline explained, and disappeared into the kitchen.

"How are you getting along with Apollo?" Sadie asked when she was back in the dining room.

Madeline froze with the pepper bottle mid air. "Fine?" she said in the form of a question.

Sadie didn't seem to notice and continued chatting. "That's good. I'm glad you like him. I hope to see a lot more of him. As a matter of fact, I plan to talk to him about it after dinner today. I want more than just two hours on Sunday afternoons. We've been seeing each other long enough to take this to the next level. If he's not ready to bring up the matter, then I will."

Madeline filled the pepper shaker and cowered in her chair. She clutched her hands together in her lap to stop their trembling, her stomach crested and plummeted like waves at high tide.

"For someone who arrived at the dinner table before our guest, you sure are quiet."

Madeline stared at her place mat. "I have a lot on my mind."

"Have you thought any more about what you're going to do after graduation?"

If she weren't so terrified at what was about to take place, she'd have rolled her eyes and sucked her teeth. Sadie asked about her post-graduation plans at least once a week. What was the rush? She probably just wants me out of the house so she can date without me getting in the way.

"Not yet," she answered, seething with exasperation.

Sadie glanced at the clock. "Apollo's usually early. I wonder what's holding him up?"

Madeline crossed her fingers under the table. "*Maybe he decided to listen to me and put this thing off.*" Twelve minutes, thirteen minutes, fourteen… *he isn't coming!*

"I'll eat something later. I'm not hungry." Just as Madeline stood to leave, there was a knock at the door. Her palms were suddenly wet and her knees unsteady. She dropped back down on her chair with a noisy groan.

"Good afternoon, Sadie. Madeline." Apollo spoke properly and stood at the dining room entrance, his shoulders back, almost at attention.

"Have a seat, honey." Sadie sat at one end of the table and Madeline sat at the other end, with Apollo between them. *How ironic*, Madeline thought.

"You haven't acted so formally since our very first dinner date. All of a sudden you need an invitation to take your seat?" Sadie laughed. Sadie filled her plate and passed the serving dish to Apollo.

"How's the yard work coming along?"

Apollo had dug up the overgrown hedges on his front lawn.

"Fine."

"Have you decided what you're going to plant in place of the hedges? The azalea bushes are on sale at the garden center."

"Not yet," he answered.

Sadie frowned. "You're acting strangely too. Must be a full moon."

She passed the remaining serving platter, and Apollo and Madeline filled their plates. Sadie continued her feeble attempts at small talk but soon ran out of things to say. Since no one else initiated conversation, they sat around the table in silence. The bell-like clink of silverware contacting plates the only sound filling the room.

"I may as well be eating alone," she finally blurted out in frustration. And indeed she was. Apollo's plate was still full, his fork in its original place setting, and Madeline's food was all mixed together in a heap from moving it around on her plate.

"Did you both get up on the wrong side of the bed this morning?" she joked. But no one laughed along with her. Sadie looked from one to the other several times, then her mouth fell open and remained locked for several seconds. Recognition altered her face. Apollo rose to his feet, speaking fast.

"Sadie, you're a wonderful woman and you were the first person to welcome me to the neighborhood and I thank you for that. It's just that... I've fallen in love with your daughter. Madeline and I have been dating and I plan to continue seeing her. We kept our relationship a secret and it was wrong. For that, I'm sorry. I should have come forward sooner. It was never my intention to hurt you."

Sadie looked at him wide-eyed and unblinking like a child trying on prescription glasses for the first time, however, as she digested the news, her face hardened into a grotesque mask.

"What a fool I've been!" she choked. "How could I have missed it? I brought home a lover for my daughter?"

Madeline hollered something about needing some air and ran from the house. A few large strides and Apollo was right at her heels calling out to her. Sadie raced to the front door.

"How could you let this happen!" she cried out to Apollo.

He stopped and turned around.

"I'm sorry about this Sadie, but I've wanted Madeline since the day I first laid eyes on her."

"This has all been a lie?"

"I enjoyed your company but I never wanted anything more. My fault in this is not telling you sooner." He turned his back to her and followed Madeline into the night.

***

Sadie slammed the door so hard, a diagonal crack splintered the window pane. A tunnel of heat encased her. Sweat poured from her scalp, trickling down her face and staining the sexy sweater she'd worn for Apollo. She lunged toward the kitchen, reaching for furniture along the way to steady herself, and stumbled to the open window over the sink for cool air. Sadie flipped on the faucet, cupped her hands under the running water and splashed handfuls onto her face. From the rack, alongside the sink, she snatched a towel to dry. She clung to the window sill and squeezed her eyes shut. Burning bile crept into her throat and threatened to erupt in her mouth.

Sadie's mind replayed all the images of the past several months. With disturbing vividness she recalled and finally comprehended the meaning behind all the stolen glances, ambiguous pleasantries and whispered conversations shared between Madeline and Apollo. Their affair unfolded right before her eyes and she was too interested in her own desires to notice her only child falling in love under her roof with the man she herself had chosen.

"I've been such a fool!"

She ran to Madeline's room and unearthed all the clues - the delicate charm bracelet, the anonymous greeting card, the fresh roses in a vase on her dresser, and even the new perfume with the musky, earthy fragrance Madeline dotted behind her ears. She now understood the reason behind Madeline's sophisticated new 'up do' with pins holding perfect curls piled high atop her head, and the care with which she applied her make-up.

"Damn fool," she berated herself.

Apollo's engine revved then idled on the street below. Sadie peered out of Madeline's bedroom window. Madeline sat in the passenger seat, her shoulders rose and fell, her head resting in her hands. Apollo laced his fingers through her hair as he rained tender kisses on her face. Repulsed by his gentle, loving gesture, Sadie tore her eyes away.

How did I miss this? She turned back to the car just in time to watch Apollo drive off with Madeline by his side. Sadie shook her head in disgust, confusion and understanding taking root all at once.

For hours, she kept vigil, listening for the familiar rev of Apollo's engine, waiting for her daughter to return. Soon, Madeline's curfew slipped by and the neighbors' homes grew dark as their lights turned off one after another, the road lit solely by street lamps and the moon.

"She's not coming home," Sadie said aloud and was somewhat relieved.

She didn't know what to say to her anyway. She knew what she wanted to say as a mother – *you haven't known this man long enough to run off with him, you're too young to be tied down, he's too old to date a young girl your age* – but that in no way reflected how she felt as the woman who was not chosen. And as for Apollo, he was deceptive in the worst way. He masked his deceitfulness behind a guise of gentlemanly manners and kindness, a trap many a careless woman fell victim to. Sadie hated that she too was among the careless.

THEIR RETURN TO SADIE'S HOUSE THE following morning was as somber as a funeral procession. Apollo's previous bravado absent, his shoulders hunched forward, white knuckles grasped the steering wheel. Madeline's head bowed, she prayed that Sadie wouldn't be there, so she could pack her things and leave without incident, but when the car turned the corner, there Sadie sat on the front porch rocking back and forth in her chair. She wore the same clothing from the day before, a colorful knit shawl draped over her shoulders, the back of her hair flattened.

"What's she doing here? She never misses work. Do you think she's sitting there waiting for me?" She asked Apollo.

"It doesn't matter. Just get your things and let's go."

"I can't go in there. Keep driving," she told Apollo.

"Maddy, you're blowing this out of proportion. Regardless of the circumstance, she's still your mother. She may be angry but she can't abandon you."

"Obviously, you don't know Sadie well," Madeline smirked.

He coaxed Madeline out of the car and nodded to Sadie. Although she looked him straight in the eye, she registered no response.

"Hello Mother, I've come for my things."

"Just get them and leave." Sadie answered, her voice void of emotion.

Madeline darted past her into the house, much the same way a naughty child skirts by her angry belt-wielding mother.

The dining room had not changed since the night before. As if they'd all stepped out for just a few seconds, plates and platters were still in their place on the table. Glasses were half full and soiled silverware and serving spoons remained submerged in dried over food. Crumpled napkins scattered at random.

Madeline hurried to her bedroom to pack. She wouldn't miss Sadie or this house with its troublesome past, but this room she would miss. Here, she conjured her fondest memories. She closed her eyes and she was a child again, snug under her blanket while Tucker sat bedside reading her a story. He wished her sweet dreams, blew a kiss and said goodnight for the last time. She wrapped her arms around herself, squeezed tight and whispered goodbye to the child she was. After taking a final look around, she lugged her suitcase down the stairs, the wheels striking each step.

Back on the porch, Madeline faced her mother who still rocked in her chair, her speed increasing the longer Madeline stood facing her. There was a change in Sadie. No longer domineering and strong, the brick wall sat crumbled before her.

Sadie would never be fulfilled. She wasted most of her life looking for that which stood beckoning before her, and Madeline had no intention of making the same mistake and ending up like her.

"I'm sorry," Madeline began to explain, "I didn't…"

"Go," Sadie spoke, barely above a whisper. "I don't want to hear anything you have to say."

"But mom, please listen to me for a moment."

"Leave my porch," she said, barely moving her lips and pointing in the direction of the road.

Madeline turned, descended the steps and got into the car waiting by the curb.

S adie unrolled *The News Lane*, West Oak Lane's weekly newspaper. Just beneath the birth announcements was Apollo and Madeline's wedding announcement. Above the caption was a photo of the soon-to-be newlyweds, holding hands while gazing into each other's eyes. In the distance, a brilliant sun hovered between them.

Sadie ripped the newspaper into tiny shreds, crumpled them into a ball and hurled it into the waste basket.

"What made you think I'd want to read this?" she questioned Pearl.

"You were going to find out eventually, so when I saw the announcement first thing this morning, I figured I'd bring it over so you can find out from me rather than one of our gossiping neighbors."

Sadie still wore her nightgown and her face was lined from wrinkled sheets. The coffee pot emitted a series of beeps when finished brewing. Sadie poured them both a steaming cup and settled in the chair across from Pearl.

"Why did Madeline take this so far? She should never have agreed to marry that man. If he deceived me, then how does she think he's gonna treat her? Girl, I'm telling you, it's just a matter of time before he throws her by the wayside and finds another woman to use."

"You're going to the wedding aren't you?" Pearl asked.

Sadie stared into her cup.

"She's your daughter, Sadie. You have to go," Pearl urged. "Granted Apollo isn't what you want for her, but in the grand scheme of things, a mother has to go to her own daughter's wedding."

"I've been disgraced, Pearl. I'm a woman scorned who's been disgraced by her own child. It doesn't get any worse than that."

"You weren't engaged to the man, and from what you told me, he hadn't made any commitment to you. There's no disgrace in that."

Sadie added sugar to her coffee and stirred. The sweet sediment scraped the bottom of the mug.

"Tell me you'll go," Pearl insisted.

"I'll think about it," she said.

"This isn't something you consider at your leisure. It's a 'must do' kind of thing."

Sadie continued stirring, even though the coffee had absorbed every bit of sugar.

"Have you heard from her since she left?"

"She mailed me an invitation a while ago with a letter begging me to participate in the ceremony."

"You didn't answer, did you?"

Sadie shook her head.

"The wedding's in just a few weeks. Give me the phone. I'll call Madeline and find out her colors and you and I are going shopping for your dress today!"

Sadie folded her arms across her chest and looked the other way.

"Then I'll get it, myself." Pearl found the phone and dialed Madeline.

"Hello, Madeline? This is Auntie Pearl. Just fine, thank you. She's fine too. Listen, I wanna take your mama shopping for the dress for your wedding so I need to know your colors. Oh, that's beautiful... ok... you wanna talk to her?"

"No," Sadie mouthed.

"She's tied up right now. I'll have her call you back... yes, I promise... bye." She hung up the phone.

"Sadie, how long are you gonna avoid talking to her?"

"I'm not ready, Pearl. I don't even know what to say to her."

"You can start with 'hello, how are you'. Anything's better than this angry silence. Anyway, her colors are turquoise and white. Get some clothes on! We're going shopping for a dress and shoes! And when we get home, please call that child."

At twelve sharp, the wedding coordinator, an anxious apple-shaped woman with a clip-on fall reaching the middle of her back, gave Madeline a firm nod, then cued the organist. Chords resonated throughout the sanctuary. Tucker stood by Madeline's side, their arms linked at the elbow.

I hope my wedding goes better than last night's rehearsal dinner, she thought. She'd met Apollo's mother, Rosa Evers, for the first time. It was a complete disaster.

"So nice to finally meet you," Madeline said sweetly with her best smile.

Rosa walked around Madeline in a circle, as if sizing up a purchase.

"Exactly how old is she?" Rosa asked Apollo, while Madeline stood less than three feet away.

"Old enough to get married, Mother."

"Maybe she's ready to get married, but is she ready for you?"

"Enough!" Apollo told her, a flash of anger in his eyes.

"What does it matter anyway, apparently she's what you want," she said as she glanced over Madeline one last time before sauntering away, "and you always manage to get what you want, regardless of the cost."

He took Madeline by the hand and led her to her place at the table.

"What did she mean by that?" Madeline asked Apollo.

"Don't worry about her, today's about you and me. Nothing else matters." He brought her hand to his lips, sending shivers down Madeline's spine.

Apollo tapped his fork on a glass until the wedding party quieted.

"Everyone please stand and introduce yourselves one by one. We'll start at the opposite end of the table."

Although Rosa was not at the opposite end of the table, she stood anyway.

"Before we get to that," she said with both hands on her hips, "where is the mother of this lovely bride?"

Madeline stammered something vague about a scheduling conflict and fled to the restroom where she stayed for most of the dinner. Not even Apollo could persuade her to emerge. It was Tucker who finally coaxed her back to the table, but by then, dinner was over. Madeline shuddered at the memory of it.

After the organist banged out the introductory notes, the wedding coordinator signaled Rosa to begin.

Rosa waited for the crowd to turn and face the rear of the church before beginning her descent down the aisle. Although Madeline fervently insisted, she'd refused an escort and walked down the aisle alone. Disregarding the turquoise and white wedding colors Madeline selected, she graced down the aisle like royalty, dignified and majestic in a gold beaded form fitting gown with an elaborate gold head wrap in the African tradition. She swung her arms with the fluidity and grace of a dancer, and crossed her feet slightly, one in front of the other, like a model gracing the catwalk. Had she worn a white gown, a stranger who happened upon the wedding would have mistaken her for the bride, so grand and flamboyant was her entrance.

With great flourish Rosa took her place at the end of the first row, then turned along with the crowd to face the rear of the church.

The music changed for the mother of the bride. It was an elegant, stirring melody that brought forth fond sentiments. The guests held their collective breaths and craned their necks in anticipation of Sadie's entrance. The music continued for a spell, then faded away when it was apparent the mother of the bride had no intention of making an appearance. An undercurrent of whispering and speculating buzzed in the chapel like a swarm of bees gathering for honey.

Madeline stood on her toes so she could get a clear view of the pews at the front of the church. Apollo's mother, Rosa, stood on one side. She nodded at Madeline and adjusted her head wrap. The pew on the opposite side, the very seat reserved for Sadie, was vacant. Her head dropped to her chest.

"Why did you put yourself through this? I told you she wasn't coming," Tucker whispered.

"I left her a message last night and again this morning. I told her to let me know if she wasn't coming. I didn't hear back so I thought there might be a chance."

"Don't let this ruin your day." Her head remained down. He lifted her chin. "I mean it."

Madeline squared her shoulders.

"That's my Maddy," Tucker smiled.

The music changed again and the room grew silent as the bridesmaids advanced to the front of the chapel in tempo, followed by the lovely flower girl, wearing a tiara befitting a princess. Cameras flashed and clicked at random.

There was a brief interlude, after which the traditional, yet nostalgic Wedding March began, tentative at first, then loud and certain. The guests rose to their feet and turned to the rear of the church. Tucker and Madeline approached the altar where Tucker presented her to her husband to be. Gallantly, he extended his arm as Madeline walked forward and took her place alongside Apollo.

Tucker held her face in his hands and gazed at Madeline as if she were the only person that mattered in this world. Madeline blushed under his scrutiny. When Tucker turned his gaze toward Apollo, his kind face turned to ice. Madeline knew he didn't approve of Apollo as a suitable mate for her. It was understandable given the love triangle leading to their union. But Tucker wasn't the only person who disapproved of their nuptials. Rosa didn't exactly embrace the matter with open arms either. Her words still rung in Madeline's ears, 'you always manage to get what you want, regardless of the cost'. Madeline shook her head to clear her mind and directed her attention to the ceremony.

THE FLIGHT ATTENDANT SECURED THE COCKPIT and conducted the safety demonstration in grand fashion. The engine roared awake, its vibrations rattling the seats as the pilot announced preparations for takeoff. The plane inched forward, increasing its speed until it lifted from the ground with ease. Caught off guard by the sudden rush of exhilaration, Madeline squealed while clutching Apollo's hand.

"It's hard to believe you've never been on a plane before. How's your first ride above terra firma?"

"This is amazing!" she said with a child's enthusiasm. She released the shade, craning to see out the window. "We're actually flying above the clouds.

Enjoying the sensation of floating generated by the plane's movement Madeline reclined her chair and closed her eyes. Her hand flicking a tear from her eye caught Apollo's attention.

"What is it?" he asked

"She never came! She missed all of it, Apollo. A mother dreams of the day of her daughter's wedding, but for Sadie, it was just another ordinary day."

"Why rehash it, Maddy. It's over. Let it go."

"But Apollo, how could she? She's angry, I'll give her that, but this is beyond anger. This is… vindication. Parents forgive their children for far worse crimes. Was it really so bad that she had to miss it? What kind of mother does such a thing?" Her eyes welled again.

"You're on your way to a spectacular honeymoon on the spectacular island of Jamaica. Put it aside for now. There'll be time to deal with that business later on, Mrs. Evers," he spoke in an exaggerated Jamaican accent.

"Alright, mon," she wiped her eyes with the back of her hand.

"What is the first thing you're gonna do when we return to the states? Before you answer, no serious talk, mon."

"Apollo, the house is horrendous."

"What do you mean?" His phony accent was gone.

"You have a good business mind, and a knack for turning a penny into a dollar but interior decorating is certainly not your forte. And don't you dare look surprised! The carpet in the living room is orange."

"Rust," he corrected her.

"No, my dear, it's flaming orange. The sofa's charcoal gray and the throw pillows are blue-green. All of the walls and ceilings are in need of a fresh coat of paint and the room is overcrowded."

"What do you suggest my sweet interior decorator?"

"I have a few ideas.... you'll soon see. When I finish working my magic in the living room, you'll fall to your knees begging me to redo the rest of the house."

TRUE TO HER WORD, MADELINE BEGAN planning the living room overhaul the minute they were back in the states. On the way home from the airport, she grabbed a handful of the most recent home decorating magazines from the news stand and perused their contents while still in the backseat of the taxicab. Within a week, she'd cut out the photos she liked best and pasted them into a scrapbook. From these she took the ideas that began the transformation of their home.

Madeline had a good eye for detail and she enjoyed experimenting with fabrics of varying texture and style. From craft stores, she bought fabric swatches and held them up against a window or chair needing upholstery, and she lined the wall with paint samples in varying shades of earth tones. After she selected her color palette, fabrics and furniture style, she combined all the elements to create the look she dreamed of.

First she added a soft, neutral to the walls with a contrasting neutral on the trim, then hung coordinating sheers. Next she tore out the carpets and hired a contractor to strip and finish the wood floors. In little over a month, the background for her canvas was complete. Apollo had seen bits and pieces of the plan, but he hadn't seen the finished product. She waited until Apollo was gone for the entire day and part of the evening to add the accessories and have the furniture delivered, so that when he returned home that evening, he'd see the final transformation all at once.

She'd just hung the last painting on the wall, when she heard Apollo's car door slam shut. He walked no slower than usual, but to Madeline it took an eternity for him to get from the car to the front door.

"Welcome home!" She greeted him with a celebratory glass of Champagne. He stepped inside, then turned from left to right in what seemed like slow motion.

The centerpiece of the living room was a solid pine armoire, hand painted in Italy in the artisan tradition of the fifteenth century, or at least that's what it looked like. It was actually a consignment shop replica of the original she saw photographed in a home decorating magazine. She complimented the armoire with a butter-colored twill sofa and an olive oversized chair with rolled arms and matching ottoman. The solid brass lamp with an antique bronze finish of winding green leaves and deep red cherries, she found at a house sale. Potted cactus accented the wrought iron coffee table and sofa table, and wheat-colored draperies she'd sewn herself graced the floor to ceiling windows. She finished the look with an area rug of the classic vine and floral design in washed shades of beige, garnet and loden. The end result was magnificent.

"Maddy, this is spectacular. This must have cost me an entire years' salary! It looks just like a room in one of those high-end design magazines."

"If these were original pieces they would have cost a fortune, but your clever wife found replicas at mere pennies on the dollar." She reached over her shoulder to pat herself on the back.

"You, my dear, have a talent. I can't wait to see what you do with the other rooms."

"So I have your permission to continue spending your hard-earned money to turn the rest of this house into a castle?"

"Permission is granted." His smile waned as he sat on the ottoman beside her. He set his glass of Champagne on the end table, careful to use the new coaster. It matched the sofa and appeared to be wrapped in leather, but knowing Madeline, it was probably some other textile made to replicate the original.

"I have news and it's not good."

Madeline put down her glass.

"My ship sets sail October fifteenth. I put in a request for more time off, but it was denied. I want more than anything to stay home a little while longer but I can't extend my leave any more."

"October fifteenth! That's less than a month from now!"

"I've been home for more than a year. If I'm not on that ship, I could lose my seniority and maybe even my job."

"How long will you be gone?"

"Six months, Maddy, but then I'll be home for six months. Remember, we talked about this when we were dating?"

She was still living with Sadie then. The prospect of Apollo setting sail seemed reasonable at the time. Now that they were married, and she'd be, in essence, a lonely newlywed, his return to sea so soon no longer seemed logical. All she could think of was the six months of days and nights without her new husband, stretched before her.

"We just got married! What am I gonna do here all by my-self?"

"It sounds like a long time but it'll fly by fast. Spring will be here before you know it." He took her hands. "I'll call as often as I can and send you plenty of money to pay bills."

Madeline moved from her parent's home to her husband's home. She'd never paid a bill in her life and didn't even know how to fill out a personal check. But she no longer had the luxury of having others take care of these things for her.

"I'll keep the money straight" she said, more to assure herself than Apollo. "But what about other household emergencies, like a leaky roof, or a burst pipe, or what if the heater breaks in the middle of the winter, or..."

"I'll leave you a number - Tony's General Contracting - you can call him if anything goes wrong."

"Who's going to cut the grass?"

"I'll do it before I leave and it shouldn't grow much during the winter. When it's time to rake the leaves, call that same number. Tony will take care of whatever comes up."

"And the snow?"

"Stop your worrying. It will all be fine."

"I don't want to be here without you." She'd never slept in a house by herself all night. She'd have to be sure to lock all the windows and bolt lock the front and back doors. The neighborhood was getting rough lately. During the past week, someone broke into the corner house through a downstairs open window while the family slept, there were news reports of gun violence just blocks away, and a rash of stolen cars, one of which belonged to the neighbor three houses down.

"You'll survive it," he told her.

"Promise you'll write me every day?"

"I promise to write you every week," he grinned.

MADELINE VISUALIZED HERSELF POISED AND STRONG the morning of Apollo's departure. She repeated the affirmation she'd recited over and over the past three weeks. *I am ready for this. I am calm,* she told herself. *I will not be emotional. In six months he'll be home.* But the mere sight of his luggage sitting by the front door as she descended the stairs, brought forth a sudden torrent of tears.

Apollo stood at the bottom of the landing, his arms open.

"I can't make the tears stop. I thought I'd be brave about this but as you can see, I'm a mess." She attempted a smile but instead a fresh swell of tears broke free.

"I love you too, Maddy."

The two embraced, enjoying the warmth of their bodies touching for one final time before the taxi's horn interrupted them. They'd both agreed that a long drawn out emotional scene at the airport wouldn't benefit either of them, so after they said their long goodbye on the front porch, Apollo rode off in the back of the cab.

"Just six months," she said as the taxi rounded the corner. "I just have to make it one hundred eighty days."

She looked up at their two-story home. It was warm and inviting when Apollo was there, but now it loomed enormous and empty. Back inside, she closed all the windows and locked the doors, providing some measure of security, but not nearly as much as if Apollo were there. She walked from room to room feeling the emptiness of it. Her footsteps echoed on the stairs.

Never in her life had she been so completely and utterly alone. Never had she existed in a house so still. Even though it was early morning, Madeline had a sudden urge to go to bed. She put on her pajamas, got under the covers and slept the entire day and through the night. Once she came to the realization that sleeping helped pass the time, round the clock slumber became her daily habit. She rose only for food, water, and bathing. The blinds and shades remained drawn at all times, and daylight touched her face solely when she retrieved the mail or picked up the pile of newspapers accumulating on the front porch.

Apollo's weekly letters provided some comfort to her days, as did his occasional phone calls. She read his letters over and over and the most romantic she memorized and recited when she was feeling especially alone.

Apollo's gift packages helped ease her solitude, too. Whenever he docked at a new port, he shipped Madeline a gift native to the region. Some were personal and sentimental, like the replica of a sapphire emblazoned tiara on which he carved 'my dear princess bride'. Others were historical artifacts aesthetically pleasing enough to mount and display around their home, like the paintings of great emperors or a handwoven basket. Her most memorable gift was an 1830 gold-gilded sword from Kaohsiung, in Taiwan, that once belonged to a sea captain. Madeline mounted the sword on a wooden display rack and hung it on the wall over the living room sofa. The magnificent twenty-eight inch blade bounced light throughout the room when kissed by the sun. She thought it an odd gift for a man to give to a woman but she loved it nonetheless.

After a month of seclusion, weary of counting the miserable days until Apollo's return, Madeline made up her mind to get out and meet new friends. What better place to start than her own neighborhood?

She'd already met the woman who lived in the house immediately to the right. Her name was Evangeline. She'd recently had a stroke and moved around on a walker with wheels. Her slurred speech was difficult to understand and her memory so impaired she'd asked Madeline her name a dozen times.

Another woman, not much older than Madeline, lived in the house on the left. They had exchanged many a pleasant 'good morning' but had never actually met. She was a tall caramel-colored woman who pranced around the neighborhood showcasing her hourglass figure in miniskirts, shorts that barely covered her panties and shirts so tight her breasts bulged from the top. She wore a heavy dark liner and smoky shadow, giving her an aura of sexiness bordering on desperation. On the surface, she didn't appear to be the type of woman Madeline would normally seek to be friends with, but hungry for companionship, she was willing to give it a try. She stepped over the low brick wall that separated their porches.

Dried leaves and yellowed newspapers, still rolled and bound with rubber bands, littered the porch, and the storm door was slightly ajar. A holiday wreath hung on a hook under the peephole. Madeline knocked. The woman opened the door just enough to peek through. She wore gray fleece pants and a simple white, cotton crew neck shirt. Her face scrubbed clean of layers of make-up, Madeline was surprised at how pretty she was.

"May I help you?"

"I thought I'd stop by and introduce myself. I'm Madeline. I live next door."

She smiled when she recognized her neighbor.

"Coletta Pierce," she announced as she extended her hand and motioned for her to come in.

"Something smells good."

"I just made cocoa. I'll pour you a cup." Coletta cleared the stacks of mail and papers off the kitchen table. From the sink, she pulled saucers and cups and washed them by hand. She poured two cups, and pulled up a chair.

"So tell me about yourself," they both said at the same time. The two giggled like adolescent girls.

"After you," Madeline said.

"I'll give you the Reader's Digest version." Coletta talked with her hands. "Born and raised in Jacksonville, Florida and the first in my family to go to college. Fell desperately in love my sophomore year and dropped out to get married. This is where it gets good." She stopped to light a cigarette.

Madeline leaned in.

"Mom said she was ashamed of me, and cut me out of her will and her life. Wonderful hubby," she made quotation marks in the air when she said wonderful, "took a job here in Pennsylvania shortly after we were married, and convinced me to move. A few months later, he left for a younger fresher version of me. Now I'm on the prowl for a replacement hubby."

Madeline couldn't comprehend the idea of any man walking away from Coletta.

"Landed a job as a receptionist at a car dealership," Coletta went on, "it pays the bills but if I'd listened to my mother and finished school, I'd likely have a better job. But that's another chapter altogether. So there you have it." Coletta blew a puff of smoke. "So what's your story?"

Madeline squirmed in her chair. "Married mom's boyfriend, mom has essentially abandoned me, and the husband's out to sea."

"You stole your mom's boyfriend? Scandalous! That's the stuff of soap operas. I love a juicy story."

"I didn't go after him. It just sort of happened."

"Regardless, it's juicy."

They talked until dinnertime but neither wanted to end the best conversation they'd had in a long time, so they ordered take out Chinese and continued chatting over dinner.

Madeline liked Coletta, although she seemed to be worldlier than anyone she'd ever met. On the end table was a magazine open to a nude male centerfold, and the T.V. cabinet held a stack of VCR tapes with a triple X rating. Madeline shrugged it off. Just because Coletta was into that sort of thing didn't mean she had to do it too. She just wouldn't be involved in that side of Coletta's life.

"So what are you doing next Friday night?" Coletta asked.

"I've been cooped up in the house for the last couple of weeks. I'd like to do something fun, maybe go skating at the ice rink in Oak Lane."

"That's not quite what I had in mind for a Friday night but it sounds like fun enough. How about I join you?"

MELANCHOLY ROSE TO GREET MADELINE ON Christmas morning. It was her first Christmas away from her parents' home, and she awakened wistful, yearning for her old life. She missed hearing her father whistle Christmas tunes an octave too high, the gifts he piled under the tree, all of which he signed "love Santa" long after she ceased believing in Santa Claus, and the sweet nutmeg-like aroma of eggnog slow-simmering on the stove.

Madeline was seriously considering going back to bed to sleep through the day when the key turned in the lock followed by the ringing of bells. Before he left, Apollo hung a row of tiny bells on the doorknob, so she'd always hear the front door opening and closing. It was Coletta. She was the only person with a spare key. Madeline had a spare key to Coletta's house too. They'd had so much fun ice skating the week after they met, they'd hung out together every weekend since.

"I'm in the kitchen!" Madeline dried her hands on a towel. She'd just washed a week's worth of dishes.

"Are you as miserable as I am?" Coletta asked. Coletta wore a dress so short it barely covered her behind. Madeline prayed she had no need to bend over.

"Worse," Madeline told her. "My father stopped by early this morning to drop off my Christmas present - a crock pot I have no idea how to operate. I was glad to see him on one hand, but on the other hand it made me sad. Christmas will never be the same as I remember it. I called my mother right after he left, but Sadie doesn't answer the phone and never bothers to turn on her answering machine. I couldn't even leave her a message so she'd know I was thinking about her."

"Look, Madeline, how about we forget our troubles and cook our own holiday dinner, like our parents did when we were growing up."

"Who would we invite?" Madeline asked.

"Just us, silly."

"That's absurd," Madeline said at first, but a mischievous smile lit her face, "so let's do it anyway."

Coletta roasted a thirteen pound turkey and a half ham, and baked macaroni and cheese. Madeline steamed the green beans and heated a tray of brown-and -serve rolls. She found the recipe for peach cobbler that Rosa gave Apollo, and Coletta thawed out a frozen apple pie. They drank store-bought eggnog with a little too much rum and played carols so loud Evangeline banged on the door and asked them to quiet down.

WINTER LOOSENED ITS GRASP AND SPRING crept timidly forward. With Coletta kneeling alongside her, Madeline set to work in her garden, clearing the weeds and turning the soil in the flower beds.

"I'll plant the hydrangeas here in front of the porch and alternate them with the juniper. The hostas will look nice along the side of the house but I'm sure I bought way too many. Do you wanna take the extras for your yard?"

Coletta didn't answer. Madeline turned and found her sitting on her heels. Her garden shears lay on the ground in front of her, her hands hung at their sides.

"What's wrong?" Madeline asked.

"You're my only friend, Madeline. I worry about what's gonna happen to us when Apollo gets home. You know how you married women get when your men are around. You won't have any use for me then."

Madeline pitied Coletta. They were both without their husbands but at least her husband was coming home. But the fact that Coletta had no friends was another story altogether. Who wanted a woman wearing clothes resembling lingerie, prancing around her husband? Now wasn't the time to bring it up, but she made a mental note to address the issue with Coletta at a later date.

"What do you think I'm gonna do? Drop you like a hot potato?" They both laughed.

"Seriously, Madeline, you're lucky to have your husband even if it's just for half of the year. My husband walked out on me and never looked back. It's like I didn't mean anything to him at all."

"Would you take him back if he returned?"

"My head says no, but my heart says take whatever you can get."

Madeline reached over and put an arm around Coletta's shoulders.

"I'm not going anywhere when Apollo gets home. Besides, who says I can't have a husband and a best friend. There's plenty room for all of us, but this friendship is history if you don't pick up those shears and get to working!" she teased.

All the talk about husbands made Madeline miss her own. "When I get in the house I have to check the calendar and see how many days are left before Apollo comes home."

"Well let me know because we still have plans to squeeze in."

"Like what?"

"On Thursday night, manicures are half off at the nail salon, and Saturday there's that sale at the linen store. Saturday night I'm going to Club Taboo. Are you sure you don't want to come with me?"

"It's a strip club!"

"That's not *all* it is. There's a dance floor, and a café with great wings and beer."

"No thanks," Madeline said, her nose crinkled.

"You don't know what you're missing," Coletta went on. "Oh, and we get in free at the Art Gallery on Sunday morning before noon. That was your idea of course, and don't forget my family reunion in Florida. Are you still coming?"

"Wouldn't miss it for the world but let me check my calendar to make sure the reunion doesn't overlap with Apollo coming home." Madeline slipped inside and returned with a wall calendar rolled up like a scroll. She unfolded it to the month of April and counted the days.

"Thirty-two," she announced.

"The reunion is in two weeks so we're all set to go. I'm glad you're coming. I didn't want t go by myself."

"Will your mother be there?"

"I'm afraid to ask but my aunt is hosting the reunion so it's possible."

"Do you think she'll talk to you?"

"I doubt it. She's pretty stubborn. By the way, I'll take you up on those extra hostas but I expect the same services."

"What services?"

"Get your tail over to my yard and help me plant them. You're the one with the green thumb. Everything I plant turns from green to brown and just curls up and dies."

THE FLIGHT FROM PHILADELPHIA TO Jacksonville took less than two hours. The plane touched down to a blazing sun and a stifling ninety degrees. Madeline and Coletta shed their winter jackets before leaving the airport, Coletta hailed a taxi.

"How far from the airport to the reunion?" Madeline hoisted her suitcase into the trunk of the cab and stopped to catch her breath. It was hard, at first, to adjust to the thick, wet air. The heat seared her lungs. She scowled at the driver who leaned against the car with his arms folded, his only contribution the thud of the trunk locking once the suitcase was securely inside.

"Fifteen minutes."

"Where to ma'am?" the cabbie asked. Coletta gave him the address. The car accelerated fast and didn't slow down, not even through steep curves, until they stopped at a red light. Their luggage slid from side to side in the trunk.

"Oh my God! Palm trees in the states?" Madeline blurted out.

"You don't get out much, huh?" Coletta laughed

"Shut up girl. How much longer is the drive?"

"About ten minutes."

"Are we there yet?" Madeline asked five minutes later.

"You sound like a kid!"

Madeline was too excited to be offended. She waited a little while longer then asked again.

"Now?"

"There, the house with the burgundy shutters."

It was a ranch style home with a long, winding driveway. Cars lined both sides. Madeline and Coletta retrieved their bags from the trunk of the taxi, walked along the side of the house to the backyard, and left the cabbie standing alongside the car, his palm facing up for the tip he'd never receive.

"Smells like ribs on the grill. I hope it's ready. I'm starving."

"Hey, Coletta." A woman approached. She looked so much like Coletta, Madeline thought she was her mother.

"Hey, Aunt Roberta. This is my friend, Madeline."

"Hi honey."

Behind Aunt Roberta came the entire legion of family in a swarm of hugging and kissing. Unaccustomed to the overt affection of so many strangers, Madeline's face grew hot.

The women were tall, shapely and brash, like Coletta, with wide hips and ample bosoms. The men, frail and subdued after years of being ruled by the domineering Pierce women, stood in the background. But one in particular, Coletta's cousin Nash, was more outgoing than the rest. He stepped forward to greet Madeline.

"It's a pleasure to meet you." He said meet like 'mate'.

"Nice to meet you too," Madeline giggled.

"I didn't know my cousin had such good taste in friends," he said as his eyes swept over her from head to toe.

"Why, thank you."

He walked in a circle around Madeline, taking her all in. "You are one gorgeous lady."

"She's not your type," Coletta stepped in front of Madeline, blocking Nash's view. "You know you like round shapely women like me." She placed her hand on her right hip and struck a pose.

"I see you haven't changed," Nash countered, his delight turned into disgust. "You still need to be the center of everyone's world." He walked off leaving Coletta standing there with her hand still on her hip.

The exchange left Madeline feeling uneasy, yet it wasn't Nash that put her ill at ease, it was Coletta.

"Come on, I'll introduce you to the rest of the family." Coletta went on, making no effort to hide her sudden displeasure.

Madeline met aunts, nieces, nephews and countless cousins. She was amazed at how easily the Pierce women, with their alpha personalities, all interacted. Conversation flowed easily, and they basked in each other's company as they caught up on the details of their lives. And although Madeline was the only person at the reunion who wasn't a blood relative, the Pierce clan drew her in. She imagined what it would be like to be part of a kinship of women such as this. Could she and Sadie foster the kind of bonds that came so easily to the Pierce clan?

"I wonder how Sadie would react if I showed up on her doorstep," Madeline wondered. They settled at a picnic table in the shade, their plates overflowing with ribs, corn on the cob and baked beans.

"As you can see, my mother avoided the reunion." Coletta shooed away a bee. "It was easier for her to hold a grudge than come here and deal with me face to face, so I'm afraid I don't have any words of encouragement for you."

"One of these days, I'm gonna get up the nerve to drop in on Sadie unannounced."

"Good luck!"

"Really, Coletta, to have to go the rest of my life and not fix this thing between us is unbearable."

"Like me and my mother? It hurt in the beginning. If I called her, she hung up on me. If I tried to visit, she wouldn't open the door."

"How did you deal with that?"

"I just went on with my life. It's her choice, not mine," she said matter-of-factly. "If you do decide to call Sadie, how do you know she wants you back in her life?"

"I don't know, Coletta, I really don't know."

"I say move on and don't look back."

COLETTA AND MADELINE TOOK THE LAST plane out of Jacksonville the following evening. Madeline was relieved when Coletta napped through the entire flight. She didn't feel much like talking anyway, her mind preoccupied with thoughts of family and reconciliation. She envied Coletta's simple acceptance of her mother's absence. Madeline, however, couldn't make peace with the absence of hers. She feared a lifetime of separation from Sadie, but more importantly, she feared realizing too late that she'd never tried hard enough to make things right

Madeline arrived home just after midnight and lay in bed tossing and turning with Sadie still on her mind. She rehearsed attempts at reconciliation and pondered possible outcomes. When she did manage to fall asleep, in the wee hours of the morning, her dreams were fragmented images of Sadie, like flipping through a photo album of partial pictures – glimpses of the ruffled sleeve of her favorite blouse, the pendant of a necklace she wore on her birthday, eyebrows expertly tweezed, the delicate folds of her ear.

When the seven a.m. alarm buzzed in three second intervals, Madeline scowled. She hated the sound. It was not conducive to gentle waking, yet it was the only way to ensure she didn't sleep until noon. She disabled the annoying buzzer and picked up her bedside calendar.

Two weeks until my hubby's home. Madeline yawned and stretched with all four limbs reaching toward the ceiling. She'd been living like a teenager. It was time to tidy up the house before Apollo got home. God forbid he witnessed how sloppy she'd been. She made a mental list of all the things she had to do in the next fourteen days. Go to the market and stock the fridge, take the drapes and rugs to the cleaners, call Tony to clear out the yard and fix the leaky sink in the basement, mop the kitchen and bathroom, scrub the baseboards… and of course a man away at sea so long certainly deserves to see his wife in sexy lingerie, so a trip to the department store was in order, too.

"There's no way I can get this all done in two weeks." She picked up the phone to call Coletta and beg for help when the bells on the door knob jingled.

"Coletta!" she called out, "I was just about to dial your number. I'm upstairs." She placed the phone back on the receiver. "I need help getting this house back to perfect before Apollo comes home. Give me a hand and I'll spring for pizza tonight."

Coletta knew what it was like to live alone and afraid so she was always careful to yell 'it's me!' when she came over unannounced with her spare key. Madeline listened for Coletta's familiar voice, yet heard nothing.

"Coletta!" she called out again.

There was a loud thump in the living room, like a heavy box falling to the floor.

"Who's there?" she yelled.

Paper rustled, then footsteps began. They were measured, even, and heavy like work boots hitting the floor. This most certainly was not Coletta. The footsteps moved toward the staircase, then paused. Madeline opened her mouth to call out again but no words escaped. She sat frozen. When she heard the footsteps ascend the stairs, fear propelled her into action. She lunged from the bed, slammed the door and rushed to set the bolt lock when the bedroom door flung wide open. Madeline covered her face with her hands and screamed while backing away from the door.

"Maddy, it's me!"

She uncovered her eyes and gaped at the apparition before her. Surely she was still sleeping, the figure before her a figment of her dreams.

"Apollo!" she shouted and jumped into his arms, her terror now pure delight. He enveloped her entirely, wrapping her in a safety and security she hadn't felt since the day he set sail. "You weren't supposed to be here for another two weeks!"

"I wanted to surprise you."

"Surprise me? You nearly scared me to death!"

"I've missed you so." He stood back and took her all in. "Maddy, you're beautiful."

She frowned, then erupted into giggles. "You've got to be kidding me." She wore her flannel granny nightgown, the one that covered her to the ankles. It was warm and comfortable, yet earned zero points in the seduction category.

"You'd look beautiful in a hard hat and overalls." He picked her up and carried her downstairs, like a groom carrying his bride over the threshold. Gift boxes of various sizes, wrapped in red and green paper, crowded the landing.

"Merry Christmas, Madeline!"

"Christmas in April!" she squealed.

Madeline tore open the boxes to pink and blue satin lingerie trimmed in lace with matching thigh-length robes, a tennis bracelet accentuated with white gold, and lavender and primrose essential oils in decorative glass bottles.

"I love all of it!"

"You are most deserving." Apollo took off an imaginary hat and with a flourish, held it over his chest and bowed like the cowboys in the old Westerns.

"Oh no!" She stood up and frowned.

"What's wrong?"

"Everything's a wreck. I wanted to clean the house before you came home but..."

"All of that can wait. I'm just glad to be home where I can finally get some rest." He sighed and leaned against the wall. She finally got a good look at him.

Ill fitting clothing dwarfed his frame, his shoulders sloped forward and his eyes were bloodshot and squinting in the bright morning light filtering through the blinds.

"Didn't they feed you on that ship? There's hardly anything left of you."

"It's nothing a little bit of rest, lovin' and home cookin' can't cure." He pulled her into his arms again.

APOLLO AND MADELINE WERE NEW lovers, touching, exploring, savoring, heedless of the passage of time or the concerns of the world around them, with pleasure as their sole aimless guide. Days, they were one, bodies intertwined, yearning and fulfilling, aching and releasing. Nights they lay awake in each other's arms speaking the language of affection and adulation, dreaming of what the future held until morning infused their nest with the radiant light of day. Apollo's entire world was Madeline and Madeline's world was Apollo, until the grinding rev of a lawn mower's engine turning over yanked Madeline from slumber and reminded her of the life she readily abandoned. She shot up in bed so fast the room spun.

"Coletta!"

"Who?" Apollo opened his eyes and yawned.

"I forgot about Coletta. We had so many things to do before you returned, and I never explained why I wasn't around. I just up and forgot about her. Apollo, are you listening?" Apollo's eyes slowly closed again, and his breathing grew measured. She continued talking anyway.

"I haven't called, or stopped by or anything!" She slipped on a bathrobe and slippers and ran down the front steps. Outdoors, it was mild. A warm breeze set the wind chimes clinging.

Coletta stood on her porch watching the landscaper push the noisy mower across her lawn. Blades of grass circled tunnel-like behind him. She wore her usual stilettos and shorts, the pink lace of her panties peeking at the hem.

"Coletta, I know I haven't called. We had so many plans but Apollo came home earlier than expected and..."

"That's how you lovesick women are when your man's around. Who needs friends when you have a man? Dropped like a hot potato after all." Coletta folded her arms across her chest, her lips pursed.

"Coletta, I'm so sorry. You know I love you girl."

Coletta grinned. "I'm just kidding. If my man were home, I'd lock him up in my bedroom too. Go on girl. Enjoy that hunk of a husband. I'll catch up with you later."

"Is that a new landscaper? What happened to the old one?" Madeline marveled at how Coletta always had the hottest, buffest men tending to her yard.

"The old one outlived his usefulness," Coletta winked.

"You didn't!" Madeline gasped.

"You couldn't possibly expect me to keep my hands off of a man who looks that good!"

Before going back indoors, Madeline picked up the handful of envelopes in the mailbox. Perhaps Sadie would have a change of heart and at least send her a card or letter if she wouldn't answer her phone. She flipped through the pile. All of it was addressed to Apollo. *She'll never change. Why do I keep looking?*

She turned around to the lumbering growl of a big rig creeping down the roadway. It was an oddity to see such an overlarge vehicle on their tiny residential street. It came to a stop in front of her home, brakes screeching to a slow halt. The logo on the truck read *Millshore Meats*.

"Must be going to the house across the street," she told Coletta.

The driver jumped from the high seat with a clipboard tucked under his arm, and took the steps to Madeline's porch.

"I have a delivery for the Evers residence," he said.

"Apollo," she yelled into the house. "Did you arrange for a meat delivery?"

Apollo hurried down the stairs tying his bathrobe. "You can bring that right in," he told the driver.

The driver rolled up the rear lid of the truck and piled six boxes onto a hand cart.

"That's an awful lot of meat all at one time. Where are we going to store it?"

"In the deep freezer in the basement."

She'd forgotten about the deep freezer. While Apollo was at sea, what little she bought for herself fit into the refrigerator.

Apollo signed the delivery slip and unpacked the boxes. "Chicken breast, lamb, beef ribs, pork roast, you name it, we got it."

"I don't even know how to cook all of that." The sight of all the meat intimidated Madeline. She could roast a chicken and fry pork chops, but had never attempted the other meats stacked on the counter. When she lived with her parents, Sadie did all the cooking.

"How about we fire up the grill this afternoon?"

"Who do you want to invite?"

"No guests, just the two of us."

Apollo stacked half the shipment in the deep freezer. The remainder he prepped for the barbecue. He pulled spices from the pantry and whisked together a tangy barbecue sauce with brown sugar, spicy mustard, honey, ketchup, and was that cumin? Madeline tried to make note of all the spices and seasonings but she couldn't keep up. Apollo measured nothing, and mixed the ingredients quickly, as if he'd done it a thousand times. He smothered the ribs and steaks with rich sauces then fired up the charcoal grill. Once the fire died down and the embers glowed, he set the meats on the grill in a row. Smothered in the tangy marinade, they sizzled over the fire, smoke spiraling up from even rows of char marks. Pungent spices tickled her nose.

"I thought we were starting the barbecue this afternoon?"

"It's almost noon."

"It's ten forty five."

"That's close enough."

"I'll pick up potato salad from the deli," she offered.

"Store bought potato salad?" Apollo frowned. "Oh no sweetheart, I'll grill a batch of new potatoes."

"Potatoes on the grill?"

"You have lots to learn, my dear, but the grill master is here to show you the way."

"Whatever, Apollo. Is there anything else I can pick up that you can't possibly throw on that grill?"

"Salad greens," he told her.

She left Apollo basting the meats and wrapping ears of corn in aluminum foil. When she came home just an hour later, he'd already started filling his plate with steak, potatoes and corn. A rack of ribs he stacked on a second plate, and on a third plate he piled the salad Madeline picked up from the deli. Before Madeline could fix her own plate of food, half of Apollo's steak was gone. He ate so fast, he barely chewed his food and had to swallow hard – hard enough for Madeline to hear it clear across the table – to digest it. He did not speak. His head down, inches from his plate, he shoveled forkfuls into his mouth. He mopped the sauces on his plate with a slice of bread before forcing the slice into his already full mouth. All three of his plates now clean, Apollo helped himself to seconds and thirds before guzzling bourbon straight from the bottle.

Her own appetite gone, Madeline stared at Apollo as if he were mad. She cleared her throat noisily.

He looked up as if noticing her at the table for the first time.

"I've never seen you eat like that," she said warily.

He opened his mouth to answer then sat suddenly still, color draining from his cheeks. He jerked to standing and hurried upstairs. Footsteps pounded the floor from the hallway to the bathroom, followed by the sound of Apollo's gagging as he vomited the contents of his over full stomach. Madeline hurried up the stairs behind him and knocked on the bathroom door.

"Are you okay?"

"Fine," he said, after which he wretched and vomited again. Immediately afterwards, he scoured the kitchen for more food. He filled a plate with the leftover grilled meats and ate as if he hadn't had a bite to eat at all.

"Shouldn't you wait awhile?" Madeline asked. "You were just sick!"

"I'm starved."

MADELINE COULDN'T SLEEP WITH THE CONTINUOUS thud of Apollo's footsteps pacing throughout the house. He walked from the living room to the kitchen, and up and down the stairs. He walked outdoors from corner to corner, providing some respite from the annoying pacing, but soon afterward his footsteps resumed in the house. She sat up in bed just as the minute hand on the clocked ticked forward. Four minutes after three. She met him in the living room just as he came indoors.

"Why are you still up?"

Apollo shrugged his shoulders and continued past her.

"There must be something bothering you."

"I'll be fine."

"But Apollo, you haven't slept at all tonight."

Apollo shot daggers back at Madeline.

"I've heard chamomile helps. I'll brew a pot." She poured a cup for both of them, hoping Apollo would at least sit down and perhaps talk about what worried him, but Apollo kept walking, cup in hand. Madeline intended to walk alongside him and keep him company, but fatigue quickly overcame her. She kept vigil on the living room sofa for a short time, however, by four in the morning her chin dropped to her chest and her eyes closed of their own will.

"I'm going back to bed. Hopefully you'll sleep better tomorrow night."

But he didn't sleep any better the subsequent nights either. Neither did Madeline. On the fifth consecutive restless night, she confronted him again after his trek outdoors.

"Apollo, this is getting serious. You have to get some rest. Maybe you should see a doctor. I can make an appointment for you."

"No need to see a doctor."

How long can you go on like this?" Madeline questioned. *How long can I go on without a good night's rest?*

"It's not a big deal. It's just a little trouble sleeping."

"It's more than not sleeping. You're exhausted during the day, you gorge on food, you're irritable…"

"I'm okay. Just give me some time."

"You talk as if you know what the problem is. Tell me!"

"Just bear with me. I'll be back to my old self again soon."

"And this will all magically go away?"

"I've been at sea for six months, Madeline. It takes some time to adjust to the routine of home."

Was it really because of being away at sea? What if this is some sort of early midlife crisis? Or is this just the real Apollo, the Apollo she didn't know? What else didn't she know about her husband? She didn't recall any of these problems during their courtship, but she had to admit the courtship was too brief to know for sure.

"Madeline, stop worrying. I'll pull it together," he told her as he went out the door for the umpteenth time.

"No sense in going back to bed now," she sighed. "The sun's coming up. I'll get a head start on the laundry before it gets hot. The dryer makes the whole house an inferno."

While she sorted and folded a load of clothes, Apollo wandered back inside and turned on the television. A news reporter interviewed a prominent, wealthy businessman about his secret to profitable investing. It was one of Apollo's favorite topics. He pulled a chair up close, sitting inches from the screen.

"Did you hear that, Madeline? He invested in aggressive stocks and hit the big time! Remember, we talked about that?" He was more alert than he'd been in days.

It was all gibberish to Madeline. There was food on the table, a roof over their heads, and money in the bank. How that money came about was of no interest to her, especially not at that hour of the morning.

"The key to being successful is not pulling out when the going gets tough," he adjusted his chair closer, "although it's hard standing by and doing nothing when your hard earned money shrinks. Do you know what I mean?"

Madeline picked up a handful of folded hand towels to stack in the linen closet.

"Uh-huh."

"Are you listening?"

Madeline nodded. She didn't want to admit she hadn't heard a word, so she changed the subject fast.

"Sure, but did you see the painting I bought for the foyer?"

Apollo refused to let go of the matter. "I'm no idiot, Madeline. I'm not talking about a damn painting. Why can't you pay attention?"

Madeline didn't know what to say.

"Answer the question!" he shrieked. She jumped, dropping the pile of laundry in a heap on the floor.

"I'm sorry," she told him. "I just didn't hear you."

Apollo stood over her, a vein protruding from his temple. His chest pumped up and down, as if he were bursting to say more, then he abruptly left the room. The front door slammed and his car roared away, tires screeching around the corner.

A sharp pain shot through the palms of her hands. Madeline opened her fists, realizing only then how tightly they were clenched. Blood dripped from the cuts made by her own fingernails. She wrapped her hands in paper towels and called Coletta.

"I know it's early, but I need to talk. I'm coming over."

They sat on Coletta's new porch furniture, a sofa and two chairs. Coletta called the floral sofa a "glider", footrests popped out from underneath the chairs.

"Coletta, my husband is going crazy and he's taking me there with him. He doesn't sleep, he's up pacing most of the night, and the lack of sleep is making him irritable. Just this morning, he yelled at me for not paying attention while he was talking, and he wasn't even talking about anything interesting. I mean, who cares about investing money?"

"So he yelled. What's the big deal?"

"The punishment didn't fit the crime. He was so worked up afterwards, he drove off in a huff."

"Is that all?"

"There's more. He's eats enough for three people then vomits it all up."

"Maybe you should buy more groceries. Clearly the man is hungry."

Madeline rolled her eyes. "You don't understand just how serious it is. There's no use talking to you about it."

"I'm just joking, go on."

"When you put it all together, it doesn't make for a pretty picture."

"Is this all new? I mean, didn't you see any of this before you were married?"

"We dated less than a year. I don't know if this is just a temporary thing or if this is just a part of him I never knew."

"Don't jump to any conclusions. It'll probably blow over."

COLETTA TOLD EVERYONE IT WAS A SMALL intimate gathering, but Coletta didn't know how to have a get together and not have it turn into a raucous, full-blown backyard bash.

It was a boiling Fourth of July. The air was heavy with humidity, leaving a damp sheen on the skin, and rendering even the sheerest of clothing heavy as wool. Clouds obscured the sun intermittently, providing some relief from the scorching rays, but the dogged humidity persisted.

Music blared from speakers on opposite sides of the yard and guests clustered in small groups. Some huddled together at tables, trying to comprehend each other over the noisy crowd. Others moved to the beat of the music balancing drinks in one hand and snapping fingers with the other. Apollo and Madeline mingled in separate groups. Apollo stood by the fence with some of the other men, swallowed up in a cloud of cigar smoke. Madeline sat at a round resin table with Coletta and a handful of neighbors. Plastic cups filled with a red punch scattered the table. A mere whiff at the rim revealed the alcohol content was far greater than its mixer.

Madeline's chair was adjacent to a stereo speaker. Aside from the elevated voices of the folks sitting at her table, she couldn't hear much else above the music. Madeline laughed at a joke one of the women failed miserably at telling, when all at once, Apollo was behind her grabbing her arm near her wrist, and pulling upward until she rose to her feet.

"Why are you ignoring me? I'm ready to go!" he bellowed.

She jerked her arm free and rubbed her wrist. "What are you talking about?"

"Three times I said 'come on Madeline, let' go' and you ignored me!"

"Stop being a jerk! I didn't hear you!" She stood on her toes and yelled, inches from his face, then turned to Coletta, "I gotta go, honey. Apollo's in one of his moods." She held both hands up and made quotation marks in the air when she said the word 'moods'. Madeline drank the rest of her soda - the fruit punch was too potent - and trudged behind Apollo over to her back yard.

"What the hell is wrong with you?" she argued. "Living with you is like living with two different people - nice one day and stark raving mad the next. You don't sleep, you eat like you're starving to death then throw up like an anorexic, or is it bulimic? I told you to see a doctor, but you refused. If you can't pull yourself together, maybe you need to get a regular job like everyone else. This six month on, six month off thing is making you crazy. Or maybe I'm the one who needs to see a doctor to find out why I keep putting up with this."

She flung open the back door so hard it struck the stone wall. Before her eyes could adjust to the darkness in the basement, Apollo grabbed her shoulders, and spun her around. She never saw Apollo raise his fist but it was instantly in her face, striking her jaw. She shoved him as hard as she could. He stumbled backward over the side of the futon and struck his head on the deep freezer. Unfazed, Apollo got up and clamored toward her, his face contorted and unrecognizable, veins bulging at the temple, eyes nearly popping out of their sockets. Madeline turned to run but Apollo caught up with her again, striking her a second time. Her head snapped back and her body slackened. The blows came fast and hard, one after the other, her face growing increasingly numb with each blow until the world went dark.

She came to seconds later. Apollo stood over her menacingly, until the realization of what he'd done bought him to his knees.

"What did I do?" He lifted her head. "Madeline?"

Her right eye was so engorged it opened only a tiny slit.

"I didn't mean it. I lost control."

Dazed, Madeline's only thought was getting off of the cold concrete floor. "Help me up," she said.

He picked her up and carried her outside to the car. He raced to the hospital, disregarding stop signs and red lights and leaving a trail of beeping horns behind him.

"Help me!" he implored the hospital staff, "my wife is hurt!"

Madeline's arms and legs dangled. Blood oozed from her nose.

"A bay is available over here, sir," a nurse told him. Apollo lowered her onto the hospital bed and tenderly swept the hair from her face.

"Sir, we'll take care of her. If you'll come with me please and fill out the paperwork."

The E.R. physician examined Madeline while Apollo filled out forms in the waiting area. "What happened, Mrs. Evers?"

"I was standing on a ladder hanging drapes," she could barely form the words through her swollen lips, "and I lost my balance and fell." She stared straight ahead, too embarrassed to look in the doctor's eyes.

"Where does it hurt?"

"My eyes, cheek and wrist." He held her arm below the wrist and rotated her hand back and forth and side to side. Madeline winced and cried out. He sent her for X-rays to make sure there weren't any fractures, and when she was back in the bay, he questioned her again.

"Tell me again. What happened?"

She repeated the same explanation verbatim as if rehearsing her part in a play.

He looked Madeline in the eyes long after she finished her explanation, as if giving her ample time to recant her story.

"Apply ice as needed for the swelling. If your eye is sensitive to light, wear this patch for the next forty eight hours." He removed the protective covering and unwrapped the paper strings. "Your wrist isn't broken but it's badly sprained. The nurse will wrap it in a bandage to limit movement. Keep it on for about two weeks. I'm writing you a prescription for pain medicine." He scratched something illegible on a pad, tore off the sheet and handed it to Madeline. "Follow up with your family doctor if the pain and swelling persist."

When he left the room, the nurse came in with the wrist bandages.

"Tell my husband that I'm fine. He can go on home." The nurse left, then returned right away.

"He refuses to leave, ma'am. He says he'll wait for you in the waiting area."

After her wrist was wrapped, Madeline signed discharge papers ducked out of the side entrance and hailed a cab. She read the paperwork while in the backseat. The attending physician had stapled a pamphlet about domestic abuse to her discharge papers. On the front of the pamphlet was a photo of a young woman, both eyes blackened, her arm in a cast. Listed beneath the photo was a 1-800 number to call for counseling or shelter.

Madeline tossed the pamphlet out of the window. *How did it all come to this? Me, the battered wife.*

"I don't need this crap," she mumbled, "I'll kill him first!"

"What was that, miss?" the cabbie asked, while looking at her through the rearview mirror.

"Nothing, just pull over up ahead. My house is there on the right."

She paid the driver and went inside. She straightened the pillows on the sofa, stacked the dishes in the dishwasher, wiped off the table and took the roast pork out of the freezer to thaw for dinner the next day. When Apollo finally arrived, she was the picture of serenity, sitting at the dining room table flipping through a magazine.

"Maddy, this will never happen again. I'm so sorry."

She held up her hand. "I don't want to talk about it right now." Her voice held no anger or sadness, just a strange calm.

"I made a serious mistake. I snapped."

She held up her hand again.

"I understand if you don't want to discuss this right now, but can we talk in the morning after we both get some rest?"

Madeline nodded.

"I'm turning in early. I have a lot of thinking to do to get my head on straight."

Then Madeline waited. She waited through Apollo's shower and shave, she waited while he rummaged through the drawers for a pair of pajamas, then she waited until she heard him snoring. She thought it odd that Apollo had so much trouble sleeping in previous weeks, yet slept sound as a newborn on the night he brutally beat her. She walked into the living room and dismounted the beautiful antique sword Apollo sent her from Taiwan. She removed it from its case and rotated the polished, deadly blade admiring it from all angles. She listened at the bottom of the stairs until she heard his measured, heavy breathing. Avoiding the creaky places, she crept up the stairs one by one, and slipped into the bathroom to gaze at herself in the mirror. Her face was a swollen mask of bruises. Both eyes were reddish purple and rimmed in black, and her distended lip and swollen cheek were a hideous mound of discolored, bruised flesh. She brushed her finger over her cheek. The skin stretched tight, and the area just under her eye was so engorged, it was numb. She shut off the bathroom light and entered the bedroom with the sword by her side. Madeline walked over to the side of the bed nearest to where Apollo slept and gazed down upon this man she loved so dearly. With both hands, she brandished the sleek blade high over her head, inhaled, and then dropped it with all her strength. Just before the blade pierced the soft flesh below his Adam's apple, Apollo's eyes flew open. He rolled off the bed and crawled into the hallway. As if someone were in hot pursuit, he grasped the railing and shot down the stairs and out into the night.

"You crazy woman! What the hell is wrong with you?" Madeline heard him yell from outdoors.

The bed linens and mattress were in pieces, sliced by the sword clean through. Madeline lifted the bedroom window and stuck her head out. "Damn you!" she yelled. "Those were my favorite sheets. If you'd kept still I'd only have to wash them. Now I'll have to throw them out!"

"To hell with the sheets! You could have killed me!" Apollo roared. He didn't come inside right away, he called from a pay phone first.

"Maddy, I'm sorry. I promise I'll never touch you again," he told her. This was the plea of many an abusive husband. Nearly all of them lived to beat their women again, in spite of their earnest proclamations of sorrow and regret. Would he, too, raise his hand again?

"I will not be a victim on a pamphlet praying and hoping that you don't take my life one day because you can't control your temper. I will fight back, Apollo!"

IT WAS THE TIME OF YEAR KNOWN as Indian summer, the season's final farewell. After an early, biting frost, the newscasters warned of seven days of stifling heat. Air conditioners and window fans whirred nonstop throughout the night and day. Birds and squirrels ceased their scurrying, and the roads were sparsely travelled as folks stayed indoors to escape the sweltering. There was no air. Even the leaves and branches were still. Madeline lounged in the upstairs rear bedroom listening to a talk show on the radio while sipping ice water. Apollo was in the back yard, washing his car.

"Not the kind of day for yard work," she heard Apollo say.

Madeline turned off the radio and looked outside.

"Somebody has to pull up these weeds." Coletta bent slowly over the hostas Madeline helped her plant near the back fence, her shapely behind perched high.

"Loving that rear view," Apollo whistled.

Coletta glanced back at him admiring her and smiled. Apollo licked his lips, a gesture that seemed obscene to Madeline.

"You better hope your wife doesn't catch you checking me out." Her words were harsh but her smile inviting.

Apollo turned and looked up at the house. Madeline ducked inside before he noticed her.

That bastard has the nerve to flirt with her right from our own backyard, with me here in the house nonetheless!

She waited until Coletta went indoors to pop over. "How are you managing in this heat?" Madeline asked.

"All the fans are turned on at full blast and it's still muggy in the house. I have no intention of going outside today."

"I saw you gardening this morning," Madeline baited her.

"Not very wise in this weather. I'll finish the yard when this heat wave lifts."

"Anything going on?" Madeline asked.

"Perhaps on a cooler day, but today all is still. She flopped onto her sofa six feet in front of an oscillating fan. Her thin blouse ballooned in the air.

"Well, I'll see you tomorrow. Try to stay cool."

Perhaps she was making a big deal out of nothing. However inappropriate, it was just a remark. It wasn't as if she caught them touching or kissing. Madeline walked back home and carried on with the day. Rather than turn on the oven, she opted for cold cut sandwiches for dinner, after which Apollo grabbed his car keys while murmuring something about errands to run. It was six thirty and almost everything in West Oak Lane shut down by six o'clock on Sundays, but Apollo drove off before she could question him.

By eleven, Apollo still wasn't home. Madeline had no reason to worry, no cause for curiosity. She knew exactly where he was. She left the house through the basement door and stepped over the low fence. She used her spare key to get into Coletta's house through the back door, walked through the kitchen and stood at the foot of the stairs. There was no need to go any further. She heard Apollo making love to Coletta, whispering all those things he once said to her.

"I need you," he told her.

"Take me," Coletta whispered back, the bed springs keeping pace, the headboard banging against the wall.

Madeline listened in Coletta's living room until she could bear it no longer, then covered her ears with her hands and fled.

"God help me. I've married a monster."

Apollo must have heard her running from Coletta's house, for within seconds he was behind her, breathless and shouting her name.

Madeline waited until she was in the safety of her own home before turning to confront him. His fly gaped open and his shirt hung crooked, his collar draped around his shoulder.

"I heard you, Apollo. I stood in Coletta's living room and I heard you making love to her. I heard all of it!" Her hands shielded her ears as if the echoes of their lovemaking still haunted her.

"I didn't plan it Madeline. It just happened. We weren't having an affair or anything, I just got caught up. It was the first time, the only time, and it will never happen again."

"And you think that matters? I don't care if it was planned, unplanned, the first time or the tenth time, it's wrong! I've put up with a lot from you, but this... I never thought you capable of this!"

He stepped forward and reached for Madeline's hands. "I haven't been myself lately. This isn't like me."

Madeline inhaled a sweet flowery scent. She covered her nose and took two steps backward, averting her face. "I smell her perfume. It's all over you."

Apollo walked toward her anyway.

"Don't touch me. Don't even come near me."

"Madeline, I think I need help, maybe some sort of counseling."

"You don't need any doggone counseling. What you need is to learn how to practice self control. All that crap about being on the ship and having that affect your eating and sleeping and temper is one thing, but this? You can't blame this on that damn ship. " She backed up and turned to leave. "I need to get out of here." She pointed a finger at Apollo. "And don't you dare stop me!"

"Please don't go. Not while you're upset." Apollo stretched his arms wide, blocking her exit.

"Get out of my way!" she yelled.

Apollo didn't move. Madeline' sight shifted to the sword from Taiwan. Apollo followed her gaze then his eyes met hers.

"Get out of my way," she said again, this time even and firm.

Apollo stepped aside.

"Where are you going?" he called after her.

Madeline didn't answer. Her elusiveness wasn't deliberate, she simply had no idea where she was going. She walked to the end of the street, turned right until she reached the main road, and walked. Past schools, playgrounds, store fronts and dozens of row houses, she walked. She walked with determination and purpose, as if training for a race. She walked until her calves ached and the pounding of her shoes on the concrete rubbed painfully against the ball of her foot.

She walked until an old familiar yearning enveloped her, a yearning that hadn't visited since childhood. It started gently, softly, like the petals of a rose brushing against her cheek, then it grew like a massive oak with branches spreading tall and wide, nearly swallowing her whole. It was a ridiculous yearning for a young woman, yet for Madeline, it was present and real. The weight of it would no longer allow her to put one foot in front of the other, and forced her to her knees in a patch of grass by a curb.

"I need my mother! Where has she been and why won't she come?" She screamed out onto the roadway. "Where is my mother?" She cried out, hands and knees dampened by the soil.

Cars slowed but none stopped. Spent, she let go and lay face down in the grass. "Mommy, where are you?"

Long after the sobbing ceased, she lay there, until the beep of a car's horn startled her. Madeline struggled to her feet. She had no idea where she was or what time it was. She checked her wrist. It was bare. She'd neglected to slip on her watch. For some gauge of the time, she lifted her eyes to the sky, but could discern nothing from the layers of pitch-darkness. She spotted a phone booth on the corner at the end of a row of stores. It held a single bench with an empty beer can tucked in the corner. Madeline sat on the bench, arms wrapped around herself, until the sun crept into the sky. She searched her pockets for a case quarter and dropped it into the pay phone.

"Daddy?"

"Maddy, are you alright? It's six in the morning." Tucker's voice was fresh like he'd been up for hours. He was probably on his way to the diner. Madeline imagined his life simpler, perhaps even happier, without Sadie.

"I hope I didn't wake you." She cleared her throat and fought to make her voice sound as normal as possible.

"Already up. What's on your mind?"

"You know how mom can hold a grudge."

"For the rest of this life, through death and the resurrection and still not speak to the person who wronged her."

"Daddy I'm gonna try to talk to her. She's mad at me and Apollo, but there's more to it than just being mad at the fact that we got married. She's been mad at me for a long time, since I was a little girl. I don't remember a time when she wasn't angry with me and I don't know why. What did I do wrong?"

Tucker didn't answer, so she went on.

"I don't expect her to change after all these years but I need her, and I won't have a chance to get what I need if I don't at least try to find out why she closed herself to me."

"Maddy, she's a hard woman. I'm not saying people can't change but don't get your hopes up. For years, I tried to reason with her and got nowhere at all. As a matter of fact, my insistence on getting to the heart of the matter likely made things worse."

"I have to at least try."

"It's hard to hear you. Sounds like traffic in the background. Are you outside?"

"I'm at a pay phone."

"Did something happen with Apollo?"

Madeline didn't answer. If she didn't speak it aloud perhaps some shred of dignity remained.

"When you're ready to talk about it, you call me back. Take care of yourself, Maddy."

"Bye Daddy."

"And let me know how things turn out with Sadie."

***

MADELINE ENVIED THE BONDS BETWEEN other young women and their mothers. Their bonds were holy and righteous, like a covenant, with no conditions or barriers, and endurance in the face of great turbulence. These mothers were gallant, unselfish women who loved their children more than themselves. Some measured their very existence by their children. But Sadie wasn't made of the substance of these noble women. Sadie was self-serving, ignorant of the higher purpose, the greater need. Was it even worth the effort to attempt to forge such a sacred covenant with the likes of Sadie? Madeline wanted nothing more than to face her life with an 'I never needed her anyway', attitude that would allow her to simply move on and not give Sadie another thought. But life had brought her to her knees and she ached for the solace that only a mother could provide. It was time to go after what she needed. What did she have to lose? Today would be the day to make things right. She would take the first step and call Sadie. If Sadie didn't answer the phone, Madeline would show up at her front door. If she refused to open the door, Madeline would camp out on her porch until they got to the bottom of whatever caused Sadie's lifelong hostility.

Of course there was still the issue of Apollo's infidelity to resolve. Madeline wasn't running from the matter, but there was a block of sorts. She wasn't able to see through to dealing with Apollo's wrongdoing without first fixing this thing with Sadie.

The order of it made sense. Sadie, first and foremost and later, she would focus her sights on Apollo. She imagined what she would say to her mother.

I'm sorry about what happened with me and Apollo. Neither of us planned it. We just fell in love. You've been angry at me for a long time, since I was a little girl. I don't understand why and maybe it doesn't matter anymore. Right now, I need you in my life. I'm all grown up but I still need my mother. Can we make a fresh start? Please, please talk to me.

MADELINE DECIDED AGAINST BREAKFAST. The mere thought of putting anything in her mouth made her stomach churn. She rehearsed her speech one last time in front of a mirror, and called Sadie. As expected, Sadie didn't pick up, so that meant she'd have to confront her face-to-face. Before heading out, she passed by Apollo sprawled on the sofa. He must have fallen asleep there while waiting for her to come home last night.

She searched through her bag for the key to lock the house, when the telephone rang. She didn't really want to answer it, but it was unusual for anyone to call so early in the morning. *It must be important. I better pick up.*

"Hello?"

"Madeline, it's Pearl. I'm so sorry honey." Pearl's pitch was high and her words flowed together making it hard to understand where one word ended and the next word began.

"Auntie Pearl, why are you crying?"

"Your mother and I were supposed to go to a yard sale this morning. I rang the bell and knocked but she didn't come to the door. I knew she was home because her car was still parked in the driveway. I was worried she might be sick or hurt, so I called the police. They broke into the house." There was a heavy silence. Madeline was too afraid of what was coming next to encourage her to go on.

"Honey, your mother didn't wake up this morning. She was still in her bed, peaceful. It could have been her heart, or a clot on the brain, we don't know yet. But she's gone, Madeline."

"She's dead? My mother's dead?"

"It doesn't make sense. She was healthy and young and strong, but sometimes these things happen out of the blue."

Pain radiated from Madeline's chest to her limbs and extremities and released from her body in uncontrolled spasms.

"No!" She cried out. She cried out over the torment of her mother's scorn, the guilt of her own betrayal, the shock of Sadie's sudden death, and the anguish at never having had the chance to make it all right. The phone slipped from her hand and she collapsed to the floor.

APOLLO AWAKENED TO MADELINE'S CRIES. He ran to the kitchen so fast, he nearly tripped over her limbs.

"Madeline, what happened?" Her eyes were open and she breathed freely, yet she was unresponsive and still. Apollo grabbed the phone which swayed back and forth on its cord.

"Hello?" A dial tone greeted him. He tossed the phone aside.

"Maddy, talk to me." He patted the side of her face. "Can you tell me what happened?"

Madeline didn't answer because she couldn't hear him. Her mind was in a place of nothingness.

He grabbed her shoulders and shook her, gently at first, then with increased fervor. Her body flopped back and forth.

"Talk to me!"

When he lifted her to a sitting position, her body slumped to the floor. Apollo checked her arms, legs and head for wounds, and searched the windows and doors for signs of an intruder.

"Hang on, baby. I'm calling for help!"

After calling an ambulance, he crouched alongside Madeline and cradled her head in his arms, all the while coaxing her to open her eyes. He strained to hear the sirens of the ambulance. Only the customary sounds of traffic - accelerating car engines, an occasional horn, or the screech of brakes applied too swiftly, met his ears. Precious seconds ticked by... minutes... *I can't wait any longer.*

He drove off with Madeline in the backseat of his mustang. Just as he sped around the corner, he passed the ambulance.

"What the hell took you so long?" he yelled out the window.

He raced through red lights and stop signs and parked in the one of the hospital's handicapped spaces. Apollo burst into the emergency room with Madeline in his arms. The attending physician examined her and asked a series of basic questions.

"What's your name? How old are you? Do you know where you are?"

Madeline's silence and her empty, glazed-over eyes said it all. The doctor ordered a brain CT and an MRI, and tested several vials of blood. A few hours later, he returned with the results.

"Physically, she's fine," he explained, yet he was checking her arms and legs again. Apollo hung his head in shame. He was likely checking for bruises considering Madeline's last visit to the E.R. "And all of her neurological tests came back normal. Has she experienced any unusual or extraordinary emotional stress lately?"

Not yet knowing of Sadie's death, Apollo suspected that he was the cause.

"Nothing out of the ordinary that I can think of," he answered.

"We're admitting her overnight for observation. If she shows no signs of improvement, a psychological consult would be the next logical step."

Apollo remained by her side until visiting hours were over, and carried on a conversation with Madeline as if all were well. It didn't matter that she couldn't respond. He just wanted to make sure she didn't slip farther into the dark place.

***

By daybreak, Madeline was alert and oriented, and answered all the doctor's questions. She told him she'd been under a lot of stress lately, and even though she spoke without emotion or inflection, the physician appeared satisfied with her quick progress. She was discharged from the hospital with a diagnosis of depression, a referral for outpatient counseling - her visit with a therapist was already scheduled for the following day - and a ten day supply of Valium. Apollo wasn't pleased that they released her so soon but he felt powerless to act on his apprehensions considering he was the one that likely drove her to her current mental state in the first place.

Back home, he tucked her into bed and checked in on her several times an hour. His guilt knew no bounds for he was certain he was the sole cause of Madeline's distress.

Although she had spoken briefly to the doctors at the hospital that morning, she had no words for Apollo. His attempts to engage her in conversation resulted in her staring past him at some distant and far more interesting object in space.

"Maddy, talk to me," he pleaded. "I could tell you I'm sorry every day 'till the day I died and it wouldn't be enough."

Madeline would not even look into his eyes.

"Listen, it's almost lunchtime. Stay here and relax and I'll go to the market for a few things. When I get back, I'll fix your favorite, potato soup. I'll be back in about an hour."

Before he left, he placed a pitcher of water and a glass on the night and watched Madeline take one of the Valiums prescribed to her at the hospital.

"A nap will do you good, and later on when you're ready, we'll talk."

His first stop was the market for a few groceries, followed by the gift shop for a dozen red heart shaped balloons with 'I love you' in calligraphy. He also picked up a card, the heartfelt kind that professed apology and appreciation.

Back home, he fixed Madeline a large bowl of potato soup, placed it on a tray with the card, and set the tray on the nightstand.

"Maddy, your soup's here. Wake up and eat before it gets cold."

Madeline did not stir.

"That medication is really strong. Wake up Maddy," he said a little louder, shaking her from side to side. In spite of the jostling, she remained eerily still. All at once, like a chameleon adapting instantly to its environment, her Mahogany skin grew ashen. As if beckoned, Apollo turned to the bottle of Valium on the nightstand. There was no need to pick up the tiny brown plastic container and inspect its contents. He already knew it was empty. Apollo backed away from the bed.

"Maddy, what did you do?" The pounding in his chest was louder than the sound of his own cracking voice. Apollo wasn't sure if Madeline was alive or dead. He called for an ambulance yet again, except this time he waited motionless by the door.

Waking

Her forefinger was numb, pinched tight by a cold, plastic clamp of some sort. Madeline was too weak and exhausted to open her eyes and see what it was. She wiggled her finger out while pushing it off with her thumb. She drifted to sleep but awakened to the cold numbness again. When she popped her finger out if its grip, the door creaked open. Footsteps entered the room, and the device found its way back to its place.

"Get it off," Madeline mumbled.

"We have to monitor your heart rate and blood pressure, and we can't do that if you keep taking this off."

Madeline opened her eyes. A nurse stood over her rearranging the spread and propping her pillow. She was tall and broad with a masculine face and a soft German accent, her hands both gentle and firm.

"Good to see you're awake."

"What day is it?"

"Wednesday. You came Monday afternoon."

"Am I going home today?" She lifted her head. It pounded at the temples. Her tongue, dry and pasty, stuck to the roof of her mouth.

"Not yet. Must get well first."

"Good." Her head dropped back into the deep, plush pillow and she slept.

For days she hovered between sleep and wakefulness, taking no heed of dawn, dusk, time or place. She heard muffled voices and felt capable hands, but none of it warranted attentiveness. All that mattered was the comfort of rest with no interruption by thoughts or worries or fears.

It was several days later, when her body and mind were fully rested, that she emerged entirely from her slumber. Curious about her surroundings and the circumstances that led her there, Madeline sat up in bed. It was a box of a room with one window, and a television mounted high in the corner. Generic prints of a sun in various stages of setting over the water, hung on three of the four walls.

She swung her legs over the side of the bed, her toes grazing the cold, marble floor. Holding on to the bedrail, she pushed her body to stand, then struggled to steady herself, as vertigo swayed her back and forth. Once the dizziness subsided, Madeline walked to the door. She thought it odd that it was closed and had been so every time she awakened. That explained the lack of noise. Madeline had never been in a hospital so quiet. Sweating from the effort, her gown lay glued to her back and ribs. She welcomed the cool air streaming on her forehead from the vents overhead. She paused at the door to catch her breath, then grasped the door-knob with both hands and pulled. The door was much too heavy. Madeline planted her feet firmly on the ground to gain leverage, grit her teeth and yanked the door as hard as she could.

Is this door locked? What kind of hospital is this? She yanked the knob harder. "I can't be locked in here! Somebody open this door!" *Think, Madeline. There must be a bell or something.* Madeline found the call button on her bed clipped to the side of her blanket. She pushed the lit red button. A nurse stuck her head through the door.

"You rang?"

"What kind of hospital locks patients in their room?"

"All the doors were locked momentarily. It was for your safety. One of the patients threatened to harm someone."

She was about to ask the nurse what made her so sick she had to be admitted to the hospital, when she heard a woman's high pitched shriek, followed by the thud of someone striking a wall. Madeline was riveted to the spot. It was then that she understood precisely where she was. This was no regular hospital room. This was either a room on the psychiatric ward or she'd been admitted to a psychiatric hospital. Either way it was bad.

"If Apollo had anything to do with this I'll kill him!" she went on. "There's no way I'm staying in this place! What am I doing here? Did my husband have me committed?"

"Try to remain calm," the German nurse told her. "I'll get the doctor straight away. He can explain everything."

"Well you better tell him to hurry up! I don't need or want to be here!"

Within seconds, the doctor walked into the room with her chart. He was perfect - far too young and handsome to be a doctor. As a matter of fact, he was the best looking blue-eyed blond haired man she had ever seen. He belonged on the cover of a magazine, or the runways of Paris, not standing in her hospital room in a white coat perusing her health history. He smiled, displaying his perfect teeth.

"I'm Dr. Austin. How are you feeling today, Mrs. Evers?"

"I'm just fine Dr. Austin," Madeline said as she shook his hand, "but I don't understand why I'm here."

He flipped a page over and skimmed its contents.

"What is the last thing you remember?" he asked.

Madeline frowned. She hated when someone answered a question with another question.

"After I heard the news of my mother's death," she paused to absorb the impact of her own words, "my husband took me to the hospital. The emergency room doctor told me I might be depressed and wrote a prescription for Valium. That same day, about noon, I took one of the pills and fell asleep. I guess it must have made me sick or something because the only other thing I remember is waking up here in the middle of the night."

"How many Valium did the doctor prescribe?"

"I was supposed to take two a day for about ten days, so there were about twenty pills in the jar altogether."

"And once again, how many do you recall taking?" He spoke in the condescending tone one used when addressing an errant child.

"I swallowed one Valium with a glass of water."

"Do you recall taking any more that day?"

"No."

"Just one?"

A coolness snaked down her spine. "I told you, just one. I was supposed to take one in the morning and another at bedtime. I had just started the prescription and that was the first one of the day."

"Madeline, there weren't any pills left in that bottle," he said in a direct, yet gentle voice.

"What happened to the others?" Her question was met with silence.

Madeline grasped the bedrails. "But I only remember taking one," she said, her voice dwindling. "Are you sure?"

She didn't expect him to answer. If he weren't sure, she wouldn't be listening to the mad woman shrieking down the hall.

"I would never try to kill myself. No matter how bad things got, I would never try to kill myself."

She knew from the pity in his eyes he didn't believe her, and if Apollo told them about the sword incident, too, she wasn't going home anytime soon.

He clicked his pen and jotted notes on her chart. "We'll talk more about this, Mrs. Evers. You'll undergo one-on-one counseling sessions every day, and..."

"Any idea how long I have to stay here?" she interrupted.

"We can't predict that right now. It all depends on your progress."

"I'm telling you I'm fine."

"I'll see you first thing tomorrow morning. I encourage you to take part in the daily patient activities this afternoon." He tucked her chart under his arm and left the room.

THE GERMAN NURSE ARRIVED EARLY AFTERNOON to show Madeline to the community room. The patients were engaged in the 'daily patient activities' Dr. Austin spoke of. It wasn't the organized activity she'd imagined, but rather free time, a recess of sorts. The patients chose what they wanted to do and socialized with whomever they pleased. They could choose to watch television, play cards or board games, or just hang out and talk. She would have preferred to remain alone in her room, but the more opportunities she had to prove she was not a danger to herself, the sooner she would be released.

The room was brightly lit with small round tables clustered in the center. Bordering them on one side were two L -shaped sectionals. White bookshelves against the wall overflowed with magazines, newspapers, books and board games.

Madeline spotted a pile of home decorating magazines and headed in that direction. She grabbed a handful and turned to find an empty spot on the sofa when a tall, stunning dark-haired woman with perfect cheekbones and a frail frame approached her.

"You must be new," she said. "I'm Margo." She extended her hand.

"I'm Madeline."

Margo stood out amidst the other patients. She wore the required pale blue hospital gown, except that hers was atop her fabulous designer clothing - chocolate wool gabardine pants, a crème cashmere sweater, and off-white suede pumps. A rhinestone sat atop each freshly manicured nail and her jet black hair fell in long cascading curls to the middle of her back. Margo wore a matte finish foundation with coordinating rouge and shadow artfully applied to her lids. Liner accentuated her bronze lips.

"Come, my dear. Have a seat." She followed Margo to the closest sectional.

Margo sat close to Madeline - a little too close for her liking - and leaned in.

"You want to know, don't you?" she asked.

Madeline looked around. She had no idea what the woman was talking about.

"It's the question everyone's dying to know when they come here."

"Ah, what question is that?"

"How did I end up here! That is the unspoken question that's burning through everyone's minds." She clapped as if she'd solved a riddle.

It was *not* the uppermost question on Madeline's mind but she was curious.

"Besides," Margo went on, "you make friends faster here when you confess your nuttiness up front instead of existing as if you landed here by some strange twist of fate."

Unsolicited, and before Madeline could get in a word edge-wise, Margo told the story of how she came to the hospital.

"My husband and I owned a beautiful split level home in Northern Jersey. A professional designer decorated the interior and a renowned landscape architect designed and maintained the grounds. The home was featured in several home decorating magazines and two years earlier won the 'Design of the Year' award. I cleaned my showcase home every day and employed a full-time housekeeper to help me with all the scrubbing and scouring. But in spite of our combined efforts, the house was never quite clean enough. I soon fired the housekeeper and hired a professional cleaning service, but I still managed to find dust or dirt in some hidden crack or crevice, or a streak in the glass coffee table. I prayed for the day when I woke up to the perfect home, but the light of each morning revealed new blemishes." She spoke with great drama, as if she'd recited her story a thousand times. "Nights I wrote lists of chores for the following day. It wasn't unusual for me to get up at three in the morning to get a head start on my cleaning. I was so obsessed with having the perfect home, I'd forget to eat and drink. I lost twenty-five pounds and suffered the early effects of dehydration."

"On New Years' Day, I sent my husband to the store for more cleanser and disinfectant. As soon as he backed his car out of the driveway, I lugged a container of gasoline from the garage, and sprinkled its contents over the furniture, down the drapes and onto the floors. Just before I was overcome by fumes, I lit a match and tossed it onto the sofa. Beautiful tongues of orange-red flames demolished everything. From the front lawn, I watched the windows burst and the siding melt. The chimney crumbled and caved into a disintegrating mass of brick, and mortar. I was finally liberated. I was weightless and finally at peace." She paused for some time while looking up toward the ceiling, a half smile formed on her lips then vanished as she went on with her story. "I never heard the fire truck coming, but all at once a fireman was standing beside me. 'What happened ma'am?' he asked me. I told him I decided to burn the dirty house to the ground and was looking forward to a fresh new start."

"He said 'you set fire to your own house?' It was a shock, you know, and I've been here ever since. I miss being in my own home, but it's a relief not having to worry about all the upkeep. This place is a holiday for me," she said, flipping her luscious hair out of her face.

Madeline was at a loss as to what to say, but it didn't matter. Margo kept right on chatting.

"Have you met Darren?" Margo asked, pointing to the chair opposite Madeline's. "He's our baby."

Madeline looked Darren over.

"You're just a kid. What are you? Thirteen? Twelve?" Madeline asked.

"Almost eighteen," Darren said with a smile, a dimple on each cheek.

"Someone your age should be picking a prom date and getting a driver's license. Why are you here?"

Darren blinked and his eyes grew blank, as if he were swept into a daydream.

"I'll fill you in." Margo said pointing both index fingers at herself.

"Darren's heard voices since he was a little boy. No one believed him until the day the voices told him to push his two-year old brother out of a window. Darren listened to the voices and the kid fell twelve stories."

Darren finally focused back on the two. "After Jacob's funeral, my parents finally understood me," he said with great reverence and awe, but not a shred of remorse. Darren sat tall with his shoulders back and his chest puffed out, as if he'd finally been validated.

"Next to Darren," Margo went on, "is Aretha. Aretha, this is Madeline."

The two greeted each other with a nod.

"Aretha goes home this week. Her story is fascinating, too. She…"

"I can speak for myself," Aretha interrupted with much attitude. "I tried to conceive for over fifteen years and found out I was pregnant on my forty-second birthday. A complication during the delivery resulted in a hysterectomy right after I had my baby boy, but it didn't matter, I finally had the baby I dreamed of." She looked off in the distance, as if seeing her past laid out before her.

"My mother had nearly given up on the prospect of a grandchild and was so happy about the baby, you'd have thought he was hers. She called me every day for an update. 'Did he smile yet? Does he look at you when you talk? How's his appetite?' She wanted to know every detail." Aretha shifted in her chair, then her head fell to one side, nearly resting on her shoulder.

"My boy didn't cry for his feeding." Her voice grew heavy and resonated with a slight tremor. "I found him dead in his crib, and I shut down. When my mother came, I was in my rocking chair singing to my boy. He'd already been gone for a week. I fought when they tried to take him away. They carried me off with my arms and legs bound."

Aretha spoke as if it had all taken place the day before, so fresh and immediate was her grief, and although they'd all heard the story of her loss countless times before, a hush fell over the room when she spoke.

Margo's head was down for a few moments, then it popped up. "What about you?" she asked. "Tell us!"

After hearing their stories, her own was miniscule, unwarranted even. She wanted to say something profound and inspiring, but Madeline struggled to find the right words. Perhaps I'm sorry for your... madness? What she found most frightening was that at one time, they all lived normal lives. What brought them to the precipice? Madeline wanted to know more about Margo, Darren and Aretha, but she also feared ending up like them. In the end, fear won out over her curiosity.

"If you'll excuse me for a moment," she told them with her best smile, and retreated to her room.

I have to get out of here.

MADELINE IMAGINED HER ONE-ON-ONE SESSION with Dr. Austin in a cozy masculine office centered by a wide mahogany desk and matching shelves filled with leather bound books, the room lit by a single Tiffany lamp with a pull chain dangling beneath the shade. She reclined on a lounge chair, set to the lowest point, so that she lay nearly flat while pouring out her secrets to the handsome Dr. Austin, her feet propped on a footstool, shoes resting on the ornate Persian rug.

To her dismay, her imagination could not have been farther away from reality. The sessions were held in an eight by eight room, smelling mildly of bleach, with a single chair on each side of a square table. Abstract photos on two opposite walls were the room's only adornments, an industrial rug in grays and blues underfoot. After obligatory small talk and a few ice-breaker questions, Dr. Austin dived right into the middle of Madeline's mess.

"Tell me about your relationship with your husband," he began.

Madeline talked about their whirlwind courtship and how she didn't believe in love at first sight until she met Apollo. She left out the part about Sadie's involvement with Apollo. It wasn't relevant. She'd tell him about that part of her life only if he probed.

Dr. Austin allowed her to talk at length without interruption. After going on for what seemed like hours, Madeline ran out of things to say. They sat in silence while Dr. Austin took notes on a yellow tablet.

"Now tell me about your mother."

"My mother died. She died the moment I needed her the most."

"Why did you need her in that moment?"

"I had just stumbled onto Apollo's affair, but not in the traditional sense when you find lipstick on the collar, or a receipt from a hotel or an unfamiliar phone number on a slip of paper in a jacket pocket. I walked into my best friend's house and heard them having sex. He told her what he used to tell me. I was hurting – I am hurting - and I wanted my mother."

"The need for your mother when something goes wrong is a child's response."

"But it's how I felt nonetheless."

"Why do you think you wanted your mother, as opposed to calling a friend or maybe talking to your father?"

"I needed her to do what mothers are supposed to do. Console, reassure, hold my hand, tell me I'll be alright, tell me I didn't need him anyway, tell me I still meant something to somebody. I wanted Sadie to tell me all those things you already know but need to be reminded of."

"Why did you think she would be there for you as an adult? Was she there for you when you were a child?"

Madeline pondered her little girl self.

"I was strong and brave on the outside, but on the inside there was nothing but shame. I craved validation so hard. I wanted her to love me entirely, but she never did. Up until the day she died, I hoped there was still a chance."

She understood Dr. Austin's next words before he finished speaking them.

"Madeline, Sadie was dead to you a long time ago. What made you think she'd suddenly assume the role of a mother after the incident with Apollo?"

"What did I have to lose? I wanted to give it a chance. As long as she was alive there was the possibility. Now that she's gone, I'll never have that chance."

"Think beyond the fact that Sadie's gone. Think about how you feel now and how you want those feelings to change, and tell me what is it you want most out of all of this?"

"As a little girl, every single day, I woke up to my mother's scorn. I thought being the best daughter I could be might change her, but no matter how hard I tried, it was her scorn that defined me. After Apollo and I were married, I was happy for a time but now I wake up to his betrayal. Just once I'd like that warm protected feeling of waking up to home. I want to wake up to loving and nurturing and safety and… warmth."

"Does Apollo provide nurturing and safety?"

"How can I feel safe when there's no trust? I haven't even trusted Apollo enough to tell him one of my most coveted secrets. Why? Because he isn't worthy of knowing. He's lost all rights to my secrets."

"What would that secret be?"

"I want to have a baby, a baby girl." Madeline lowered her voice, as if someone forbidden might be listening. "I think about it all the time. I even dream about it. And when I wake up and realize it's not real, I'm heartbroken. But there's no trust, so my secret remains buried. If you can't share your most treasured desires with the one you love, then where do you start? How could I possibly get to that feeling of 'waking up to home' with Apollo when we don't even have a basic foundation of trust and sharing?"

"You don't just stumble upon this 'waking up to home' you speak of. It's a decision that has to be conscious, deliberate. You make it happen. You create the circumstance."

"How?"

"If the right variables are not present in your life, you must remove them and seek out all that which brings you closer to what you want."

"Seek out all that which brings you closer to what you want," Madeline mimicked. "Exactly how am I supposed to do that?"

Dr. Austin suppressed a chuckle at her impersonation attempt.

"You create the circumstance of this 'waking up to home'. You don't wait for the outside world to bestow it upon you. You act on it."

"Great," Madeline mumbled. "I'll never get out of here because I have no clue as to what I'm supposed to do."

"When you're ready, you'll know how to create it. You're farther ahead than you think." Dr. Austin stood and shook her hand.

"See you at the next session."

"Since I'll be here in this hospital for the rest of my life trying to figure out whatever it is you just told me, when can I have visitors?"

"You have two downstairs in the waiting area."

"Who is it?" She brightened.

"Check at the nurse's station on the way back to your room."

She'd barely reached the station when the German nurse stood, waving a small slip of paper. "You have two visitors, can I let them up?" She was as excited as Madeline.

"Do you know who it is?"

"Stovall and Evers," she read from the paper.

"One at a time please, Stovall first," she said while heading back to her room.

Tucker rushed in. He sat beside her and folded her into his arms. In those first few minutes, there were no words, just clinging in silence.

"Daddy, I'm so sorry to worry you."

The whites of his eyes were crimson, a salt and pepper beard shadowed his face.

"You told me to come to you if I needed help and I didn't."

"No, Maddy, I am the one who should be sorry."

"You did all you could. You protected me from my mother and you warned me about Apollo. What more could you do?"

"There's something I should have told you a long time ago. If I'd had this conversation with you sooner, you might have understood Sadie a little better and you might not be here in this predicament."

Tucker slid backward a little so he faced her fully, then he took a deep breath and paused as he contemplated how best to deliver the news.

"When Sadie was pregnant, you weren't our only baby." He took another deep breath. "She was carrying twins."

Madeline's mouth dropped open.

"You had a brother who we named Marcus."

"Marcus was my brother? I remember hearing that name. You and mommy argued about him. I wondered who he was and why the mention of his name made her so angry. What happened to him?"

"You were a strong, robust baby. Marcus wasn't like you. He was fragile and weak. He lived for just a few moments after birth and died right in your mother's arms. It was a difficult time for Sadie. She never got over losing him, and because Marcus didn't make it, she somehow had a hard time showing you that she loved you."

Madeline's chest rose and fell fast, like she just ran a race. "She blamed me for it, didn't she? She blamed be because he died!"

"She never outright admitted it but I believe it to be the truth."

"But I was just a baby. How could she think it was my fault?"

"Her mind was all screwed up, Maddy. I tried reasoning with your mother, but I could never get through to her."

"All these years! It wasn't me after all. It wasn't me, daddy!" Her face brightened, and she nearly smiled.

"What wasn't you?"

"I thought I was the one who made her so unhappy."

"It wasn't you. It wasn't me. It wasn't my relationship with you, as much as she tried to convince me it was. It was Sadie's way of thinking." He went on. "I never thought knowing about Marcus would help you until that night you called and talked about wanting to connect with Sadie. I felt so helpless because I knew she couldn't give you what you needed. Once you ended up here in this hospital after taking all those pills, I felt responsible. I'm so sorry I didn't tell you sooner, and Madeline," he moved in closer, "tell me you'll never try to hurt yourself again."

"I wasn't trying to hurt myself. It was an accident. I had some kind of breakdown, a lapse. I don't know how to explain it but I assure you it wasn't deliberate."

"Are you comfortable here?"

"I'd rather be home, of course, but it's okay."

Tucker stood. "Good… now, let's try this again. If you need someone to talk to, promise you'll come to me."

"This time I promise, but is there anything else about Sadie I should know?"

"What you now know is all that matters." He planted a kiss on her forehead.

"Love you, daddy."

"Apollo's in the waiting room. Don't let him upset you, Maddy. If you feel overwhelmed, ring for the nurse to show him out."

"Tell him to give me about fifteen minutes. I want to rest a bit."

To be angry at a dead person was pointless, but Madeline was angry anyway. So many wasted years, feeling guilty for no reason at all. So many years of shouldering the blame for Sadie's unhappiness, years of not fighting for herself because she thought she was somehow deserving of Sadie's vile treatment. Madeline's mind raced through all the slights, reproach and self-loathing she'd endured.

"I am not to blame for Sadie's unhappiness," she spoke aloud to the empty room. "My marriage to Apollo did not cause her unhappiness. Sadie was already unhappy and I am not to blame."

Madeline closed her eyes and exhaled slowly. Every muscle in her tense body unraveled, her mind, her thoughts stopped their racing. She released the guilt and everything else that bound her. Her life stretched ahead, seemingly just beginning, her slate of sins wiped clean.

It was then that Apollo walked into the room, tentative at first, as if expecting her to pounce.

Here comes my only remaining thorn.

He wore a long sleeved striped polo shirt, wrinkled and stained at the wrists. His jeans, normally ironed and crisp, held no creases, a small Afro framed his face.

"How are you feeling?" Apollo asked. He moved around the room cautiously, as if walking too hard might startle her.

"Better, thank you."

"Maddy, you scared the heck out of me. I wasn't sure if you were alive or…" he couldn't bring himself to speak the next word.

"Madeline, I loved you from the moment I set eyes on you. I don't set out to deliberately hurt you, and I'm not making up excuses. It's just that I don't always stop to think before I act. Rest assured I will make this all up to you. Please forgive me, for everything."

Madeline stared at Apollo, as if she couldn't even comprehend the meaning of forgiveness.

He paused then blurted out quickly, "I assume Tucker told you about Sadie's death?"

"I'm dealing with it," she said, although she thought it ludicrous that after all this time he still had no idea that it was the news of Sadie's death that caused her collapse.

"Does the counseling help?"

"I only had one session, but I've learned from it."

"The thing with the pills… were you trying to…" He shifted his weight from one foot to the other.

"No, Apollo, I was not trying to kill myself. I have no memory of taking all those pills."

"When are you coming home?"

Madeline shrugged her shoulders. "I'd like to know the answer to that question too. I'm told it depends on my progress."

Apollo looked down at his scuffed Oxfords, seemingly at a loss as to what else to say, and Madeline wasn't making any effort to keep the conversation going.

"You get some rest. I'll be back to visit tomorrow, and Madeline?"

She looked up at Apollo.

"I'll make this right."

She realized after he was gone, that she had no desire to see him, and felt no remorse at his departure.

DOCTOR AUSTIN DISCHARGED MADELINE FROM care, with a prescription for an antidepressant. Madeline couldn't remember the name - it started with a "P". He also arranged for outpatient psychiatric counseling and gave her a twenty-four hour phone number she could call in the event of a crisis. She agreed to the counseling during her last session but only to expedite her release. She had no intention at all of attending any follow-up treatment. After enduring the nearly two weeks of daily counseling with Dr. Austin, she'd had her fill of it. As far as Madeline was concerned, she shouldn't have been admitted to the hospital in the first place. Margo, Darren and Aretha – their stays were warranted. Madeline's was the result of an unfortunate turn of events. And as for the antidepressant, that prescription would never be filled.

Madeline felt the need to say goodbye or at the very least, good luck to the other residents, but reconsidered. Maybe it was best to just leave it alone. It wasn't like she was going to keep in touch. She gathered her few belongings and left unnoticed.

The wind whipped up the leaves on that blustery October day, pitching them in loops through the air. Frost on the shrubbery glimmered in the sun like specks of diamonds. Madeline pulled her sweater tight around her, the sudden frigid air left her teeth chattering.

For the last time, she looked up at the hospital from which she'd just been set free. It resembled a retirement home, its façade revealing nothing of its troubled patients or their heartbreaking stories, their secrets guarded behind the brick and mortar walls.

"Thank God for getting me out of there," she said aloud, then cringed. "I better not let anyone see me out here talking to myself, or they might just drag me back in."

She'd declined Apollo's offer to drive her home and had already arranged a ride with Tucker. Apollo told her it was ridiculous to bother Tucker when he, himself, had a well running car at home, but he was in no position to dissent. He agreed to Madeline's request, absurd as it was, and stood on his front porch shaking his head in exasperation, when Tucker pulled up in front of the house with Madeline in the passenger seat.

She walked past Apollo and stood in the center of the living room with her arms folded over her chest.

"Before you settle in, how about I take you to lunch?" Apollo asked. He shuffled back and forth from one foot to the other, his shoulders bunched nearly up to his ears.

"I'm not up for lunch today, but I have something to say and it's time to clear the air. I had a lot of time to think while sitting in that hospital room all this time, and I've come to the conclusion that I will no longer put up with how you treat me. In the space of our brief marriage, you have raised your hand at me, verbally abused me, and if that weren't enough, you had sex with my friend and neighbor and didn't even have enough decency to be discreet about it. I didn't deserve any of it."

"You're not the first person I've allowed to treat me poorly. My mother treated me poorly, too. It took some time, but I understand now that I didn't deserve it from her either. And that damn Coletta, she was my friend one day and the next day a total stranger screwing the husband I thought I knew. I didn't deserve it. But you," she pointed at Apollo, "you have disappointed me the most because you took a vow to love and honor me. You are all I have but if you can't treat me the way I deserve to be treated, love me the way I need to be loved, then we're through. I can be alone if I have to. I've played the dutiful wife and you give me crap in return. I will no longer allow you or anyone else to run over me. It stops today."

Apollo stood before her like a berated puppy with his head down and his tail between his legs. He nodded his agreement and occasionally mumbled, 'I'm sorry' or 'you're right', but that was the extent of his exchange.

"If you hurt me again, our marriage, as you know it, will be over."

She turned her back to Apollo. He shuffled out of the room, his head still bowed.

APOLLO WATCHED MADELINE WHILE SHE SLEPT. It was during this time, when darkness enveloped the earth, and she peacefully slept, her face a picture of simplicity and naivete that he loved her most. When she was awake, contempt and disgust shot from her eyes like daggers. She armed herself for disappointment, tense and ready to snap at any slight.

He missed the way she looked up to him, adored him. This woman-child who once admired him, now berated him, her innocence to the ways of men gone. And it was all because of him, he who vowed to honor and protect her.

I have to change my ways. I am all she has. I have to make this work. There was no use telling her he was going to change, how much he loved her, how sorry he was and how he never intended to hurt her. There was no use proclaiming his loyalty, his earnestness from this day forward. His words no longer held any power. His actions were his sole redeemer.

He had little time, however, to put his intentions into practice. Within just a few weeks he returned to sea.

After six months at sea, Apollo returned home to the same Madeline he'd left, a bitter, resentful and hardened woman. He didn't expect her to run and jump into his arms, but couldn't she at least summon a hint of appreciation for his safe return? After all, he was still her husband.

She didn't even bother to open the gifts he hauled from halfway around the world. She said she'd open them when she had some time, after which she sat at the dining room table looking over design school brochures. How much effort could it possibly take to pick a school, a design school nonetheless? He'd be a fool to believe their lives would immediately return to normal after he raised his hand to her. Certainly not after the way she found out about Coletta, but how much longer was she going to make him pay?

If Madeline weren't going to celebrate his return, he'd celebrate it by himself. He left the house and drove around until he came across one of his old haunts, The Star Mist. It was the last place in town a married man should frequent alone, but Apollo was hungry for good company, and The Star Mist had a way of making anyone feel at home.

He didn't recall the Star Mist looking so vulgar when he frequented it years earlier. It was dated back then, but now it was downright decrepit. White puffs of stuffing oozed from the torn overstuffed leather seats of the booths, dark curtains blanketed the windows which were sorely in need of replacement, and the deep crack that crept down the center of the ceiling remained, except it was now longer and wider, the room nearly split in two.

The crowd was thin, just the way he liked it, the dance floor sparsely occupied. He sat on a stool at the bar and ordered a shot of Jack Daniels and a beer. He pondered his marriage for a time but found it hard to order his thoughts after the third round. His only measurement of the passing of time were the empty beer mugs and shot glasses lined in front of him. Hunched over his glass, he debated over whether or not to order yet another round when the room pulsated and swerved to the left. Apollo grasped the counter edge to steady himself.

"You okay there, man?" the bartender asked.

"I better hold off on that next drink," he chuckled. "Nothing but ice water for me."

The first few notes of Marvin Gaye's *What's Going On* filtered through the sound system. Apollo snapped his fingers and pat his foot to the beat, when a beautiful, dark- eyed woman caught his eye. Her angelic face wore a practiced modesty. Her clothing, in stark contrast, betrayed her blatant sexuality. She wore a knit beige dress that plunged at the neckline and clung to her round hips and thighs. Her bare legs were crossed, accentuating full, round calves and the straps of her sandals wrapped around her delicate ankles. Her hair was course and wild. She looked his way, batted her long thick lashes, and turned away. When she glanced back with a sultry half smile, Apollo knew the game had begun. Blood coursed alive in his veins, his pulse quickened, and his palms grew wet. He sat up in his chair to get a closer look, then motioned for her to come forward. She did so, swaying her hips to the rhythm of seduction. Apollo stood when she arrived by his side and fumbled for something clever to say. The seductress took the lead and introduced herself.

"My name is Sybil. Sybil Taylor." She flashed a coy smile and sat on the bar stool to his left.

Apollo," he said with a slight bow of his head.

"I've never seen you here before."

"It's been awhile since I've hung out in this area of town."

"Do you live here in Nicetown?" she asked.

"Not too far." Apollo was careful not to reveal too much.

The bartender walked over.

"What are you drinking?" she asked, glancing at the row of empty glasses in front of Apollo.

"Jack."

"I'll take that," she told the bartender.

She took the glass before he set it on the counter and finished it off.

"Not many women can keep up with me and Jack," Apollo joked.

"I can definitely hold my own." She flashed her sexy smile again and ordered another.

The lights dimmed. A stream of steamy love songs thickened the atmosphere.

"Dance with me?" Apollo asked. He was prepared for a 'no', most women played hard to get, but the seductress surprised him by taking his hand and leading him to the dance floor. She danced slowly with her eyes closed, fully aware of the effect she had on him. He felt the soft curves of her warm body pressed into his and he knew there was no backing out now. The game was in full swing.

"I should leave," he said to himself but Jack Daniels told him he'd be a fool to walk out on the game. As Apollo caressed her hips, she swayed into the bend of his hands. They danced close and hot with limbs touching until long after midnight staring into each other's eyes like longtime lovers.

"Let's get out of here," she whispered, her lips grazing his ear.

"I'll drive you home."

"I live close by. We'll walk."

By hand, she led him to her place and beckoned him in. The soothing scent of lilacs filled the air, slow jazz piped low. Aside from two candles flickering shadows on the ceiling, the room was dark.

"Were you already expecting someone or was I just seduced?"

Sybil moved her body side to side, then stepped closer until they were inches apart. He closed his eyes and lost himself in the music, her hot curves arching into his ready body. The pace of the game quickened but Apollo was a most willing pawn. She acquiesced when he pulled her into his arms.

He lowered her to the sofa and stripped off her knit dress. Her body responded to his. In a wild, fast frenzy, she bucked up against him until Apollo slowed her to a steady pace. *At last, desire.*

Madeline once desired him but he'd ruined it. She didn't deny him sex but their lovemaking had become mechanical, obligatory. 'There is no trust', she kept telling him. 'I don't feel safe'. But lying beneath him, in that moment, was a woman who made love to him out of neither obligation nor necessity.

Hours later, Sybil kissed him awake. His head pounded just above his eyes, his tongue was thick, his mouth cottony.

"Way too much to drink," he murmured. "Sybil, I have to go."

Naked, she led him to the door and blew him a kiss. He pulled her close, enjoying the contours of her body molding into his one last time.

"I'll see you again?" he whispered. Although he was doubtful he could pull it off.

"I'm sure you will," she told him.

Apollo raced home and crept in the back door just as the sun crested the horizon. He tiptoed upstairs for a shower to rid himself of the remains of his rendezvous, and after an aspirin and a cup of coffee, crashed on the sofa. His thoughts turned to Sybil. He rehearsed every detail of their encounter - her skin, her body, the alluring way she talked - until Madeline stirred.

It was a one night fling and it will not happen again. Madeline can never find out.

But Apollo returned to the Star Mist again and again waiting for the woman who seduced him, hoping for an encore. He sat directly across from the entrance so he'd see everyone entering and exiting. Every time the door opened, Apollo jerked to attention, craning his neck for a sight of the temptress. After weeks of failing to see Sybil again, he gave up. He ordered a shot of Jack Daniels, gave a toast to old times at the Star Mist, and chalked it up to his most memorable one night stand.

"Let's stop in the Star Mist this time," Madeline suggested.

"Ah... there are nicer places if you want to travel a bit farther. What about Aminah's, that sweet little café where I won your heart?"

"It's my choice tonight, remember? The Star Mist it is! The place is hard on the eyes but they have the best music in the city."

Date night Friday was Madeline's idea. It was her attempt at repairing their troubled marriage. They took turns choosing the evening's events. Tonight was Madeline's turn. Apollo racked his brain for an excuse not to go in but could think of nothing convincing enough. He parked the car and followed Madeline inside.

"I'll find a spot at the bar," she said as she slipped out of her jacket, "while you hang up our coats."

Apollo was just about to join Madeline when he noticed that she and all of the other patrons at the bar were riveted to the T.V. For a few seconds, each was frozen, oblivious to their surroundings, eyes focused solely on the screen. It was a news report about a man who fired dozens of shots on the White House. *Who would want to kill Bill Clinton? Everybody loved the guy.*

Out of the corner of his eye, Apollo saw a fluttering. He turned to see a hand waving back and forth. It was Sybil. Seated at a booth, she motioned for him to come over.

Damn! He shook his head 'no' and pointed in Madeline's direction. Sybil rolled her eyes in fake disgust then rewarded him with a coy smile. His pulse soared.

"Something wrong?" Madeline asked when he joined her.

"Uh… stomach's bothering me."

"Was it something you ate?"

"I hope it's not that bug going around. How about we take a rain check on drinks today and get out of here."

"Aw, we just got here. I was really looking forward to this."

With great drama, Apollo rubbed his stomach and grunted.

"Ok," Madeline pat his hand, "let's go."

Outside, Apollo searched his pockets for his car keys.

"Did you pick them up?" he asked.

"You probably left them on the bar. I'll get them."

"Oh no," Apollo yelled, then lowered his voice. "You stay here. I'll go back in and look for them."

After Apollo scooped up the keys he strategically left on the counter, he found Sybil. Her elbows rested on the table, her chin nestled in her hands. A massive plate of food sat before her.

She won't keep those lovely curves for long with an appetite like that.

"I knew you'd come back for me," she teased.

"It's been five, maybe six months. Where've you been? I came here looking for you a few times."

"Well now I'm found! You should give me your number or an address so we can keep in touch."

"That was my wife, Sybil. I can't just give you my number."

"I don't want to marry you, Apollo. I just want to stay connected."

He loved the way she said his name, with a perfect roll of her tongue.

"How about I take *your* number?" he suggested. He jotted it down on a napkin.

"Call me as soon as you can," she said pointedly, "I don't want any more time to go by without seeing you... alone... perhaps at my place again?"

On the way home, Apollo stopped for an antacid. He made sure to take a tablespoon while Madeline was watching and announced he was retiring early because of his horribly upset stomach.

Madeline left him to nurse whatever ailed him, and retreated to the dining room to pour over college brochures and course descriptions for interior design programs. In fact, she had already registered for the Philadelphia Design School's open house the following day.

Upstairs, Apollo called Sybil from the bedroom phone with the door closed. He whispered low with his hand cupped over the receiver.

"What took you so long to call?" she joked.

"Can we meet at your place tomorrow?" The timing was perfect. Madeline would be gone all afternoon.

"Come over around six. I'll cook you up a nice dinner and then afterward, we'll just see what happens."

I can't risk Madeline finding out about this. This visit with Sybil will be my last. After tomorrow, I'll bid her farewell forever.

APOLLO SPRUNG INTO ACTION THE MOMENT Madeline left for the open house. He grabbed a bottle of wine from his own private stash, and chose a bouquet of petite red roses from a street vendor. Although he'd been there before, the street Sybil lived on wasn't familiar at all. Neither was the old high rise building in dire need of a host of repairs. He recalled none of it from the night they met. After she buzzed him into the main entrance, Apollo knocked on the apartment door. He heard Sybil walking toward the door. It was more like sliding. It reminded him of his grandmother padding around the kitchen in her slippers when he was a child.

Sybil opened the door and stared Apollo steadily in the eye. There was no smile to greet him, no warm words, just a probing stare. Stunned by the chilly reception, Apollo stood back and looked at her from head to toe. He gasped. Her belly was barely contained in a T-shirt several sizes too small. His mouth dropped open and the bouquet of flowers tumbled to the dingy carpet.

"Your mouth is open," she snapped as she grabbed the bottle of wine and turned on her heel. Apollo followed her into the apartment.

"I'll get right to the point. I'm nearly six months pregnant and yes, it's your child."

The room spun, only this time he was fully sober. Apollo reached for the arm of the sofa like a blind man, and eased himself down onto the chair. It was the very sofa he made love to her on the evening they met. He didn't recall the cushions being worn flat. Pillar candles perched on milk crates, sat at opposite ends of the room, and a can of lilac air freshener sat atop the television set. A little girl watched cartoons cross-legged on the floor, the volume turned too high.

"I cannot afford to feed another child by myself," Sybil went on, "and I'm not getting rid of it so I suggest you start explaining how you're gonna support your baby."

A roach crawling on the wall behind her grabbed Apollo's attention. She turned around to see what distracted him, snatched a slipper from her foot and smashed the roach dead on the wall. Its liquid innards slid down the faded gray paint.

Is this the same seductress I desired all these months?

Circles under her eyes were deep, dark ridges, and acne scars speckled her cheeks. She wore a baseball cap facing backwards, unkempt hair sticking out of the sides. Her belly hung over a pair of unzipped, cutoff denim shorts. There was no hint of the exotic beauty he remembered. Sybil was just another ordinary, brown woman, raving about how she could not afford to feed another child. Apollo's throat tightened, a fit of coughing racked his frame.

"May I have a glass of water?"

Sybil went into the kitchen as if it were a great inconvenience and emerged with a greasy glass of water. Apollo put the glass aside.

"Sybil, I'm a married man."

"That's not my problem. You figure out how you're gonna chip in to provide for this baby or I'll sue your ass for child support."

"We were only together once. How do I know the baby's mine?"

"If you put me through the humiliation of a paternity test, your wife gets the results delivered in person."

Apollo had nothing more to say. He drove the long way home and sat in his car a long time before going inside.

How the hell am I going to tell Madeline this?

Madeline switched on the bedside lamp.

"Wake up, Apollo."

Cringing, Apollo cupped his hands over his burning eyes.

"Ok baby. Just don't talk so loud, and can you turn off the light?"

"If you weren't courting a hangover, yet again, the light and my voice wouldn't be so painful. It's the same old light and I am not raising my voice."

"It's the middle of the night."

"It can't wait until morning. I can't rest until I get this off of my chest."

Apollo yawned and rubbed his eyes.

"You've been sneaking out of here at night and creeping home in the wee hours of the morning for weeks now. I never let on that I know but I am fully aware of what's going on."

Apollo sat up. *Did she know? Did she know about Sybil and the baby?* He no longer saw Sybil in the biblical sense but he did go out nights to see the baby.

"I think I understand why you have to leave some nights," she sighed, "you do it to get away from me."

Apollo didn't realize he was holding his breath until he exhaled.

"You hurt me more than I can ever explain, and for a long time I treated you terribly because of it. I probably shouldn't, but I believe you when you say you won't hurt me again. I want to trust again and I've decided to allow myself that chance. I have you, a beautiful home, I'm going back to school and will one day have a job doing what I love. We have our health and money in the bank. For all that, I should be enjoying life and giving thanks. I'm sorry, Apollo. I'm sorry we stopped talking, touching and loving, all because I couldn't forgive and move on."

"No need to ask for forgiveness." Apollo caressed her face. "We all have our sins."

"Let's start all over again. No more lies and no more secrets, starting with me." She put a hand on his forearm. It was the first time she'd deliberately touched him in months. "I've kept a secret. For a long time I couldn't share it with you because I didn't trust you. I'm ready now, to speak it aloud." There was a long pause.

"Tell me," Apollo encouraged, leaning forward.

"Apollo, I want to have a baby. Not now, of course. We have some things to work out, but maybe we can consider it once I finish school."

"You enrolled?"

"I start in just a few weeks." She sat up a little taller.

"You went after what you wanted. Good for you, Maddy."

Apollo's mind raced through the past four years - their court-ship, the wedding, Madeline's hospitalization, his vow to love her anew, his willful acquiescence to Sybil's seduction, Sybil's banal proclamation of her pregnancy, and finally Madeline's plea for a new beginning. Madeline had made a deliberate decision to be content in spite of all he'd put her through. It pained him that her serenity was so transient. She deserved so much more.

"What about you?" she asked, "do you have any secrets?"

"I'm an open book," he lied.

SAME DAY SALON APPOINTMENTS USUALLY MEANT your stylist barely squeezed you into her already overbooked schedule, so you'd likely sit in the waiting area idle for an hour or so before even getting to the shampoo bowl, but Madeline's name was called within seconds of her arrival.

She wanted something special to commemorate her new beginning with Apollo. An outfit was nice but he barely noticed a new blouse or slacks. She decided on a new haircut, something bold and original, a stark departure from her current look, a haircut that signified daring, and chance.

"Cut it off low like a boy's so I can just get up in the morning, shampoo, and accentuate the curls with a little gel," she told Nikki, her stylist. Nikki's own sleek haircut feathered lightly around her face and tapered at the nape.

"It's taken me forever to get your hair to grow past your shoulders. Why would you want to cut it all off now?" Nikki complained while popping gum.

"You can't be the only one around here with a fierce cut. Make me as sharp as you," she joked.

With each clip of the scissors, long thick locks of hair fell to the floor. It was alarming to see her hair underfoot, but with Nikki's skill with the scissors, it would be worth it in the end.

She spun the chair around so Madeline faced the mirror. "I'm done, take a look."

The back and sides of her hair were trimmed close and the top spiked in a windblown kind of way. She liked the way her cheekbones stood out now that all the thick hair was gone, but she didn't like the fact that her face had become so plump. If only she could lose a few pounds. She'd been in a cycle of losing and gaining. At last tally, she'd gained over twenty-five pounds. She called them 'Apollo pounds' because the scale inched higher with each stressful episode he dragged her through. *The next few weeks are about relaxation, diet and exercise.*

"You've worked your magic once again," Madeline exclaimed as she slipped Nikki a generous tip.

From the display stand near the cash register, Madeline selected a pair of silver hoops to compliment her new hairdo, and strutted out of the salon with a swagger worthy of the new look.

The haircut wasn't all that Madeline had in mind that day. A new beginning certainly warranted a celebratory meal, too. She drove to the fish market to pick up a few pounds of Whiting. Apollo loved it battered with corn meal and deep fried and would eat it for breakfast lunch and dinner if she let him. The produce stand was two blocks over so she grabbed a few bunches of fresh broccoli, then made a third stop at the deli for cole slaw. Her last stop was the music store. She bought Smokey Robinson's *Greatest Hits* on cassette. *Ooh Baby Baby* was Apollo's favorite oldie. He hummed it every morning off key in the shower. It was a love song - the romantic kind. She imagined making love to Apollo while Smokey sang his soulful lyrics in the background.

Back home, she heated the oil and boiled water to steam the vegetables. It was a balmy yet breezy late summer afternoon. The windows were open and the curtains blew into the room, rising midway with the breeze then drifting down to the sill. Madeline slipped a smooth jazz cassette into the boom box and swayed to the beat of the music while the fish fried.

As she put the bread pudding in the oven and set the table with a fruit bowl and yogurt dip, the storm door opened and closed.

"Just in time," she said with a sly smile, imagining the look on his face when he saw the feast she prepared for him. Madeline stood over the stove, stirring vanilla sauce with one hand, her other hand rested on her hip.

"Hi honey!" She stood on her toes to plant a kiss on his cheek when she caught sight of the tiny infant he carried in his arms.

"Whose baby is this?" She lifted the white cotton blanket from the infant's eyes. "Hello there," she said with a tenderness reserved solely for the newborn and the very old. She washed her hands at the sink, then reached out to take the baby from Apollo. Madeline cooed, making silly faces. The child inadvertently made faces back at her.

"You are the sweetest thing I've seen all day," she gushed. "Boy or girl?

Apollo stood rigid and silent.

"Whose beautiful baby is this?"

"Madeline, this is my child."

She lifted the baby close to her face, her nose grazing its forehead. "You are so precious," she whispered.

"Madeline, this child is mine." He said again, louder this time.

"What do you m… mean?"

"This is my baby and I've brought her home."

"Your baby! How can this be?"

Madeline shoved the infant back into Apollo's arms and stepped backwards. She wiped her hands on her apron and wrapped her arms around her chest, as if keeping herself warm.

"I don't understand this at all?" She searched his face, frantic for some sign that perhaps she'd misunderstood. He stood firm, taking back none of what he said.

***

Earlier that morning he'd stopped by Sybil's place to see the baby. The door was unlocked so he let himself in. The baby slept in her bassinet, a pacifier in her mouth. Brianna watched cartoons a few feet away.

"Sybil," he called out. The bedroom and bathroom doors were open, so he peeked in. Sybil wasn't there.

"Where's your mother?" he asked Brianna.

"Outside somewhere."

"How long has she been gone?"

Brianna shrugged her shoulders, never once taking her eyes off of a colorful cartoon character scaling a ridiculously tall building.

"Do you mind if I hang out here with you and the baby until your mom comes home?"

"I don't care."

The apartment smelled of sour milk and rancid diapers. Apollo busied himself putting out the trash and lining the cans with fresh bags. He sprayed each with disinfectant to minimize the odor.

It was a half hour before the door popped open. Sybil strolled past Apollo into the kitchen.

"How could you leave these kids here alone?" Apollo bellowed.

Sybil raced back to the living room, her hand over her chest.

"Did you just get here? I didn't see you?"

"I've been here half an hour. What were you thinking leaving Brianna to look after the baby? How old is she... four, maybe five years old? She isn't ready for that kind of responsibility!"

"I wasn't gone that long. The baby naps for an hour anyway, and she's perfectly safe in her bassinet."

"The door was unlocked. Anyone could have come in here and done harm to these children."

"I was just around the corner. You're making a big deal about nothing."

"Where's Terri? I thought she was helping you with the kids?"

"She's in the hospital again, problems with her liver, maybe her kidneys too."

"I send you enough money for a sitter. Why don't you hire help?"

The baby stirred. He picked her up and caught a whiff of her soiled diaper. He changed her and cleaned her bottom with a wet wipe, then grabbed a few more wipes to clean the dirt caked in the crevices of her navel and between her toes. She appeared thinner since her first few days home from the hospital.

"Has she been eating?"

"Are you now accusing me of starving my own child?"

"Sybil, I don't like what I see here. This isn't the first time I've come here and you've not adequately taken care of her. She's not clean, no one interacts with her, you leave her here alone. What if something terrible happens?"

She rolled her eyes and stumbled. High or drunk, he couldn't tell, but she was under the influence of something at that early hour.

"I'm taking Jana home." He packed her diaper bag with bottles, pampers and the undershirts and socks piled on the end table. From the fridge he grabbed a can of formula.

"You can't just walk out of here with my baby!"

"You were around the corner and left an infant unattended. I can't leave her here in good conscience. I'm not saying this is permanent - maybe we do this until Terri comes home - but today, right now, Jana comes home with me."

She made no further protest. If he were not mistaken, she sighed like she'd just unburdened a heavy load, and simply closed the door behind him.

***

Watching Madeline's demeanor transform was like watching a train speeding toward a car stalled on a railroad track. She looked from him to the baby, back to him. In an instant, peace fled and Madeline raged. The pots on the stove, she dumped one by one into the garbage. She snatched the bread pudding from the oven and hurled it out the open window, pan and all.

"Who is she!" she screamed, "and why did you have to bring your bastard child here!" Her body shook with rage. "I know I took awhile, but I was coming around! I was coming around, Apollo! I put the past behind us and I forgave you!"

Even though there was nothing he could say to placate her, she waited for some justification, some explanation.

"Say something!" she demanded.

"I can't ask you for forgiveness or understanding, nor do I expect it. I have nowhere else to take her and her mother isn't fit to raise her right now."

"That's not my problem. Get out and take that baby with you. I don't want it in this house. Take it out of here!" she shrieked.

As she charged past Apollo, her shoulder struck his arm so hard it spun him around. She continued up the stairs and locked herself in the guest bedroom.

Apollo followed her, but there was no use trying to talk her into unlocking the door. She'd already forgiven him for the most hideous of sins and now he'd ruined it. She was now lost to him. He could see it in her eyes. His only recourse, this time, was prayer. The first was a prayer of thanks, that he was able to rescue his only child from neglect. The second was a prayer of forgiveness, for he knew he had deeply and irreparably wounded his undeserving wife.

A CAR SCREECHED AROUND THE CORNER and accelerated, the engine revving high. It whizzed down Cedar Crest Road, swerving out of control, the piercing scream of brakes growing louder. A deafening crash finally ended its course. Apollo's footsteps raced to the front door. A string of angry curses ensued.

Madeline opened the window overlooking the street. The white sedan had crashed into the driver's side rear of Apollo's car. Smoke poured from the engine, strips of rubber adhered to the roadway. The car jerked as the gears shifted, then went in reverse. The driver straightened the wheel, floored the gas and sped off.

Apollo ran outside and jumped in his car. Madeline hurried after him.

"Take this baby with you. Apollo, I am *not* taking care of this child!"

Apollo turned the key in the ignition and raced after the white sedan.

"Don't leave this baby here!" Madeline screamed after the car, but Apollo was already in hot pursuit.

"Who the hell does he think he is?" she spoke into the air.

Another car pulled up. The door popped open and stilettos appeared, followed by endless legs and topped off with a most inappropriate mini skirt. It was Coletta. She ascended the steps to her house as if the streets were lined with suitors.

"And to hell with you too, Coletta! To hell with you!"

Her nose in the air, Coletta ignored her old friend and continued her high stepping. Madeline glared at the side of her face, daring her to say a word so she'd have a reason to release her seething rage. Coletta didn't entertain her with so much as a glance and disappeared into her home.

Madeline's eyes swept the neighborhood. It was a Friday morning and the street was quiet. Most of the neighbors were heading to work, some to the shore for a long weekend during the final weeks of summer. Madeline welcomed any distraction from her thoughts – a meddling neighbor, a stray cat, anything to quiet the thoughts bombarding her mind. *How much more can I take from this man? I've already suffered through so much, and now this too?*

Then she heard an unusual sound. At first she couldn't identify it. Was it the faint faraway purr of a kitten, or the sweet whimper of a newborn puppy? She stood still, her ears straining for another inkling of the odd noise. It surfaced again, only this time it was crisp. Seconds later, the whimper grew louder and more distinct. Madeline spun around. It was coming from right behind her. The baby! She ran with leaps until indoors. The baby lay on the middle cushion of the sofa on her tummy, head bobbing up and down, cries alternately muffled then clear.

"Babies cry all the time," she yelled at the infant. "So go ahead, scream."

Relentless in its discontent, the pitch of the baby's wail heightened.

"I don't even want to be in the same room with you!" She paced back and forth in front of the baby, then came to a dead stop in her tracks. *The diaper bag!*

She found the diaper bag in the dining room draped over a chair. She searched it for any clues as to where this child came from. If she could find an address, phone number or even a last name, she'd take the baby back to its mother. She turned the bag upside down spilling the contents in a heap on the table - diapers, undershirts, socks, wipes, a can of formula and two bottles. There were no clues.

"I'm stuck with you!" she fussed. "If you're hungry, I have to feed you. If you need changing, I have to change you. I have to take care of you until Apollo comes home and I have no idea when that is." She wrung her hands to stop their shaking. "This is insane!"

"I'm just gonna feed and change you so you stop crying. Apollo can take you back to wherever you belong when he gets back. If you want to scream after you're fed and dry then that's fine with me!" Her yelling caused the infant even more distress. Red splotches formed on each cheek.

She rinsed a bottle from the diaper bag and filled it with formula. Bottle in hand, she watched the bobbing infant for several moments. If the baby were older, it could hold its own bottle. Exasperated, Madeline picked the baby up and shoved the bottle into her mouth, careful to extend her arm so their bodies touched as little as possible. The baby suckled, letting out a series of pleasurable grunts and staring without blinking into Madeline's face, as if trying to figure out who she was.

"You can't be more than a few weeks old," Madeline's voice softened. "You should be home, bonding with your mother yet here you are, a motherless child with a whore for a father. Damn you Apollo!"

After the baby was fed, she changed her diaper. *A girl. I always wanted a baby girl.* Madeline didn't even know she was crying until her teardrops wet the baby's yellow sleeper.

Damn you to hell, Apollo!

The baby slept in her arms but awakened, crying, two hours later. Madeline repeated the feeding and changing but this time she held her close. Her head nestled in the crook of her arm, her tiny warm body touching from head to foot.

"We are both so needy, you and I," she whispered, "you in need of a mother and I in need of someone who's deserving of me, and your father's the monster that binds this all together.

Why couldn't you be my baby," she lamented, "the baby I had with Apollo?"

She never heard Apollo's key in the lock or the creaking of the door inching open, but there he was standing over her while the infant nestled against her bosom. She tried but failed to erase the sad longing from her face.

"You left me with this baby on purpose. You're crueler than I ever imagined." There was no anger in her voice, just grief. She eased the sleeping baby onto the sofa.

"It all happened so fast. I couldn't let the guy just hit my car and take off. I followed him until I flagged down a patrol car. He was drunk, you know, said he hadn't slept a wink all night. I hung around until the officer impounded the car and finished the report."

"I could care less about your damn car. When is she coming to get her baby?" she asked.

Apollo sat down next to her. "Her name is Jana and no one's coming."

"You had a baby with a woman who doesn't want her own child?"

"It's not a matter of whether or not she wanted her, she just wasn't taking good enough care of her."

"What are you going to do with her?"

"I'm not taking her back until her mother can do a better job with her."

"What about me?"

"I'm sorry Madeline, I screwed up and I'm trying to make it right. This is where I need to start. I know I've messed things up between us, probably forever, but I can't mess up Jana's life too."

"We've been married almost five years and I've had to deal with so much crap! And now you expect me to put up with this, too?"

Apollo hung his head.

"How long is this baby gonna be here?"

"I don't know. Could be days or could be months."

"You brought another woman's baby into our home. How could you? Especially knowing I wanted to have a baby, too. For a long time, I kept it a secret because I didn't think you were ready and I wanted to spare myself the heartbreak." She threw her hands in the air. "As it turns out, I walked right back into the center of more heartbreak, and once again I owe it all to you. For my sake, you have to find another way to accommodate this child."

"I can't give her back to Sybil, not now."

"So that's the woman's name. Sybil," she said as if she had a bad taste in her mouth. "Doesn't Sybil have family who can take her?"

Apollo shook his head. "For now, she stays. It's unfair and cruel but it's the only way I know how to fix all of this."

"It may fix things for this baby, but it doesn't fix us."

"I'm old, but I damn sure ain't stupid. Where is she, Sybil?"

Terri pulled herself to standing with her walker and moved around at a snail's pace, her limbs heavy with excess fluid.

"What are you talking about now?" Sybil asked. She said goodnight to Brianna and closed her bedroom door before turning to deal with Terri. She wasn't at all pleased with the direction of the conversation.

"Don't pretend as if you don't know what I'm talking about. Where's Jana? Did you follow in my footsteps and abandon your own baby?"

"I did *not* abandon her," she shot back, "not like you abandoned Shane. She's visiting her father."

"Visiting? I've been out of the hospital for well over a month, now. You mean to tell me she's visiting her father for three whole weeks? You go and get that baby!"

"But she's better off there with him. He has a home and a good job. I have nothing. Men can raise their own children, you know. There's no written rule that says only a woman can raise a child."

"There is no way a child can be better off without her mother!"

"I would have been better off without mine!"

Grandmother Rose would've had harsh words for Sybil if she heard the way she talked to Terri, but Terri wasn't fazed in the least. Her insults were like hurling a brick into a bale of cotton.

"Listen Sybil, I let my dear Shane go away and I'll probably never see him again. It was the biggest mistake of my life. You don't see it now but one day you will die on the inside for the child you let go. It's a pain that will never go away. Do you want that?"

"This is different. I know where she is and I can see her whenever I want."

"How many times have you seen Jana in the last three weeks?"

Sybil turned away.

"Have you called to check on her?" Terri ambled toward her, her walker leading the way. She stopped a foot from Sybil, leveled herself after letting go of the walker, and pulled Sybil's shoulders square.

"Don't let my mistake be yours." She accentuated every word.

"It's not a mistake. I haven't been to his house but I know from the address it's in a good neighborhood. What if Jana's better off there?"

"Do you want Jana to grow up thinking you left her?"

"But I haven't left her. She's with her father and he's her family too. He'll take good care of her. Besides, I can't afford to feed another child."

"Bull. One more mouth won't matter and if you haven't visited her by now, you had no intention of doing so. Do it now, Sybil, before she grows up not knowin' who you are. Do it now, while you're still young. You're only twenty-two years old. The older you get, and the older the baby gets, the more complicated it becomes."

The day Apollo took Jana away, Sybil felt no remorse. She shut out her feelings on purpose and made a conscious effort not to think about it ever since. But the more Terri talked, the more uneasy she became. Terri had become her conscience. She summoned all her doubts and fears and mistakes out into full view. It was as if, Terri, the most sinful of all, was her mirror.

"It hurts that I have so few memories of Shane," Terri continued, "I wish I'd spent more time with him, I wonder what kind of man he is, if he finished high school, if he will have a child that he too will one day leave behind." Her voice lowered, swollen with anguish. "He reaches out to me in my dreams, you know. I try to grab hold of him," she grasped the empty air, "only to wake up and realize I'm just reaching into nothingness. No one is there at the end of my arms. What hurts me even more is that whatever happens to him in his life is my fault. I hope good comes to him, but if bad comes, it's because of me. I changed the course of his entire life and I have only myself to blame. Sybil, look at me."

Sybil lifted her head.

"Please don't repeat my sins," Terri implored.

Sybil didn't even realize she was crying until a tear tickled her cheek.

"It's not the same. I'm not like you, Terri."

C lusters of children scattered about Cedar Crest Road. Bicycles whizzed by, a football sailed through the air and jump ropes slapped the pavement in beat to the singsong tunes that accompanied them. Sybil marched down the center of the road, her head turning from side to side as she inspected the neighborhood. New shutters and siding adorned nearly all of the two-story brick homes, lawns were lush and green, and hanging plants with bright colorful flowers dangled from porch ceilings. The street and sidewalks were clean of debris, and the children well-dressed and mannerly.

She regretted what she was about to do, but a baby needed her mother. Besides, she didn't want to end up like Terri, wondering at the light of each new day, what became of her child.

I wish it wasn't so damn hot, she thought. *It's May but it already feels like July!* Her Levis were damp with humidity, her hair clung to the back of her neck. *I should have worn something more comfortable. I'm gonna pass out from this heat.*

It was a long street and Apollo lived closer to the opposite end. She was at the halfway point and had a ways to go. She slowed her gait, yet walked onward with her head held high, for surely she was about to take on a worthy and noble cause. She was a mother coming to claim her child. She just hoped Apollo didn't start talking about a custody fight. There was no way she could afford a lawyer.

When she reached Apollo's house, she stood on the sidewalk, facing the entrance, to take it all in. A beautiful arrangement of

351

lilies and wildflowers lined the front bay window, and potted shrubs flanked the stairs. The porch held a single chair with a striped seat cushion that matched the burgundy shutters.

Why couldn't I convince a man like Apollo to marry me and put me up in a house like this?

Sybil advanced up the walkway and turned right to go up the three steps which led to the front porch. She took a deep breath and knocked on the front door. There… she made the first move. There was no turning back. A tall, solidly built woman opened the door.

"Hello, may I help you?"

"I'm Sybil. I'm looking for Apollo. Does he live here?"

"Yes," Madeline replied. "He lives here but he stepped out for a moment. Is there anything I can help you with?"

"Who are you?" Sybil asked.

"I'm Madeline, Apollo's wife."

"I'm here to take my daughter home."

Madeline stared at Sybil for several seconds, then her eyes spread wide open.

"You're *that* Sybil?"

"I'm taking her," Sybil said it as if it were a certainty. "She is here, isn't she?"

"You'll have to wait until Apollo comes home. I expect him in a couple of hours." Madeline spoke quickly and shoved the door closed, but Sybil kicked it back open before Madeline could lock it.

"I know she's in there so either bring her out her to me or I'm coming in to get her. I'm not waiting for Apollo and I don't need his permission. If he wants to see her, he knows where to find me. Now open the damn door!"

"Jana's been here almost three months. You just can't waltz in here after all this time and expect me to simply turn her over to you. If you wanted her you would have kept her in the first place. Besides, how do I know you're her mother anyway? You could be anyone!"

"I'm her mother and you know it. I have every right in the world!" Sybil screamed, louder this time. "Why are you defending a man who screwed another woman behind your back? What kind of woman are you anyway to allow him back into your little love nest with a baby he had with someone else?"

Sybil's eyes darted all over the room looking for her child. Jana was right there in the room sleeping in her bassinet but Sybil couldn't see her because the height of the bassinet was flush with the rear of the sofa.

"Come back later and discuss it with Apollo. You may be her mother, but he's her father and he has a right to her too."

"So you've been playing house with my baby? You must be pretty damn desperate to put up with that crap. Can't you have babies of your own? Either bring Jana to me or I'll get her myself!"

Before Madeline could respond, Sybil started up the stairs. She managed to get to the fourth step when Madeline grabbed her arm and yanked her backwards down the stairs.

"Get out of my house before I call the police!" Madeline lowered her voice. She didn't want her business out in the street.

"Get off me!" Sybil screeched. A small crowd formed on the sidewalk in front of the house. Jana began to whimper.

With an open palm, Sybil struck Madeline hard across the right cheek. Madeline shoved Sybil out the front door and onto the front porch. Sybil fell to the ground but she got up kicking and punching her way back into the house. The crowd at the bottom of the stairs started to disperse but when Sybil came crashing back out onto the porch again, the neighbors scurried back to their places, each jockeying for a front row view. Even the children scattered in the street stopped their playing, mesmerized by the raucous altercation.

"How dare you?" Madeline hollered.

Sybil fought back as best she could but she was no match for Madeline. Madeline attacked with something beyond mere physical prowess. She fought with a venom Sybil could have never anticipated. She left Cedar Crest Road defeated and alone, her child still in the care of another woman, a woman who fought harder for her child than she.

***

After Sybil ran off, Madeline sat on the floor in the corner of her dining room rocking Jana in her arms until they both stopped crying. Madeline's entire body shook, so frightened was she at the depth of her own fury. Wrestling to harness it took every ounce of strength and fortitude she could muster. What was happening to her?

Something had taken hold of Madeline. It snuck up on her like a predator stalking innocent prey, then pounced nearly consuming her whole. She never even saw it coming. When she held little Jana, something resounded in Madeline like the music of an entire orchestra. It reverberated wide and deep and brought forth a longing and a sorrow all at once. Not too long ago, she'd demanded that Apollo take her away. Now she fought for Jana as if her very existence depended on it.

"I've fallen in love with you," she whispered to Jana. "I can't let you go."

"Who's in my room?" Apollo bellowed in his monster voice. He'd just slipped off his shoes and sunk his feet into his slippers when he spotted Jana out of the corner of his eye, sneaking in. She'd grown so much over the past few years. It was hard to believe she was almost six. It wasn't too long ago that he'd held her, newborn, in his arms, wondering how he was going to keep her in his life.

"It's Milly the Mouse," Jana said in her best squeaky voice. Every day, Jana was a different animal. Today she ate only cheese and walked on all fours. She convinced Madeline to draw whiskers on her face and sew ears onto a hooded sweater. A paper tail taped to her bottom swung side to side.

"And who will you be tomorrow Miss Mouse?"

"I will be Lillian the Lion," she roared in her gruffest voice.

She popped up from the floor and hugged Apollo's legs. "Mommy said dinner's ready." She landed back on her hands and feet and made her way to the kitchen.

Chuckling, Apollo trailed Jana. The three of them assembled at the table.

"Did you have a good day at preschool?" Madeline asked Jana.

"I had a good day but my friend Charlie didn't." Charlie was her best friend. He was a grumpy kid who wore a permanent scowl on his face. He was known for pummeling anyone who rubbed him the wrong way. He pummeled his friends, teachers and even his own mother. Tucker was surprised that Jana talked about him more than any of the other children, especially since he'd pummeled her on occasion, too.

"Why not?"

"Charlie says his mommy and daddy are getting a deevorce and won't live together anymore. Are you and mommy getting a deevorce too?"

"It's called a divorce, and why would you think that we were getting one?"

"Because you don't sleep in the same room like other moms and dads and sometimes you're really mad at each other."

"We're not getting a divorce. We..." Madeline appeared frustrated.

"We just like to have our own room, like you have your own room," Apollo finished for her.

Madeline cradled a serving dish in her arm and spooned mixed vegetables on their plates.

"I have one more question." She held up one finger and turned her head to the side as if suddenly shy.

"What's that?"

"Do I have another mommy?"

The serving bowl slipped from Madeline's hand. It struck the floor splitting in two. Peas and carrots splattered to the far ends of the dining room.

"H... how did you know? Wh... who told you?" Madeline asked.

"We had to bring our baby pictures to school to put on the bulletin board and everybody else in my class has newborn pictures 'cept me, and I hear you and daddy talking at night time. I hear you talking about my other mommy. I even know her name. It's Sybil."

Madeline was frozen.

"Yes Jana, you have another mommy," Apollo answered.

Jana leaned back in her chair. "Everybody else has one mommy, I have two. That makes me special." She picked up her fork and resumed eating.

Madeline turned away and grabbed the broom and dust pan to sweep the vegetables from the floor.

"Oh, and mommy, have you finished sewing my lion costume? I want to wear it tomorrow."

"It… it'll be ready."

Just as Madeline emptied the dustpan into the trash can, the mail slid through the slot and landed in a messy mound on the living room floor. Madeline hastened to the living room.

"Isn't my birthday coming soon?" Jana asked.

There she is, off on another topic again. Poor Madeline's barely digested the Sybil comment and now she's talking about her birthday?

"It's less than two weeks away. Have you decided whether or not you want a party?" Madeline answered with a forced cheery attitude.

"I want a big party with a clown and a moon bounce and face painting, like at the fair."

"We'll have to send out invitations right away."

Madeline walked back to the dining room while flipping through a handful of mail. "The check from my last design gig should have been here by now. Some folks sure take their time paying," she said with fake normalcy. She reached the last envelope and stopped in her tracks. Her hand rose to her mouth, as if she were about to scream.

"Mommy, are you okay?"

"Remember what we just talked about?"

"My birthday?"

"No, your… other mommy."

Jana sat up straight.

"You got a card in the mail today. It's from Sybil. You probably have lots more questions about her. I'd like to answer all of them but I can't right now. I don't know what else to say except that I love you very much." She gave Jana the card fluttering in her hand.

"Can you read it for me?" Jana asked.

"I'll read it," Apollo offered.

"It says, *'when I thought of you today, the sun rose, the flowers bloomed and the birds sang, love Sybil and Brianna'*. It's a nice card, Jana."

"Who's Brianna?"

They both looked at Apollo.

"She's your sister," Apollo explained.

Madeline waved her hand up and down in front of her nose, as if she needed air.

"Jana, go ahead and finish your dinner. Your mom's gonna go upstairs and take a little break."

"Is mommy alright?"

"We'll talk later," Apollo said.

"But I don't want to wait to talk. Let's talk now!"

That's Jana, Apollo thought, *persistent and always living in the now. If I don't give her an explanation, she'll needle me for hours.*

"Give me a few minutes and I'll come back down so we can have a little chat," Apollo answered.

"Ok, daddy."

Halfway up the stairs, Madeline stopped and turned to Apollo. "I don't like this. I don't like this at all!"

JANA WAS SUPPOSED TO BE HELPING APOLLO and Madeline decorate the tree but her favorite Christmas carol was on the radio, *Angels We Have Heard On High*, and she was singing the 'gloria' part with her eyes closed, her mouth a perfect 'o'. The scent of Douglas-Fir filled the air, cider simmered on the stove.

"When you're done promoting your singing career, you have a package. It came in today's mail," Apollo mentioned. Song abandoned, she took off running to the stack of mail. A box sat atop.

"Pop Pop sends the coolest gifts!" Tucker didn't visit often but he was diligent about sending her a present on her birthday and at Christmas. Jana shook the silver rectangular box over her ear.

"What do you think it is?" he asked.

"A bracelet, or earrings, or maybe... a radio."

"Jana, there is no radio in the world that would fit in that size box," Apollo teased.

Jana melted into giggles, "I know, daddy, I'm just joking. Can I open it now?"

"It's Christmas Eve, wait until tomor..." Madeline began to tell her but Jana had already ripped it open.

It was a watch with a pink and white polka-dotted band and a heart on the background of the face.

"It's just like the one from the Christmas Catalog."

After Apollo fastened it on her arm, she rubbed it against her cheek.

"It's not polite to open the gift before reading the card," Madeline scolded.

"Oops," Jana exaggerated. "I forgot." She tore open the card and looked puzzled. "This isn't pop pop's handwriting. Daddy, who's this from?"

Apollo read the card. Madeline was instantly by his side.

"What is she trying to pull?" Madeline roared.

"Let's not do this in front of Jana, Madeline."

"It's happening again. First her birthday, now this! What's next?"

"We'll finish the tree and talk about it *later*," he said with a nod in Jana's direction.

Apollo climbed the ladder to set the star. "Plug in the lights."

Madeline slammed the plug in the receptacle so hard it missed. She closed her eyes, seemingly to calm her nerves, then tried again.

The lights came on steady then blinked in short intervals.

Jana clapped her hands, "It's so pretty. Even the star's blinking!"

"Well that's that. I have to check on the cider. Madeline turned off the radio and retreated to the kitchen. Apollo followed.

"It's just a gift Madeline, nothing more," Apollo whispered.

"But how do we know this isn't going to keep happening? What if she wants to do more than just send a card or gift? Have you forgotten the time I had to beat her down because she tried to come here and take Jana? We can't wait for something else to happen. Do something now!" she pleaded.

"If I shut Sybil out, she may want more. The last thing we need is a custody battle."

"What can we do?"

"If she goes too far, I'll stop it."

"She's already gone too far."

"I'll take care of it."

"You better, Apollo. You owe it to me."

"I know." He knew more than he let on, how much he owed it to her. He couldn't allow Madeline to suffer any more at his hand. Ensuring that his family remain intact and that this child

Madeline loved so hard remained in her life was the least he could do.

"She's all I have. Don't let that woman take my baby."

Apollo was lost in his thoughts.

Are you listening to me?" Madeline asked.

He nodded. He understood perfectly. Keeping Jana in Madeline's life was his redemption.

THEY WERE TALKING TOO LOUD FOR THEIR conversation to be private. Jana heard the whole thing. She didn't want to hurt her mother's feelings, but she was curious about Sybil. *How come she never comes to visit? What does she look like? Is she nice like mommy? And a sister! I always wanted a sister.*

She waited until after her bubble bath to barge into Madeline's bedroom. No matter how much Madeline scolded, she'd never complied with what her mother called 'the art of knocking before entering'.

"Come in, honey," Madeline said with a hint of sarcasm.

"I forgot to knock, didn't I?" Jana said a little too sweetly, then her face grew cautious. She sat on the bed and folded her hands in her lap. "Promise not to get mad if I ask you something?"

Madeline stood in the mirror applying moisturizer. She looked at Jana's reflection. "Go ahead, ask."

"Can I go see my other mommy?"

"You want to meet Sybil?"

Jana nodded.

"We've given you everything, we've loved you…"

"I know, but I still want to see her."

Madeline backed into a corner, a slight tremor to her hands. "I don't know about this."

Jana sort of understood why her mother was upset but why was she so afraid? Being afraid was for ghosts at Halloween, the scary house at the amusement park, and the dark. Why was she afraid right in their own house?

"Can I please go?" Jana pleaded.

"I'll talk to your father tonight and we'll see if we can take you to see her in the next couple of days."

*S*ybil hated impromptu guests and ignored the door bell whenever someone dared arrive unannounced. But this time, whoever was at the front door wasn't going away. The bell sounded, seemingly with no end, until Sybil could stand it no more. Against her better judgment, she pressed the intercom.

"Who the hell is it?" she shrieked.

"I hate to drop in on you like this but it's urgent," Apollo said.

She unlocked the door with the buzzer. "You better not be here to tell me something's happened to Jana. I should have never let you take her!"

"She wants to see you." Apollo rubbed the stubble on his chin. "Can we bring her tomorrow?"

"Jana's coming here?"

"What time is best?"

"Ah… I don't know."

"You do want to see her, I hope."

Why now? I don't want her to see me like this. I've done nothing with my life. What will she think of me?

"I don't feel ready on such short notice, and I don't have anything to wear." Her eyes made a quick circle around the apartment. "And the place is a wreck!"

"She's five, Sybil. None of that matters. She's not coming to see the house or your clothes, she's coming to see you. If you don't want me to bring her, just say so."

"How about five thirty?"

"Fine." Apollo turned and left.

Sybil's breath grew shallow, panic boiling in her belly. She was a stranger to her child, and she had no one to blame but herself. She could argue that Madeline denied her access to Jana but that was years ago, when she showed up on Apollo's doorstep and demanded that Madeline turn her over. Since then, she'd made no effort at all. If she were completely honest, there were many other, more civil ways she could have claimed her child. She simply didn't try hard enough. Because of her, the child she bore into this world knew another woman as mother.

I've become Terri.

"This is all your fault," Madeline snapped, her voice almost inaudible through her teeth. "You had an affair with that woman and brought this child into my life. I love her Apollo. I love her fiercely. If Sybil takes Jana away from me, you are to blame." She slipped a light jacket over her shoulders and searched for an umbrella. It wasn't raining yet but the air smelled of precipitation.

"Madeline. It's gonna be okay."

"It's not okay! I'm scared to death!"

"This is hard, I know, but I promise you Sybil won't try to take Jana."

"She has every right, you know."

"She won't exercise that right."

"Once again you have me right smack in the middle of a horrible circumstance. I swear if you walked out of my life and never came back I'd be okay with it. I can live without you, you know. I just don't want to live without Jana. She's *my* baby."

Jana appeared at the top of the staircase.

"Are you ready?" Apollo asked, his tone light.

Jana came down, careful not to scuff her patent leather shoes. She'd picked out her own clothes for the visit with Sybil. She wore a fancy yellow dress with matching lace socks, and handed Madeline a yellow ribbon for her hair. Madeline could barely see through her puffy eyes, yet managed to tie the ribbon perfectly.

No one spoke during the ride to Sybil's house. Even Jana, talkative to a fault, was quiet.

All too soon, the car pulled over to the curb and Apollo turned off the engine. Having arrived in less than twenty minutes, Madeline was shocked at how close Sybil lived. Her fury with Apollo crested anew.

Apollo opened the car door and reached for Jana's hand. She got out on her own and walked ahead of him with her big girl walk. She took short steps, swinging her arms close to her body, her head tilted slightly upward.

Madeline, on the other hand, could have used some assistance. Her knees were wobbly, and although the weather was mild for winter, her teeth chattered. But she dared not reach for Apollo's hand. She struggled out of the car on her own as well.

Sybil buzzed them in before Apollo had a chance to knock. A young girl, a few years older than Jana, opened the door.

I'm Brianna," she said, "you must be Jana."

"How do you know my name?"

"Because you look more like my mother than I do," Brianna giggled. She was lanky with big dark eyes. She wore hoop earrings, more suitable for an older teenager or an adult, and noisy bangles at the wrist. After the two girls embraced, Brianna led Jana to the kitchen and pointed to Sybil.

"There's your mother."

Sybil stood over the stove with her back to the girls. Hesitant, she turned around.

She looked very different from the last time Madeline had seen her, and life had not been kind. Premature lines weathered her face, her body already sagged.

"My baby!" Sybil gushed as she stepped forward and wrapped her arms around Jana. "You've grown up beautiful!"

"Thank you," Jana said, her arms still at her side. Jana looked up at Sybil as if she were trying to figure out who she was. It was the same searching look she gave Madeline that first time she held her.

"I've wanted to see you for a long time. Every year on your birthday and at Christmas I hoped to see you," she explained. "I tried to visit once and I planned to see you lots of other times but…" Sybil's voice trailed off.

Madeline took in the tiny kitchen. A mangled blind barely covered the single window and a film of grease shined the cabinets. Slats were missing from the high backed ladder style chairs.

They all stood around in an awkward silence, waiting for Sybil to say something more. It was Jana who broke the silence.

"I'm glad I met you but I want to go now."

"The paratransit bus will drop your grandmother off in about an hour. She had kidney dialysis today. I know she'd want to see you. Can Jana stay for dinner?" Sybil looked at Apollo. She'd never even acknowledged Madeline was there.

"Maybe another day," Apollo said.

"Oh, and thanks for the watch, Ms. Sybil." Jana added. Madeline didn't miss the fact that Jana called Sybil 'Miss'.

"Can I call you sometime?" Sybil asked. The desperation darkening her face terrified Madeline.

"Sure," Jana said, as she slipped her hand into Apollo's hand then reached over for Madeline's, too. She squeezed so hard the bones in Madeline's fingers throbbed.

"Bye," Jana said over her shoulder. She didn't stop pulling them until she reached the car. The minute Apollo unlocked the doors, Jana climbed into the back seat, taking Madeline along with her. She sat close with hips and knees touching.

"Mommy, let's go home." She rested her head on Madeline's arm.

Madeline nodded. "Yes, let's go home."

Quick Order Form

☐ **YES**, I want _____ copies of **The Fruits Of Our Sins** at $14.95 each plus $4.00* shipping and handling per book. Allow 15 days for delivery.

My check or money order for $_____.____ is enclosed. Please make your check payable to Red Lotus Press.

Please charge my credit card:

      ☐ Mastercard   ☐ VISA   ☐ American Express

Card # _____ Exp. Date _____ Security Code_____

Signature _____

Name _____

Address _____

City/State/Zip _____

Phone _____ E-mail _____

Please send to:
> **Red Lotus Press**
> **P.O. Box 11252**
> **Elkins Park, PA 19027**

Or order by:
Email: orders@redlotuspress.com
Phone: Call (215) 863-7562. Have your credit card ready.

International Shipping: $9.00 for the first book; $5.00 for each additional.

Quick Order Form

□ **YES**, I want _____ copies of **The Fruits Of Our Sins** at $14.95 each
plus $4.00* shipping and handling per book. Allow 15 days for delivery.

My check or money order for $_____.____ is enclosed. Please make your
check payable to Red Lotus Press.

Please charge my credit card:

□ Mastercard   □ VISA   □ American Express

Card # _____ Exp. Date _____ Security Code_____

Signature _____

Name _____

Address _____

City/State/Zip _____

Phone _____ E-mail _____

Please send to:
   Red Lotus Press
   P.O. Box 11252
   Elkins Park, PA 19027

Or order by:
Email: orders@redlotuspress.com
Phone: Call (215) 863-7562. Have your credit card ready.

*International Shipping: $9.00 for the first book; $5.00 for each
additional.